ALSO BY HEATHER CLARK

Nonfiction

Red Comet: The Short Life and Blazing Art of Sylvia Plath

The Grief of Influence: Sylvia Plath and Ted Hughes

The Ulster Renaissance: Poetry in Belfast 1962–1972

The
Scrapbook

The
Scrapbook

a novel

Heather Clark

PANTHEON BOOKS
New York

FIRST HARDCOVER EDITION
PUBLISHED BY PANTHEON BOOKS 2025

Published by Pantheon Books, a division of Penguin Random House LLC, 1745 Broadway, New York, NY 10019.

Pantheon Books and colophon are registered trademarks of Penguin Random House LLC.

Grateful acknowledgment is made to Ruth Franklin for the use of an excerpt from her translation of Tadeusz Borowski's "Light and Shadow" sequence, translation © Ruth Franklin.

Library of Congress Cataloging-in-Publication Data
Names: Clark, Heather, author.
Title: The scrapbook / Heather Clark.
Description: First edition. | New York : Pantheon Books, 2025.
Identifiers: LCCN 2024030467 (print) | LCCN 2024030468 (ebook) | ISBN 9780593701904 (hardcover) | ISBN 9780593701911 (ebook)
Classification: LCC PS3603.L36365 S27 2025 (print) | LCC PS3603.L36365 (ebook) | DDC 813/.6—dc23/eng/20240715
LC record available at https://lccn.loc.gov/2024030467
LC ebook record available at https://lccn.loc.gov/2024030468

penguinrandomhouse.com | pantheonbooks.com

Printed in the United States of America
2 4 6 8 9 7 5 3 1

The authorized representative in the EU for product safety and compliance is Penguin Random House Ireland, Morrison Chambers, 32 Nassau Street, Dublin D02 YH68, Ireland, https://eu-contact.penguin.ie.

For my grandfather,
who fought in the war

There are beings who are overwhelmed by the reality of others, their way of speaking, of crossing their legs, of lighting a cigarette. They become mired in the presence of others. One day, or rather one night, they are swept away inside the desire and the will of a single Other. Everything they believed about themselves vanishes. They dissolve and watch a reflection of themselves act, obey, swept into a course of events unknown. They trail behind the will of the Other, which is always one step ahead. They never catch up.

—ANNIE ERNAUX, *A Girl's Story*

At the end of the war I was just one year old, so I can hardly have any impressions of that period of destruction based on personal experience. Yet to this day, when I see photographs or documentary films dating from the war I feel as if I were its child, so to speak, as if those horrors I did not experience cast a shadow over me, and one from which I shall never entirely emerge.

—W. G. SEBALD, *On the Natural History of Destruction*

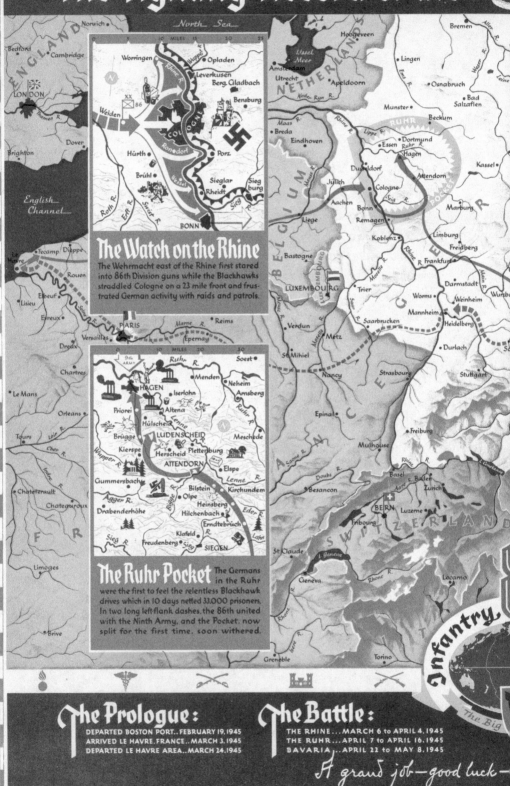

The Fighting Record of the

The Watch on the Rhine

The Wehrmacht east of the Rhine first stared into 86th Division guns while the Blackhawks straddled Cologne on a 23 mile front and frustrated German activity with raids and patrols.

The Ruhr Pocket

The Germans in the Ruhr were the first to feel the relentless Blackhawk drives which in 10 days netted 33,000 prisoners. In two long left-flank dashes, the 86th united with the Ninth Army, and the Pocket, now split for the first time, soon withered.

The Prologue:

DEPARTED BOSTON PORT.. FEBRUARY 19, 1945
ARRIVED LE HAVRE, FRANCE.. MARCH 3, 1945
DEPARTED LE HAVRE AREA... MARCH 24, 1945

The Battle:

THE RHINE... MARCH 6 to APRIL 4, 1945
THE RUHR... APRIL 7 to APRIL 16, 1945
BAVARIA.. APRIL 22 to MAY 8, 1945

A grand job — good luck —

Blackhawks in World War II

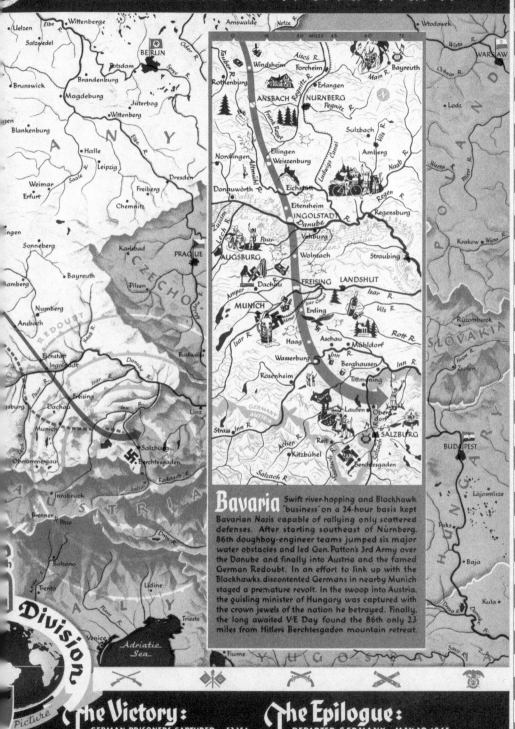

Bavaria

Swift river-hopping and Blackhawk "business" on a 24-hour basis kept Bavarian Nazis capable of rallying only scattered defenses. After starting southeast of Nürnberg, 86th doughboy-engineer teams jumped six major water obstacles and led Gen. Patton's 3rd Army over the Donube and finally into Austria and the famed German Redoubt. In an effort to link up with the Blackhawks, discontented Germans in nearby Munich staged a premature revolt. In the swoop into Austria, the quisling minister of Hungary was captured with the crown jewels of the nation he betrayed. Finally, the long awaited V-E Day found the 86th only 23 miles from Hitler's Berchtesgaden mountain retreat.

The Victory:

GERMAN PRISONERS CAPTURED... 53,354
GERMAN TERRITORY CONQUERED... 220 MILES
RIVERS FORCED..BIGGE, ALTMUHL, ISAR
DANUBE, MITTEL-ISAR, INN, SALZACH

The Epilogue:

DEPARTED GERMANY... MAY 30, 1945
DEPARTED LE HAVRE... JUNE 7, 1945
ARRIVED NEW YORK... JUNE 17, 1945

is M. Melasky - Maj. Gen. U.S.A.

Division — Picture

I crossed borders for him. To Germany. I knew nothing of the country then. We met in Cambridge, a Harvard party. The details are not important. What matters is that he was not like the others and I knew this from the beginning. For years after I tried to tell myself that what happened between us was hardly worth remembering. Others told me the same. But now I write the truth. He was everything to me then. Everything.

MY ROOMMATES DID NOT like him. They ignored him the week he stayed. You barely know him, they said, and already you're in love.

But they were wrong. I fell in love later. During that week, Christoph and I sat together by the window. We listened to music. My roommates came in and out of our suite, said quick hellos and were gone.

They don't like me, he said. It's because I'm German.

We were in bed, in my small corner room. There was a large window that looked out onto the courtyard. It was the end of spring term, the end of my senior year. Moonlight cut across my bed and illuminated our bodies like ghosts.

Probably, I said.

I don't care, he said. And then, after a silence, But they should not judge.

·   ·   ·

HE STAYED WITH ME the week before my final exams, the week I was supposed to be studying. I gave him novels to read; together we listened to Rachmaninoff, Stravinsky. When we talked, we talked mostly about music. How Bernstein conducted Beethoven's 9th Symphony before the dismantled Berlin Wall to celebrate Germany's reunification. How Shostakovich subverted Stalin's demands, how Stalin could not tell the difference between patriotic music and music that mocked patriotism.

Maybe young men like Christoph existed somewhere at Harvard, probably they did, but I never found them. I was a rower and lived half my college life at the boathouse. The other half I lived at the library. I was shy and rarely spoke up in class. At night I played in a band. My experience of love was mostly drunk nights on beaches, or some rower's dorm room.

He came to me the week I was supposed to be studying. I had to pass the English exam to graduate with honors, I had to know everything about all of English literature. We talked about Schopenhauer, Goethe, Joyce, as my roommates wandered in and out of the suite, said quick hellos and were gone. I knew he was leaving at the end of the week—he would board a plane for Germany on the day of my first exam—and so I could not concentrate. I began to care only about the sound of his voice, the movement of his hands. I forced myself to go to the library, I could hardly bear to be away from him. My world contracted: only he was real. I lay awake through our last night, committing the contours of his body to memory. Studying him.

I PASSED MY EXAMS. I graduated. I won an award for my thesis on Yeats and decided I would use the prize money to visit Christoph in Germany. I bought the ticket without asking him. I didn't want his permission.

After he left, I read novels by Günter Grass and W. G. Sebald. I only wanted to talk about Germany, history, him. My roommates said I was becoming obsessed. One had lost her extended family at Treblinka. The other's grandfather had survived Buchenwald. I knew little about the

Second World War beyond what I had learned in classrooms, movies, a few books. My own grandfather had helped liberate Dachau as a young GI, but he rarely spoke of it. I had nothing to ground my relationship to the war beyond a Nazi flag he had brought back from Hitler's summer-house in the Alps. And his scrapbook, the one with the photos.

In the days before I left for Germany, I could not sleep. I stayed awake and thought of Christoph, what it would be like to see him again. Now he knew I was coming. I had called him after my exams and told him, casually, about my plan. I had secured a job teaching English at a summer camp in Switzerland that July. I asked if I could visit him for a few days before I started work there. After all, I said, he was not so far away. I could take the train from his place to Lausanne. Would that be all right? Yes, he said, great! He wanted to see me. He would show me his university town where he lived and studied, he would take me to Heidelberg and Munich. He wanted me to meet his roommate, Matthias. He had told him about me, his American girl.

My hand, holding the phone, began to tremble.

It was strange to think that he, too, had a roommate, that he was also a student, my age, that his life had any parallels to my own. I suppose I had imagined him living a very sure and serious life in Germany, reading Wittgenstein and Goethe. But no, he told me about all-day hangovers and nights spent in muddy fields with the music pulsing through his body to the bodies dancing around him, wind and music moving through the trees. It was difficult to imagine him like this, dancing, drinking, standing close to other girls. He had been so sure and serious while he was with me, the week before my exams, the week I was supposed to be studying. We had listened to music, we had talked about the fall of Berlin, the siege of Leningrad. How Shostakovich premiered his 7th Symphony in the besieged city, how the German soldiers knew the war was lost when they heard it. And now this voice on the other end of the telephone, a casual, pleasant voice telling me about raves in moonlit fields.

My roommates said, Don't go. They had both been to Auschwitz. They would never set foot in Germany.

But I would go to him, that was the only thing I knew.

Each day they said, Don't go.

·   ·   ·

I WROTE DOWN everything that happened to me that year—May 1996
to May 1997—but I lost the journal on the metro in Prague. This happened some days after I left Christoph in Germany. When I got off the
subway and realized I did not have the battered notebook, I sat down
and cried. Trains sped by me in the tunnel. The air was hot and thick.
People poured out of the doors and walked past me, avoiding my eyes. I
would have done the same.

2

He was waiting for me in the arrivals hall at Frankfurt Airport. I lost my breath when I saw him. I remember the sensation, the tightening in my chest that I later associated with panic. There he was in a navy blue polo shirt with the collar turned up. His copper-blond hair fell over his forehead, his deep brown eyes. When he saw me, his face came alive in a wide, white smile. Such a simple thing, that smile, and yet I'll never forget it.

We pulled onto the Autobahn and drove toward his university town. In the car he kept his hand on my thigh, lifting it only to move the black leather stick shift back and forth, up and down. I looked at his muscular forearms. He is a German driver, I thought, as I watched him weave down the Autobahn at a hundred miles an hour. I leaned back in the seat and closed my eyes, tired and happy. He asked me about the flight but otherwise we did not speak much. We listened to the radio, then he put in a CD and played a song for me, something that sounded like German rap. It was "Jein," by Fettes Brot. It's good, right? he said. I asked him to play it again. He turned it up louder this time and we drove down the Autobahn, southwest, deeper into Germany.

I had never been to Europe.

When we got to his flat, he introduced me to his roommate, Matthias, who smiled and shook my hand and said I must be tired. He had short, curly brown hair and a kind smile, and he spoke English with a British accent. I liked him immediately.

I'll let you get settled, Matthias said, and then Christoph looked at me and nodded toward a door at the end of a short hallway.

Come, he said.

I followed him into his bedroom. He set my backpack on the floor, then sat down in a swivel chair and tapped a pencil on his desk. I looked around, studied the sleek, modern furniture, everything black and silver. An American flag hung on his wall. There was a small open window above his bed that looked out onto a church steeple. The sky was gray. The air was cool.

I stood next to my backpack. He looked at me, tapped his pencil on the desk.

A bird flew away from his window ledge, startling the silence. The dark outline of a cloud moved past, and suddenly I saw the weight of the sky collapse into silver. A downpour.

He stood up and shut the window.

I asked him what I should do with my backpack. He said it was fine where it was.

Do you want to shower, he asked? You must be very tired.

I did not answer him. I sat down on his bed and reached into my canvas purse and found the small hairbrush I always carried with me. I began to brush my hair. He sat down next to me and said, I would like to do that. I gave him the brush. He ran it through my long brown hair once, twice, then put the brush down and ran his hands down my shoulders, my back.

Later, after the rain stopped, we heard cathedral bells ringing through the town.

WHEN I AWOKE early the next morning I did not know where I was. And then I remembered. I looked at Christoph sleeping beside me and wondered what I had done, why I had been so foolish to end up here, in Germany, with this boy who had come to me the week I was supposed to be studying. I looked at his face in the early morning light and wondered, already, if I'd made a mistake.

He moved closer to me and said something in German. I turned toward him and touched his face. He opened his eyes and looked through me for a moment, as if I were an apparition. I wondered if he remembered who I was, why I was here.

He closed his eyes and held me close.

WE SLEPT UNTIL the bells woke us.

Sleep, he said. I'll make breakfast.

I did not go back to sleep. Through the door I heard him laughing and speaking to Matthias in German. I had never heard him speak German before. He sounded like someone else, not the boy who had talked to me in Cambridge about Gallipoli and Passchendaele and Erich Maria Remarque. I had no idea what he was saying. I sank a little as I began to understand the cost of pursuing him here, in Germany. I looked around his room, searched for something to hold on to. All the books on his shelves were in German. I felt dislodged reading the incomprehensible titles. There were notes pinned on his bulletin board, all in German. I tried to decipher them, whispered them out loud. It was useless.

Christoph opened the door, quietly, and saw that I was awake.

Coffee?

Yes, please.

I got up and walked into the bright white kitchen, small but clean. There was a table in the middle covered with what looked like blueprints. He was studying architecture.

Are these yours? I asked.

Yes. It's for a competition at the university.

What is it?

He cracked an egg into a white bowl.

A building.

I looked down at the vague lines and tried to imagine its shape.

What will it look like?

I don't know yet. Something different. New.

He cracked two more eggs into the bowl, threw the shells away, and began to whisk. When he finished, he poured the thick yellow liquid into the frying pan. I heard the butter sizzle and hiss.

Germany is a good country for architects, he said.

Suddenly there was a tap at the window, followed by another. Then another. Within a moment the taps became a single sound. We both turned and saw large silver drops running down the pane.

Damn, he said.

I don't mind the rain.

He turned back to the stove. He stood scrambling the eggs in his white terry cloth bathrobe.

We'll get wet, he said.

It's okay. I want to see the town.

He removed the blueprints from the table and set two places.

Can I help? I asked.

No, sit.

He picked up the frying pan and spatula and scooped the eggs onto our plates. He set the pan and the spatula gently in the sink, then sat down.

We began to eat.

Suddenly a bell rang. He stood up and opened the door of the small toaster oven on the counter, took out two slices of bread and set them on our plates.

He looked up at me.

Butter or jam?

Either is fine.

He reached into the refrigerator and pulled out a jar of apricot jam.

I hope you like it, he said, setting the jar down on the table. It's from Austria.

I opened the jar and spread the orange glaze on the thick white bread.

Normally we don't toast the bread, he said. We just eat it plain.

Oh.

But that's the way you have it in America, yes?

Most of the time.

I remember. We always had scrambled eggs and toast at Josh's house.

We should send him a postcard.

Yes. We can't forget.

We won't.

When we finished eating, he got up, rinsed the plates, then put them in the small dishwasher.

Could I . . . take a shower? I asked.

Of course.

I stood up. I was very close to him.

Just a moment, he said. I'll get you a towel.

He moved out into the hallway.

I looked at the tidy kitchen, the blue-and-white tea towels, the wooden dish rack, the cafetiere. A man had never made me breakfast.

He stepped back into the kitchen and handed me a soft, white, folded towel.

Danke, I said.

Bitte. He brushed my fingers, then stood back to let me pass.

HE WANTED TO show me the university where he studied architecture. He took me to his department, and I shook the hand of a professor. We had sandwiches at the canteen and I met some of his friends. Their names and faces blurred together, as such names and faces do. His university was modern, gray, concrete. Dull to the eye. The old buildings had been bombed during the war, he said, like everything else.

We had a coffee, then walked to a park. The rain came down heavier, but the linden trees formed a canopy above our heads that kept us nearly dry. I could feel the gravel through the soles of my shoes. The gravel was dark from the rain.

We sat down on a bench. The air was cool and clean. We did not speak, just listened to the rain and the sound of an occasional police siren. Nobody else was in the park. Nobody else was walking in the rain.

So, what do you think? he asked.

It's quiet here.

That's true. Even the streetcars are quiet. People get killed every year. They don't hear them coming.

You'd better warn me, then.

He smiled. Don't worry.

He took my wet hand in the rain.

THAT AFTERNOON the rain subsided, and we walked around his university town. He pointed out buildings and spoke of their histories. Nearly all of them dated from after the war.

This place was heavily bombed, he said. Almost everything you see is new.

My grandfather fought in the war, I said.

Christoph was silent for a moment, then said, Mine too. He was in the regular army. The Wehrmacht.

I nodded. We had never spoken about our grandfathers.

The Wehrmacht and the SS were different, he said. Everyone in the Wehrmacht was drafted. The SS, they were the elite soldiers, the Nazis. My grandfather was in the Wehrmacht.

We walked through a small, empty square. Suddenly he caught my arm and pulled me back as a tramcar moved silently past us, inches from our bodies.

See? he said. Everything here is quiet.

THE SUN BEGAN to shine, and we sat down at an outdoor café. He ordered two weissbiers, showed me how to pour mine into the tall glass and let the foam settle. Then he raised his glass.

Prost, he said.

Prost.

The beer was tart and refreshing, nothing like the warm, tasteless yellow liquid I'd drunk at keg parties.

Well? he said.

I like it.

Good.

We sat in silence for a moment.

You probably think he was a Nazi, Christoph said, setting down his glass. My grandfather.

No, I said. But of course, I did.

I'll tell you what I know, he said. My grandfather fought in the east. He was wounded near Minsk. This was after Stalingrad. You know about Stalingrad, yes?

A little.

Stalingrad was the worst battle of the war, the first real defeat for the Germans. Hitler ordered the Wehrmacht to fight to the death, but they surrendered. Almost all of them died. They froze or starved or died in the prison camps. The Red Army began to push back, after Stalingrad. My grandfather was stationed in Belarus then. There was fighting. The army left him for dead, and so he walked home through Poland and Slovakia. He remembered washing in a clear, blue lake, somewhere in a forest. It was early spring by then, and the air was beginning to thaw. This was in 1943. He stripped off his uniform and dove into the lake. When he told the story he always talked about that lake, how clear and blue it was. He said it was the first time he saw his reflection in two years. He vowed to join the resistance if he made it home alive.

And did he?

Yes.

I didn't know there was a German resistance.

Of course there was a German resistance. Christoph shrugged and drank his beer.

So he was a hero, your grandfather? I said.

No, I didn't say that.

My grandfather told me that when he was in Germany, in the war, he was wet and dirty and tired, I said. And afraid.

Christoph nodded, and I thought to myself how strange it was that our grandfathers had fought on opposite sides in the war. Had they encountered each other in the killing fields east of the Rhine?

Your roommates at Harvard, he said. Jess and Susie. They barely spoke to me.

They're Jewish.

I know, he said. Still, it's always the same with Americans. They see a German and think, Nazi.

I don't think that.

No, he said. Not you.

He leaned back and flashed that wide smile of his, the same one that had filled my heart at the airport. I felt sunlight warm my shoulders, and though I did not move, I felt my body rising toward his, like it had in his room, in the dark.

THE RAIN STARTED AGAIN and we walked home. It cast a gray pall over the town. We carried umbrellas but we were wet, tired from spending the day on our feet, a little drunk from the weissbier. I could tell he was glad to get back to his flat. I could tell he needed to be away from me for a while, as I needed to be away from him. He offered to cook dinner while I took a nap. I was jet-lagged. I said all right, surprised again at the thought of a man cooking for me.

I walked into his room, lay down on his bed, and stared up at the ceiling. I tried to concentrate on the whiteness of the room, the cool air coming through the open window, the soft warbling and wing flutters outside.

I thought about the first time I had seen Christoph. We had met through Josh, who knew us both. Josh and I were in a grunge band that played some of the local clubs in Cambridge. Sometimes I hung out in Josh's Lowell House room after crew practice, writing songs, jamming on my acoustic guitar. Josh, with his long hair and shy smile. Everyone thought he was a stoner, but he was acing organic chemistry and applying to medical school. I liked being with him because our friendship was based on the band. On music. I wasn't attracted to him, and he knew it and he didn't care.

Josh's family had hosted Christoph as an exchange student during his senior year at Bradfield, a Boston prep school. Christoph was visiting him that May, the week I was supposed to be studying. The first time Christoph saw me, I was onstage with the band, playing guitar and singing a Hole cover. I don't remember our first words, only that he approached me after the show, shook my hand, and started a conversation. I would never have approached him—he was too disarmingly handsome, with his lovely brown eyes and floppy gold hair. His beauty thrilled and troubled me.

After the show we went back to my room and talked all night, about Josh, Harvard, Germany. He said he tried to visit Josh at least once a year to keep his English up. He lay with me in my bed and we kissed for a long time. I wanted to sleep with him but he stopped me, gently, and said, Maybe when we know each other better. Then he laughed a little and said, We Germans have our principles.

In the morning he was quieter. By the time I got out of the shower and dressed, he was sitting on the couch in our common room reading *The Economist*. When he saw me, he put the magazine down and smiled. Shall we have breakfast? he said brightly. I was shocked to see him there. I had assumed he would be gone, out of my life forever.

We went to a local diner, a very American place he seemed to enjoy. He ordered pancakes and bacon and we drank several cups of coffee. We talked about the Russian Revolution, we talked about the Somme. After, we walked around Harvard Square. I took him down to the Radcliffe boathouse and we strolled together along the Charles. It was a warm spring day and the sun shimmered across the river in a rippling sheen. Rowing season was over, and I was glad. I wasn't used to so much free time and I wanted more of it. Christoph held my hand as we walked. A boy—a man—had never held my hand along a riverbank, and the gesture made me wild with hope. And that was how it all started, the blue hours listening to Rachmaninoff, the nights in my bed with the window open, and the moonlight, and the warm spring air.

When I told Josh what was going on, he said, Be careful. Then he picked up his guitar and started to play. That was the last time we spoke of Christoph. By then I did not care about the band, or even my exams. My mind would drift back to the blond boy lying on the mottled couch by the window, reading.

My roommates, Jess and Susie, avoided our common room when Christoph was there. They stayed in the library or sat outside in the

Kirkland House courtyard. Sometimes, when I looked out the window, I saw them lying on their stomachs, stretched out on a pink blanket, books and notebooks in disarray around them. I guessed they were talking about me, and Christoph, and how it was that they were suddenly sharing their suite with a German. I knew they were keeping their distance because of him. They avoided his eyes; they were always on their way out. When the door shut behind them, I wondered if I were somehow complicit, a conduit of the cataclysm's aftershocks.

We slept together the night before he left. He asked me if I was sure, and I said yes. By then I was very sure. He kissed me and I drew him close. I was not used to boys who waited and I was impatient for him.

He laughed. Slow down, he whispered.

Moonlight cut across our bodies.

I'm sorry. But Christoph—

Yes?

I really want to.

So do I. Let's not rush.

He was different from the others.

THAT NIGHT, Christoph, Matthias, and I packed into Christoph's black Jetta and drove to the outskirts of town, to a field pulsing with American and German hip-hop. We parked in a muddy lot and walked over to a makeshift bar under a large white tent. A deafening sound system pumped out "Return of the Mack."

Try some, Christoph said, as he handed me a white plastic cup filled with maroon juice. It's calimocho. Coke and red wine. They drink it in Spain.

I drank, dubious, but it was surprisingly good. I recalled that Christoph had spent a couple of summers in Barcelona learning Spanish.

He poured himself a drink and then wandered away from me, hollered greetings to friends halfway across the field and never looked back. I wondered if I should follow, but he didn't turn around to say, Come on. He walked straight ahead until he met the crowd. The sun had nearly set, but I could see him laughing and drinking, putting his arm around other girls. What was happening? Everyone around me was speaking German, and I was lost. I watched him dumbly until Matthias came over and asked me where Christoph had gone. He seemed surprised I was alone. I pointed to Christoph at the other end of the field.

Matthias put his hand over his forehead and scanned the crowd.

Ah yes, he said, I see him now. He looked back at me and smiled. You two met at Harvard, is that right?

I was struck, again, by his British accent.

Yes. He was visiting a friend of mine.

Matthias nodded, smiled, and snapped his fingers. Yes of course, I remember now. Josh, the friend he lived with in Boston. Christoph told me.

I thought he was lying.

Were you able to sleep this morning? he asked. You must be very jet-lagged.

No, but it's all right. I'm taking everything in.

He smiled. Of course. And what do you think of this disgusting concoction? He pointed to my plastic cup.

Oh, the cali . . .

Calimocho. I wish I didn't know.

It's not that bad.

You come all the way to Germany and your first drink is calimocho. He shook his head and smiled at me. Shameful!

I laughed. It's not my first drink. Christoph introduced me to weissbier this afternoon.

Good, he said. But let me get you something else. Wine? Beer?

I'd love a beer.

He took the plastic cup out of my hand, dumped the dark red liquid on the ground and said, Follow me. We walked over to the makeshift bar, where he pulled two cold, dark bottles of Franziskaner from a cooler. He opened one and handed it to me, then opened the other.

Prost, he said.

Prost.

We clinked our bottles and drank.

I could get used to this, I said.

Good! I don't know what Christoph was thinking, giving you that swill.

I looked out at the last place I had seen Christoph, but he wasn't there anymore.

He likes to wander, Matthias said quietly. Don't worry, he'll be back.

I nodded. I wish I spoke German, I said.

Oh there's no need. We all speak English.

You have an English accent.

So I've been told. I spent a few summers in London.

But Christoph's accent is American.

Yes? Well, that makes sense. It's hard for me to tell.

Just then Christoph returned with a small group. He began to introduce me as Matthias waved goodbye and receded into the background. I didn't want him to go. One by one, these new people shook my hand. The women all seemed to be wearing a version of the same uniform—khaki pants, white button-down shirts, silk scarves, and small gold hoop earrings. I had no idea why they had dressed up like that to stand in a field and drink beer. The young men wore short-sleeved polo shirts with the collars turned up. All of them had brilliant white smiles.

Christoph walked away again, said, I'll be right back, but I must have talked to his friends for an hour. They spoke English and asked polite questions. I was less aware of the time the more I drank. I began to laugh with them, to assume a familiarity. I looked for Matthias but couldn't find him. It was getting darker now. Christoph appeared at my side with a fresh drink every so often, but then wandered off again.

At some point, I left the group and walked back to Christoph's black Jetta. The door was locked so I sat down and leaned against the front wheel. I pulled my Discman out of my canvas purse and listened to U2's *War*.

I fell asleep. I was still jet-lagged. Suddenly I felt a hand on my shoulder. I snapped awake and saw Christoph crouched down in front of me. Small crowds were moving toward their cars in the dark.

I've been looking everywhere for you, he said.

I got tired.

I could see he was angry. But I was angry too.

Well you missed a good party, he said as he unlocked the car. Matthias and two girls climbed in. They left the front seat for me.

Shotgun, Matthias said. Isn't that what you say in America?

Christoph pulled out of the field and slid a CD into the stereo, German hip-hop again. It didn't sound right, the white voices, the wrong language. I suddenly missed my country.

Where are we going? I asked him.

What? he yelled above the music.

Where are we going now?

He kept his eyes on the dark road ahead.

Another party.

I'm tired. Can you drop me off back at your place?

Oh come on! He was playful now. He reached over and held my hand. Don't you want to experience the German party scene?

I thought I just did.

That wasn't a party. That was just a place to . . . what's the word . . . get a buzz? Come on. He squeezed my hand. Stay with me.

All right, I said. All right.

THE PARTY WAS at his *Verbindung*—his fencing club, he called it—in an old stone mansion outside town. The walls in the front room were decorated with hunting trophies, fencing swords, and medieval crests. Heavy-lidded young men lounged on couches, girls on their laps, drinking beer out of glass steins. They raised their steins at Christoph as we passed, and one of them said something about America. Christoph laughed, said *ja, ja*, and kept walking, his hand on my lower back. The place smelled of alcohol and reminded me of the Harvard finals clubs women weren't allowed to join.

He led me down to a cavernous basement with a high, arched ceiling. Striped flags with gold embroidery hung from stone walls, and brass candelabras glowed on wooden tables. Two young men wearing flat green caps and matching green jackets stood behind a bar and pulled beers for us as we approached. They looked like bellhops.

Our foxes are in for a rough night, Christoph said cheerfully, handing me a beer. No one leaves till he's been to the pope, he told the young men, who kept their eyes down.

What was that about? I asked as he led me away.

They're our foxes. Pledges, you call them. The pope is . . . never mind. He laughed. You don't want to know. Come.

He showed me around the old house, stopping to explain the significance of swords and trophies, portraits of men. We headed back down the grand stone staircase to the basement. I tried to take it all in, but I wanted to leave. He hadn't told me he was part of a fencing fraternity. This was something I didn't know about him. I was tired of smiling and meeting people and feeling the curious stares of his friends, wondering, Who is she? What is she to him? I did not know myself. I was beginning to feel disoriented with the beer coming steadily, the hall growing hot, the sound of German all around me. I knew not a word. I didn't see Matthias. I wondered where he'd gone. Someone cut the lights and soon it was so dark I could only make out the shadows of people dancing, touching each other. Christoph left me to go talk to someone. This time I did not mingle. I stood against a stone pillar and drank my beer. I had been drinking for a long time and I was tired.

I saw his silhouette walk toward me. He offered me another beer and I took it.

You didn't have to sit alone by the car, he said. I wanted you to meet people, have fun.

But you left me.

I thought you were right behind me. I turned around and you were gone.

Christoph, I don't speak German.

Everyone here speaks English. You don't need to . . . make yourself apart.

But I don't know anyone.

The music grew louder. Everyone was dancing. I could see their shadows. Christoph was now shouting over the thumping beat, but I couldn't hear him anymore.

I want to go back, I said.

What? He leaned closer.

I want to go back, I shouted.

He looked at me for a moment, then took my hand.

All right, he said. We'll go back.

WHEN WE GOT TO his flat, I undressed, threw on one of his T-shirts, and lay down on his bed. I lay there, while he was in the bathroom, and wondered what I was supposed to do now. Whether I should leave the next day, or stay. I didn't want to go. He hadn't done anything terrible. He had left me to fend for myself at a crowded party. But I wanted it to be like it was in Cambridge, when we had stayed in my bed for hours talking about Tristan Tzara, Kandinsky, the Prague Spring.

I heard the toilet flush, heard him open the bathroom door and walk down the short hallway. He came into the room and clicked off the light. I heard drawers open and shut. In a moment he was next to me in bed.

I waited for him to reach for me. But all I felt was his cool skin against my bare arm.

THE NEXT DAY the sun came out. Matthias was cheerful at breakfast, telling us stories about what had happened after we left the party. He assumed we had gone home early to be alone together. Christoph gave no hint to the contrary. Laughing, he slapped a pancake onto my plate.

Josh taught me how to make them, in America, he said.

I took a bite.

He stood over me. Well, how is it?

Good.

Ha! He clapped his hands together, energized, then poured more batter into the pan. He was talking quickly now, asking me questions about Josh, asking Matthias to give him more gossip about the party. His sullen mood had evaporated overnight.

What are you two doing today? Matthias asked.

We're going to Nuremberg, Christoph said. I'm going to give this American a history lesson.

I had not realized we were close to Nuremberg. I thought we would go to Munich or Heidelberg. Somewhere more picturesque. Nuremberg did not evoke sunny beer gardens and castles. It made me think of the war.

Nuremberg, Matthias said. Interesting choice.

I smiled and said nothing.

3

We did not speak much on the drive to Nuremberg. I was becoming tired of trying to understand Christoph's moods, tired of wishing we were back in Cambridge, where I was the one on home ground. I was too reliant on him here; I could not speak his language. Sometimes he would try to teach me German, simple phrases. *Entschuldigen Sie, bitte.* He made me say the words until I had them right. He seemed to enjoy these tutorials more than I did, for I had little interest in learning German. I could not seem to separate it from the Nazi barks I had heard in movies. I knew my resistance was ridiculous, that I had been manipulated by Hollywood, but those fricatives seemed harmful. I knew they could do harm.

I looked out the window at the passing landscape and suddenly wondered if my grandfather had traveled along this same road, or what was left of it, in the spring of 1945. How strange that he had been here, in Bavaria, half a century earlier. What had he seen as he marched toward Munich, toward Berchtesgaden? He had said the roads were empty, that everything was bombed. I imagined him in a brown-green transport truck with other soldiers seated grimly on opposite rows, their guns and canvas rucksacks at their feet. I looked at Christoph and realized he was about the age of the German soldiers my grandfather might have killed.

My grandfather's unit had been one of the first to arrive at Dachau in late April 1945. He was nineteen years old. No one in our family spoke of it and we all knew it was something we were not to bring up, ever. But in high school, for a history assignment, I found my courage and asked if I could interview him about the war. I was very nervous when I asked, aware of the magnitude of this favor. To my surprise, he said yes. By then he had mostly given up drinking. He had started drinking after the war. Always whiskey, or so I was told. I had never seen him take a drink because he always drank alone.

He sat back in his easy chair by the living room fireplace in the house north of Boston. He spoke to me about arriving at Camp Old Gold outside Le Havre in March 1945, moving on to Aachen, then a bombed-out Cologne. He remembered seeing wrecked planes in fields as his unit made its way east toward the Rhine. They crossed the Rhine at night, put pontoon bridges down. It was pitch-black and they worked in silence. It was very dangerous, he said, but they needed to take the river. The Germans were waiting for them on the other side, and there was fighting. He didn't talk much about it, whether he lost friends. But the Germans were on the run after that, he said. They no longer had the upper hand like they had in Normandy. They had lost strength, lost morale.

His unit went deeper into the Ruhr valley. He never saw a German civilian on the road. There was an eerie quiet as they passed through the bombed cities and villages. He assumed people were hiding, or dead. There were reports Hitler was raising an army in the south, and so his unit made its way down to Austria.

The GIs knew nothing about the camps, he said. Absolutely nothing. If the higher-ups knew, he said, they had kept it a secret. None of them were prepared for what they saw when they arrived at Dachau.

"Dachau, we were at the back of it. The front of it was in Munich. We were at the back of it. Dachau was a city. And all around it were houses. You can't tell me the Germans didn't know about what was happening. We saw the freight cars full of bodies, you know, sticking out. We didn't know what they did. When we were going in there, I see these two guys, they have on striped uniforms, you know, like they used to give them down south, for the chain gangs. And they were scared to death. We just looked at them, we didn't know what was happening. They stayed away from us and they hid. So we just kept going down the road until we found out there was another unit at Dachau, at the rear gate, and that's . . . when it was bad, you know."

"So you went to the rear gate and you opened it?"

"We didn't open it. Another unit had opened it. We just happened to stumble into it."

"So the guys in the chain gang uniforms, these were the Jewish prisoners?"

"Yeah, all . . . emaciated and fearful."

"They didn't know who you were, and you didn't know who they were."

"No."

"So how did you piece together what was happening to these people?"

"Stories started to come out, and the army started to find out about these places."

The trains, the freight cars, he said, were from Buchenwald.

After Dachau, his unit went south to Berchtesgaden. They kept us moving, he said. When they arrived at the Eagle's Nest, Hitler's alpine retreat, they walked in and it was empty. But someone had just left. He smelled perfume in the air. He took the Nazi flag that hung above the fireplace and a small lamp. Souvenirs, he said. His squad was small and they had the place to themselves.

He was in Austria for V-E Day. It was nothing like V-E Day in America, he said. No sailors kissing girls in Times Square. It was a quieter relief. They sent him to the Philippines then. He was on a troop ship in the Pacific when they dropped the bomb on Hiroshima.

When I interviewed my grandfather that day, he did not talk about the photographs he had taken at Dachau. But I know, now, what he saw.

A few days after my grandfather's funeral, my grandmother asked me to gather some of his old clothes in the attic for Goodwill. As I moved among the Christmas decorations and yellowing files, I saw a large cardboard box in a dark corner, its flaps open. It seemed orphaned. Curious, I knelt down beside it. Inside was a brown military jacket, neatly folded, with brass buttons. I knew it was my grandfather's. I knew he'd kept his things from the war in the attic. But I had never seen this before. I lifted the formal jacket, its spectral arms dangling. I could hardly believe it was fifty years old—it looked so clean and new. I wondered where he had worn it. Bars in Boston, girls swooning around him before he shipped out. On leave in Paris, walking down the Champs-Élysées with a bottle of champagne. But I had no idea. I was making it all up, his war.

As I folded the jacket, I saw something else in the box. A large, faded maroon album. I sat down in the dusty light and took the book in my hands.

I opened it up. There was my uncle in uniform, standing between an older man and woman in front of a three-decker house I didn't recognize. And then I realized this wasn't my uncle. This was my teenaged grandfather, and these were my great-grandparents. My grandfather was young. So young. I looked at the caption underneath—*Saying goodbye to Mom and Pop*—and recognized my great-aunt Maureen's handwriting from the birthday and Christmas cards she always sent. There were photos of my grandfather's friends, and two photos of a beautiful young woman with perfectly coiffed dark hair. In one she was sitting on the hood of a car in a knee-length dress, her legs outstretched. In the other she was in a bathing suit at the beach, lying on her stomach, eyes flirting, hands under her chin. This woman was not my grandmother. Underneath, my great-aunt had simply written, *Ruth*.

I turned the pages. There was a battered blue train ticket from Georgia to Oklahoma. A small pamphlet titled *A Camera Trip Through Camp Howze*. Two newspaper clippings from *The Boston Globe* about my grandfather's infantry division heading west. Photos of him with other uniformed men in a dry, hilly landscape, down on one knee, holding their rifles. Smiling, confident. There he was again, on top of a small mountain above those same undulating, treeless hills. *December 1944, San Luis Obispo*. Now he was on a ship, leaning against a rail, a book in his lowered hand, an expanse of ocean behind him. *Heading for France!* There were photos of men playing cards on deck, cigarettes dangling from their mouths. Men lying in undershirts on narrow bunks, dog tags hanging loosely around their necks. Men in uniform, a hundred of them, sitting shoulder to shoulder on deck, heads bent, reading letters. My grandfather, I saw, was a good photographer.

Then he was in a different landscape, posing with army buddies in front of canvas tents and long transport trucks. *March 1945, Camp Old Gold.* There were army schedules, a mimeographed camp newsletter, francs and deutschmarks, notices from General Melasky. A wide river with small supply boats. *The Rhine.* More photos of army trucks driving down dusty roads past ruined buildings. A photo of my grandfather and a teenaged boy in lederhosen, standing in front of a fountain, both of them smiling, at ease. Domed towers of a bombed-out church. Bomber planes in the sky. *April 1945, Munich—Almost Over!*

When I turned the next page, I startled to see a bright red armband embroidered with a black swastika. And underneath it, a smaller red-and-black armband that read *Deutscher Volkssturm Wehrmacht.* Two green badges decorated with gray eagles and black swastikas were stapled onto the bottom of the page. The edges of the badges were frayed, uneven, as if they had been torn off a uniform. On the mirroring page was a letter from General Melasky dated May 3, 1945, that began, *Deutschland Ist Kaput!* And below it, a small, square army pamphlet, *Special Orders for German-American Relations,* signed by General Bradley.

Never trust Germans, collectively or individually . . . The Germans have no regrets for the havoc they have wrought in the world . . . There will be attempts at proving that Nazism was never wanted by the "gentle and cultured" German people . . . We must bring home to the Germans that their support of Nazi leaders, their tolerance of racial hatreds and persecutions, and their unquestioning acceptance of the wanton aggressions on other nations, have earned for them the contempt and distrust of the civilized world . . . American soldiers must not associate with Germans . . . Give the Germans no chance to trick you into relaxing your guard.

I turned the page. Now there were photographs of a freight train. Old wooden boxcars, a long line of them, doors half-open. There was something inside. I looked closer.

I sat in the attic for a long time looking at those photos, one by one, slowly, deliberately. They were arranged in vertical rows, their corners tucked neatly into small red, white, and blue photo mounts. There were no captions, but I knew they were from Dachau. Three pages of photos, from different parts of the camp. Bodies. All bodies.

My hands shook as I closed the scrapbook and placed it back in the cardboard box where I had found it, under my grandfather's uniform. I was sure his sister had made the scrapbook. She had written the captions, lined up the photos, chosen those patriotic corner mounts. She had probably gone through his duffel bag when he came home from the war and gathered up the letters and armbands and badges. Washed and ironed his uniform. This was women's work, scrapbooking. Maybe she had even developed the photographs. Maybe my grandfather had never seen the scrapbook. But he had taken those pictures.

That afternoon, I walked down the stairs with a trash bag full of my grandfather's old clothes. I told no one what I had seen. For reasons I still don't understand, the scrapbook seemed like a secret I had to keep.

ALMOST THERE, Christoph said. You'll like Nuremberg. The cathedral is beautiful, one of the oldest in Germany.

I thought the whole city was destroyed during the war.

Most of it was. Not as bad as Dresden and Hamburg, though. You know about the firestorms, yes? Hundreds of thousands of people died. Women and children.

I know. I've read Vonnegut.

He nodded. It's actually a funny book, don't you think? He comes at it sideways. The horror of it, I mean. But later he said he was the only person to ever make money from what happened in Dresden. That he had made a few dollars for each person who died.

He already seems disgusted with himself at the beginning, I said. The part where he mocks his urge to write his own war story.

Yes.

I thought Hemingway did it better.

Hemingway?

A Farewell to Arms. The part where he writes about how the names of the villages had more dignity than words like *honor* and *glory*. I always think about that.

Shostakovich wrote a piece about Dresden, he said. Have you heard it?

No.

The Eighth Quartet. I'll play it for you.

I'd like that.

A lot of Americans don't know about Hamburg and Dresden, he said, his eyes on the road. They think we did . . . all the killing.

Well, you did most of it.

I don't know why I said this. I immediately regretted it.

I'm sorry, I said.

He was quiet for a moment, then said, Are you Jewish?

Christoph, my last name is O'Brien.

Well I don't know, he said, defensive. Maybe on your mother's side. I wondered. Because you live with two Jewish girls. And you look, maybe, Jewish.

I'm a little Italian, but I'm mostly Irish.

I wanted to ask you, back in Cambridge. I don't know why I didn't.

Would it have mattered?

Of course not.

We drove in silence for a few minutes.

Matthias fell in love with a Jewish girl in England, Christoph said, but it didn't work. She said it was because he was German.

Did he understand . . . eventually? I asked.

I don't know. He still talks about her. It upsets him. He felt . . . betrayed.

By who?

Ach, his grandparents. Germany.

His words had a finality about them, as if he shared the same thoughts and did not want to discuss the subject further. I was glad to let it go.

Wasn't Dürer from Nuremberg? I asked.

That's right. There's a museum here. We can go if you like.

Okay.

Is there anything else you want to see?

Could we go to the courthouse, the one where they held the trials?

Of course. I was planning on it. He looked at me and smiled, finally. It's all part of your history lesson.

We'll see the cathedral too, right?

Yes, and when we're too tired to walk around and admire the city we'll find a nice beer garden.

Wunderbar. I do like your weissbier.

He smiled again. Yes, I noticed. Your German education is coming along nicely.

I have a good teacher.

You do.

I laughed. Listen to you.

I *am* a good teacher, aren't I? So far you know how to prost, say a few words in German. You like German hip-hop, weissbier, you told me you liked Günter Grass . . . what else?

I like you.

He put his hand on my thigh.

I like you too.

WE ARRIVED IN the city a short time later and parked near the center. When I opened the car door I was surprised by the heat. Christoph locked the car and took my hand.

Come, he said.

He led me through a dark alley and suddenly we emerged into a large, sunny square bordered by medieval buildings and cafés. People tilted their heads back, laughing, as they lifted glasses to each other, or sat quietly alone with a book and a cigarette. Pigeons pecked at crumbs around them. I had never seen such a charming square with so many bright cafés and contented-looking people. Now I know that they are common throughout Germany, and I have seen lovelier squares. But this was my first encounter with a place so perfectly attuned to my expectations of Europe—the timber-framed houses leaning slightly forward, the narrow, cobblestone alleys, the waiters moving effortlessly between crowded tables with small silver trays. We stood in the center of a low, happy echo, laughter reverberating all around us. It was about noontime and the sun was directly overhead; there were no shadows, at least none that I could see. Everything was lit from above, the reds and yellows and greens of the café awnings intensified by the sun, their bright angles outlined against the cloudless blue sky. Light sparkled on the falling water of a nearby fountain, glinted off the metal coins thrown in for luck. Buskers stood on opposite sides of the square. One played the guitar, the other an accordion. People hovered around them, couples like us, holding hands.

Welcome to Nuremberg, Christoph said.

We sat down at a café and ordered two coffees. We drank slowly. I leaned back in my chair, closed my eyes, and felt the sun on my face. I opened my eyes and admired the shade of my bare arms, tanned golden brown from rowing. I had rowed all spring for the varsity team and my body was still strong and toned. For the first time in my life, I felt beautiful sitting there in the sun, with Christoph, at that café in Nuremberg. Maybe it had to do with the glamour of Europe, the brightness of the square, the rhythm of the fountain. I was outside my country, looking at myself from a different angle and admiring what I saw. I was startled by my own beauty. But I didn't need the moment just then. I had needed it the night before on that muddy field, or at the fencing club, or later in Christoph's bed, the two of us lying stiff and still, the cathedral bells tolling the hours through his open window. But the moment had not come to me then.

We finished our coffees and he paid the bill. When we stood up to leave, I moved gracefully out of my chair. I wondered how long this new sense of myself would last, how long I would feel in control of my movements, my words, him. For I felt, suddenly, that I belonged in this sunny European square with Christoph. It was all starting to seem more like destiny than chance. Maybe he noticed this shift too, for he stopped inside a little shop and bought me a pink chiffon scarf. He squared my shoulders with his hands, tied the scarf gently around my neck, then stood back and smiled.

Now you look like a German girl, he said.

He was right. I had noticed many women wearing elegant scarves.

I thought you liked my American style, I said.

What style?

Hey! I kicked his leg.

Here women dress up when they go out, he said. In America you wear jeans and baseball hats.

What's wrong with jeans and baseball hats? Isn't that a sexy look?

No!

I kicked him again, playfully.

You're a bit of a bastard, you know.

He smiled at me. I was enjoying this banter, happy he was in a good mood again. I thought I had ruined things on the drive. It was the same feeling I'd had the night before, lying in his bed after the party, waiting for him to touch me. I thought I had wrecked it all. But I hadn't. He was here with me now, wasn't he?

WE DECIDED TO VISIT Dürer's house first. It was in a pretty, quiet square bordered by half-timbered houses and restaurants. We opened the heavy door and stepped inside. For a few marks we could get a tour narrated by an actor in fifteenth-century costume, or we could look at the gallery for free. We decided to skip the tour and go straight to the gallery, up the creaking stairs as Mistress Dürer addressed an audience of Japanese tourists on the floor below.

The gallery was small but there were several etchings on loan from other museums in Germany. I did not know much about Dürer beyond the famous rabbit, and so I was surprised to see several darker works. *The Four Horsemen of the Apocalypse. Knight, Death, and the Devil. The Angel with the Key to the Bottomless Pit.* This last engraving intrigued me most. An angel with a large key stood in the foreground, trying to force a devilish creature into a pit. Two angels stood behind on a hill, looking down upon the scene. One pointed to a turreted city in the distance. I wondered if it was Nuremberg.

I stood a long time before it, even after Christoph had walked around the gallery, touched me on the shoulder and said, I'll be outside. I thought that maybe if I waited until the others left and I had the etching to myself, the meaning would become clear. But nothing appeared to me. There were no startling revelations, though I noticed a flock of black birds in the distance, flying away from the city toward the mountains.

As I turned to go, I read the placard next to the painting. It bore a passage from the Bible, printed in German and English:

And I saw an angel come down from heaven, having the key of the bottomless pit and a great chain in his hand.

And he laid hold on the dragon, that old serpent, which is the Devil, and Satan, and bound him a thousand years,

And cast him into the bottomless pit, and shut him up, and set a seal upon him, that he should deceive the nations no more, till the thousand years should be fulfilled: and after that he must be loosed a little season. (Rev. 20:1–3)

I left the gallery and walked outside, into the sun-filled square.

CHRISTOPH WAS SITTING on the museum steps, drinking from a bottle of water. I watched his Adam's apple as he swallowed.

How do you like Nuremberg's favorite son? he asked.

Fantastic.

That one you were looking at is usually in Karlsruhe. I've seen it at the Staatliche Kunsthalle. I like it too.

Is the city Nuremberg?

It's supposed to be Jerusalem, I think. All those woodcuts are out of Revelation. They were originally in a book called *The Apocalypse.*

Where's the rabbit?

Who knows. Come, let's have a beer.

He stood up and led me back to the main square, the *Hauptmarkt.* It was past lunchtime now. We sat down at a crowded café with a red awning. Christoph leaned back in his chair, looked down at the menu for a moment, then glanced back up at me.

Well, he said, his face bright, what would you like?

Something German.

Ha! He smiled. That can be arranged.

Christoph ordered, and the waiter brought us tall, elegant glasses of weissbier. After a few minutes he returned with two steaming plates of sausage, sauerkraut, and potatoes.

That's traditional *Nürnberger Bratwurst* with *Bratkartoffeln*. Try it, it's good.

Christoph, I can't eat all this.

Of course you can. What do you say in America? Supersize it? Well, here you go. He smiled, then picked up his fork and knife.

I began to eat. The sausages were delicious.

In the winter there's a big Christmas market here, he said. People come from all over. In December this whole square is full of stands selling ornaments, wooden toys, candles, lebkuchen, glühwein. He gave me a frank look. Mostly people come for the glühwein.

I've never had it.

You'll have to come back at Christmas. It's all part of your German education.

Does it snow here?

Of course. We're in Bavaria.

Do you ski?

Yes, but we go to Verbier, in Switzerland.

I had never heard of Verbier or lebkuchen or glühwein or Christmas markets. I was used to finding my own way, but Christoph sent my compass spinning.

I'm excited to see the Alps, I said, when I go to Switzerland.

Switzerland?

For the summer camp, where I'm working. Just a couple more days.

You've never seen the Alps?

No. This is my first time in Europe, remember?

Right.

Isn't Berchtesgaden in the Alps?

Yes, it's close to Austria.

My grandfather was there, during the war.

In Berchtesgaden?

Yes. He raided Hitler's summer house. That's what he always called it.

You mean the Kehlsteinhaus? The Eagle's Nest?

That's it.

Christoph laughed. Come on!

No, really, he did. He said that when they went inside they could still smell perfume in the air. The Nazis had just left. He took the flag that hung above the fireplace. I've seen it myself, a huge swastika. Bigger than—

I turned and saw a banner on one of the buildings that bordered the square. The banner read, "Nuremberg: City of Justice and Human Rights."

Almost as big as that banner, I said, pointing.

Christoph turned around, looked at the banner, then turned back to me.

You're telling me your grandfather captured the Eagle's Nest?

That's what he said.

And you've seen this flag?

Yes, he showed it to me.

I told Christoph the story. After I interviewed my grandfather about the war, he said he had something to show me, and led me up the stairs to the attic. I was nervous. I had never been in the attic. My grandmother had not allowed me and my cousins to play there as children. We'd trip and hurt ourselves, she said. Now I followed him up to the crowded, gloomy space and saw boxes everywhere. There were holiday decorations, mismatched dinner plates, limp dresses hooked on coatracks, empty suitcases. I could see why my grandmother had warned us away. There was barely any space to walk. But my grandfather knew where he was going.

After shuffling through some dusty debris, he found what he was looking for. Here it is, old girl, he said as he set an old square box down on the floor and lifted the lid. Carefully he took out the folded red cloth and asked me to grab a corner. I held it as he stepped away from me, and the flag unveiled itself between us. There it is, old girl, he said. Straight from the lion's den. He seemed to admire it. Not the flag itself, but the memory of capturing the flag. I think he was happy that this symbol had been reduced to such insignificance, that it was now rotting away in an attic north of Boston. Did he think he had tamed such power? I suppose if you had been nineteen years old and part of an American army unit that had seized the Eagle's Nest, you might imagine such a thing. You might. But I wrestled with this memory for years after, sometimes hating my grandfather for letting me touch the flag, other times hating myself for following him up to the attic. What had compelled me to view this unholy relic other than a morbid fascination with the power it had once commanded? For years after I had lurid nightmares in which my hand burst into flames when I touched the bloodred fabric.

Damn, Christoph said quietly when I finished the story.

My grandmother wants to burn it, but my grandfather made her promise she wouldn't. He said it's too valuable.

He's right. It should be in a museum.

You don't think she should burn it?

Of course not. We need to remember the Third Reich.

I looked out at the sunny square, the smiling young women with expensive scarves and gold earrings, designer purses on café tables. And the young men who sat opposite them, men who reminded me of Christoph in their easy confidence, the way they leaned back in their chairs and laughed, as if to say, The war?

You know, he said, we learn about the Holocaust from the time we're young. We have a word for it, this focus on our . . . past. *Vergangenheitsbewältigung*.

Say that again?

Vergangenheitsbewältigung.

I'd never heard a word so long or strange, and I was unsettled by the way it flew out of Christoph's mouth.

That's good, I said, that you learn about it in school.

Of course. But . . . This will sound . . . Please don't misunderstand me, but when something's all around you, it loses its force. It doesn't surprise . . . startle . . . it doesn't startle you anymore.

So remembering becomes a way of . . . forgetting?

No, that's not what I mean. Just that when someone else has done all the work for you, it frees you of responsibility. To remember.

He was quiet for a moment.

This is hard for me to explain, he said.

You're saying that if a historical event is remembered by the nation, then that absolves the individual from remembering?

Something like that. This country has made damn sure we don't forget what happened during the war. Last year was the fiftieth anniversary of the surrender. There were memorials . . . commemorations . . . all over Germany. There was a big exhibit about the Wehrmacht in Hamburg . . . about the atrocities it committed in the east. People were shocked. Because the Wehrmacht was the regular army. Not the SS. As I told you.

Yes, I remember.

But still, who really *talks* about it? Do you talk about Hiroshima with your friends? And listen, he whispered, leaning close, only fifty years ago this city was a wasteland of rubble and rats and rotting corpses. People who survived those bombings lived in the wreckage for months, with no electricity, no water. And now look around, a model of German order. It's as if it never happened.

He sat back, took a long drink, then set his beer down on the table.

You know, he continued, there was a big discussion here in the eighties about all this. Your president Reagan came over to Germany to lay a wreath on the graves of some Wehrmacht soldiers at a military cemetery in Bitburg, to commemorate the fortieth anniversary of the end of the war. But Waffen-SS soldiers were buried there too. There was a debate in all the newspapers. Elie Wiesel asked him not to go.

And did he?

In the end, yes. It surprised everyone. He even said the German soldiers buried there were as much victims of the Nazis as the Jews who died in the camps. Christoph shook his head. Unbelievable.

Do you think they were victims? Not the SS, I mean, but . . . the other soldiers. The ones in the regular army. Like your grandfather.

No. That's bullshit. But the visit wasn't about forgiveness. It was about the Cold War. America's way of sealing the alliance against the Russians. Anyone could see that.

He paused, then continued.

If I am honest, I will say that even I am tired of the debate, the question. Can we never look beyond the Third Reich? Can we remember nothing that came before, or after? He shrugged. But Nazism, fascism . . . I once read that it is like the . . . how do you say . . . the half-life of something radioactive. There is no point at which responsibility goes away. Reagan's visit was a farce.

It sounds like he was trying to remember to forget, like you said.

Look, this country has been to hell and back. You would think there would be some . . . wisdom that comes from such a journey. But I wonder. The historians are always coming up with reasons, justifications. How did Hitler gain power? The shame of Versailles. The stab in the back. Why did we murder the Jews? Because they sympathized with the Bolsheviks, they were a threat. Didn't you know that in 1939 Chaim Weizmann declared that all Jews would fight on the side of England? There's your answer. Why did we fight so fiercely in the east during the last days of the Reich? Because the Russians were advancing, they were raping our women. We are always looking for reasons. There must be some logic behind it all, yes? But there was no logic. It was hypnotism. That is the only way I can understand what happened here. I am aware my answer is no better than the others.

His hand shook as he lifted his beer. He drank, then set it back down.

Habermas says the Holocaust should be as fundamental to Germany's identity as it is to Israel's, he said. Have you read Habermas?

No.

He says our history must remain painful. And that even those born after the war are in a way responsible for it. He says that because we grew up in a society that supported the Nazis, we have the potential to fall back into that . . . abyss.

Do you believe that?

Yes. I do. We Germans . . . we must be careful. Do you know that when the Nazis built Buchenwald, they left Goethe's oak tree standing? The tree he wrote poetry under. They wouldn't cut it down when they cleared the forest to build the prison. There's a famous photo of it, in front of Buchenwald's barracks. For me . . . that is Germany.

I tried to imagine the photo he'd described.

A nation cannot survive without an identity, he continued. Okay. I understand this. But how do you build such a thing, after the war? It's no surprise the historians have tried to explain what happened in terms of politics rather than . . . mass delusion. But even if we say that what happened *was* the work of a madman and his hypnotized followers, well, that, too, is a kind of apology, yes? Either way, we avoid responsibility. That's what upset Habermas. We regard Auschwitz as an . . . aberration in German history. Or we look to Stalin, Pol Pot, and say we have only done what the others have done. Maybe that's too cynical. But I don't think so.

He was quiet for a moment.

I never talk like this with anyone, he said. Except you.

We talked like this in Cambridge.

We did.

I'll always listen.

He reached across the table and took my hand.

How did we end up here? he said.

My grandfather.

Ah, yes. And mine.

Isn't it strange to think about them . . .

Yes, he said. Let's not talk about it.

He let go of my hand and rubbed his face as if he were very tired. Then he looked up at me and smiled.

Do you like your bratwurst? he said.

Yes, very much.

Good. And the beer?

It's excellent.

We ate quietly as I thought about the things he had said, this strategy of remembering to forget. If the prosperity that surrounded me in this sunny Nuremberg square was the result of looking forward, why would anyone ever look back? What would compel a nation to resurrect memories of defeat and moral degradation when by burying those memories, by letting them rest quietly with the dead, that nation could—like Brueghel's ship—sail calmly on? The force of such questions bore down upon me like a heavy gust of wind that swept the lighter debris from my mind. But as luck would have it, the one thing that could resist that force happened to be sitting across from me, smiling, leaning back in his chair as if to say, The war?

AFTER LUNCH, we walked to the Frauenkirche. Before we entered, we paused at the Schöner Brunnen, an ornate, triangular fountain that looked like a church steeple. Christoph told me the fountain had been built as a spire centuries ago, but the townspeople of Nuremberg had kept it on the ground. Now tourists crowded around it, mesmerized by the cascading stream, the red and gold arches, the carved figures of knights and kings. When I asked Christoph why the Nurembergers had refused to put the spire atop the Frauenkirche, he said, It was too beautiful. They couldn't give it to God.

We left the fountain and made our way into the cathedral. I bent my head low as together we opened the heavy wooden door and stepped into the cool space. As my eyes adjusted to the darkness, I heard the sound of an organ from somewhere above. The notes lent a weight to the silence; the music made the air heavier. Tall stone pillars branched into great arches overhead. Above us, stained glass windows cast rays of light outward through the shadow. We walked slowly toward the golden altar and the tabernacle, past wrought iron chandeliers and rows of candles glowing low in small red glasses. Stone-bodied saints looked down on us, their cold hands cast in prayer. The church was nearly empty.

All of the art here is original, Christoph whispered. It was protected in wine cellars during the war.

What about the building?

Most of it was destroyed, but you would never know. They've reconstructed it. One of the kaisers built it to house his jewels.

Like a bank?

Actually there used to be a synagogue here. The church was built on its foundations. The *Hauptmarkt,* that main square outside? It used to be a Jewish quarter.

What happened to them?

The Jews? Probably they went east.

On my way out, I read a short history of the church, printed in German and English, framed by the doorway. It declared the Frauenkirche was built in the fourteenth century by the Holy Roman Emperor Karl IV and that it had been nearly destroyed during the war. There was nothing in the history about the old synagogue or the Jewish quarter.

Outside, we stopped to look at the blue-and-gold clock on the church's façade. It showed a king on his throne, Kaiser Karl, holding a scepter. The *Männleinlaufen,* Christoph called it. At noon, he said, everyone in the square stops to gaze up at the seven electors, dancing in circles round the king.

WE SAT ON the edge of a fountain and drank from our water bottles. Christoph was wearing a navy blue Red Sox T-shirt, and I let my eyes linger on his forearms. I thought back to last night, his arm against mine in his bed. How we had lain so still and stiff, barely touching. I had not slept well.

Now my body was becoming tired in the sun. I did not want to do any more sightseeing, I only wanted to sit there with Christoph on the edge of the fountain and watch people walk across the square. I was content to admire the bright awnings of the cafés and the white, half-timbered buildings. I was at ease with him here, sitting in silence. Again my mind turned back to our afternoons in Cambridge, the long days of open windows, the warm spring air. How close I had felt to him then.

We sat quietly for a few minutes, watching Japanese tourists feed the pigeons. It was the same group from the Dürer museum. I was hot, already sunburned.

He turned to me. Do you know the story of Kaspar Hauser? he asked.

No.

Really? It's quite a famous story.

Tell me.

Well, it all happened back in the 1800s. Someone found him standing near here with a letter in his hand. The letter was from a peasant, addressed to the local army captain, so that's where they took him. The peasant said someone had left Kaspar with him when he was a baby. He had kept Kaspar locked in a cellar but always made sure he had enough bread and water. The peasant apologized and said he hoped the officer would make Kaspar into a soldier. When the officer asked Kaspar if this was true, Kaspar spoke the only sentence he knew: *I want to be a horseman like my father.* That was all he said, all he could say. He had never known words, or the sun, or time.

He couldn't speak?

No.

Christoph told me the rest of the story: First they put Kaspar in jail, but the Nurembergers decided that was too cruel. A local family took him in, but he got to be a burden, and they wanted money. Eventually the townspeople adopted Kaspar and taught him to speak. It was the children, mostly, who taught him. They gave him lessons, made him recite nursery rhymes. He was a kind of pet to them. When he finally learned language, Kaspar told them he had never seen another person until the day he came out of the cellar. He remembered being dragged out of the dark room by someone, a man, he now knew, and fainting in the light. The man carried him into the mountains, and when darkness fell, he taught Kaspar to walk. Later Kaspar said he remembered seeing birds. He thought he could touch them, but when he reached into the sky all he grasped was air. He said that moment was the first time he formed a clear thought in his mind. How he'd wanted to touch the birds, the sky, the things that moved overhead. They camped out in the mountains until Kaspar could walk by himself. Then they walked to Nuremberg, where the man left him in the square.

Nobody knows who brought him out of the cellar, Christoph said. Imagine, all that time in darkness, without language.

What happened to him?

Eventually, a nobleman adopted him. And then one day he was stabbed.

Why?

Well, there's a theory that he looked just like the kaiser, that he was his heir. People said his aunt switched his body with the body of a dead peasant infant on the night he was born.

But why did they keep him in the cellar?

I don't know. None of it makes sense. He was probably an imposter.

Christoph finished the last of his water.

Time to see the courthouse, he said.

I don't know, Christoph. I'm getting tired.

He stood. Come on, up off your American ass.

He took my hand and pulled me toward him until we were standing face-to-face. He paused for a moment, and then, perhaps because we were so close, he kissed me. Behind us I heard the rhythm of falling water, the echo of laughing children.

I THOUGHT ABOUT Kaspar Hauser on the walk toward the courthouse, macabre and voyeuristic thoughts. What had it been like in the dark cellar, before he knew light or sound? What did he think about? Was he capable of thinking? How did he understand darkness if he had never known light? Did shapes have meaning? Did touch? He had known the void, but had not thought of it as such. Christoph told me that Kaspar Hauser never harmed anyone. Even when some of the local Nurembergers teased him with fire, poked his body with a candle, he did not fight back. The professors conferred. Did this not prove some inherent benevolence in human nature?

I was about to ask Christoph to tell me more about Kaspar Hauser when we turned a corner and approached a large stone building with three rows of high windows and a maroon slate roof.

Here it is, Christoph said. The Palace of Justice.

It seemed we had walked for miles. My legs were tired and I no longer wanted to see the courthouse. Now, with each step we took toward it, I wanted to pull Christoph back. But I followed.

We walked through a wrought iron gate and stepped under a low archway that led inside. A guard stopped us at the doorway and spoke to Christoph, who nodded, raised his hand, and said, *Danke.*

He says we're lucky. The room is usually closed but they opened it today. Something about a group of World War Two veterans.

Is there a tour . . . admission?

No. It's free.

I thought it would be a museum.

No, silly. It's still a courthouse.

There were no plaques on the wall, no commemorations. The interior had the clean, sterile feel of a government building. As we walked down the long, quiet hallways, I felt I could have been in any courthouse, in any country. But this was the courthouse of the world. If ever good had triumphed over evil in an official capacity, it was here, in this building. Maybe, I thought, there should be a marker. Maybe the place should have been turned into a museum. For how was anyone to learn what had happened here? I wanted to know the names of the lawyers and the judges and the SS men who were tried. Because like everybody else, I knew only bits and pieces of the story, images I had picked up from *Judgment at Nuremberg*. Now that I had come all this way, I wanted facts, and I couldn't find them. Only men and women in suits, carrying leather briefcases, nodding and smiling as they passed.

Why is it so quiet here? I said.

Christoph put his arm around my waist and whispered, Didn't I tell you? In Germany, everything is quiet.

Room 600 was in the east wing of the building. We could tell we were getting closer by the number of people who passed us from the other direction, all obviously tourists. There was a guard standing at the door, and a short line to enter. He told Christoph, in a whisper, that we must wait fifteen minutes until the group inside left. Then it would be our turn. And so we waited, corralled between two heavy red velvet ropes. In front of us was a group of older American men, all wearing navy blue hats with military insignia. They were laughing, bantering. I turned my back to them and faced Christoph. I wondered how they could be so jovial here.

Those must be the vets, he whispered. Americans.

Yes.

Just then a small group of tourists exited the room. They passed us in silence, looking straight ahead. The guard stepped away from the entrance and ushered us inside.

The group of vets hovered around their tour guide. Come, Christoph whispered, let's listen. But I led him away.

Don't you want to hear? he asked.

No. I want to experience it on my own.

He nodded. It was a reasonable answer, but it wasn't the truth. I did not want to be near the veterans. All day we had been around young people, couples, parents with children. And now this group of old men with their memories of the war. Perhaps they had killed Germans. Young German men, Christoph's age.

I sat down. My head was spinning.

Are you okay?

Yes, just tired. Jet lag.

He sat down next to me. I looked around the elegant room, set up like a church. Pews for the viewers, a wooden altar for the judge.

Christoph sat with his arms crossed, also in a daze. I wondered what he was thinking. But his presence was not enough to distract me from what had happened here, although I had no facts to aid my imagining. All I saw in my mind's eye was a man in a black suit sitting in the witness box, flanked by American MPs, giving curt answers to the prosecution. Pure Hollywood.

Christoph stirred, as if awakening.

Who was tried here? I asked.

Göring, Ribbentrop, Hess. Others too. I can't remember.

Where are the documents? The photographs?

I think everything is in the Holocaust Museum, in Washington. Have you been?

No.

It opened a few years ago. I've heard it's very good.

We sat in silence for a few more minutes. I had the strange feeling, again, that we were in a church, praying.

Soon the guard ushered us out of the room. This time the veterans were behind us. They were quiet now. There was no more laughter. I turned around and saw them walking, slow and silent, in single file down the hallway.

OUTSIDE, we stood in the sun for a moment, orienting ourselves. We began to walk toward the *Altstadt,* stopping along the way at a cart that sold souvenirs: Nuremberg T-shirts, lebkuchen, other trinkets. I saw a book displayed on a small stand. *Nuremberg Diary*.

Hold on, I said.

I picked up the book and read the back cover. It was an account of the trials, written by a famous American psychiatrist who had analyzed all the Nazi war criminals. I opened it at random.

LUNCH HOUR: There was a general letting off of steam as the defendants met and shook hands and talked for the first time since captivity, some for the first time in their lives. They ate lunch right in the courtroom after it was cleared, buzzing with released tension about all sorts of things from power politics to physical needs.

Ribbentrop was arguing with Hess but getting nowhere, since Hess has no recollection of the world events recounted in the Indictment. Ribbentrop then remarked to me, "Why all this fuss about breaking treaties? Did you ever read about the history of the British Empire? Why, it's full of broken treaties, oppression of minorities, mass murder, aggressive wars, and every-thing." I asked him whether the crimes of past history should be the accepted pattern for international law. "Well, no, but I thought that as long as the atomic bomb has made war too dangerous for nations to resort to, they will settle their differences peacefully in the future anyhow——."

Here Hess pricked up his ears. "Atomic bomb? What's that?"

"The atom-smashing bomb," Ribbentrop tried to explain.

"What does that mean?"

Ribbentrop launched into an explanation of the atomic bomb again, and asked Hess whether he really couldn't remember any of the things they were talking about today.

As I watched the others eat, several of them remarked that the food was getting better. "I suppose we'll get steak the day you hang us," von Schirach grinned.

Christoph peered over my shoulder.

Ah, the *Nuremberg Diary*.

He took the book out of my hand, paid for it, then gave it back to me.

A present, he said.

Thank you.

Bitte. It's all part of your German education.

I think I like it better than the scarf.

He smiled. You would.

What does that mean?

Just that you think about things. That's good.

But you don't approve of my fashion sense.

Come on, I was only joking.

He reached down and held my hand. I leaned into him. We were walking like lovers now, indistinguishable from the other young couples I had seen earlier in the *Hauptmarkt.*

I don't think we'll have time to see the Zeppelin Field, he said.

What's that?

The place where Hitler held the Nuremberg rallies. Book burnings, mass marches.

I think I've had enough of the Nazis for one day.

Maybe it's time for a beer, yes? Should we find a nice biergarten?

Absolutely.

He put his arms around me and drew me close.

HE KNEW A GOOD PLACE in the *Altstadt,* though he warned me it would be crowded. I didn't care. I was glad to be out of the courthouse. We turned a corner by the Frauenkirche and I thought again how the area had been a Jewish quarter in the fourteenth century. I asked Christoph if the destruction of the synagogue and the quarter had to do with the Plague.

Yes, he said. The Plague decimated the city. The Christians blamed the Jews. They burned them alive and stole their property. There were pogroms all over Germany.

Jesus. Are there any memorials?

Yes, but not to the Jews. Come.

He led me back the way we came to a small iron statue of a man holding bagpipes. It was the only statue I had seen in the city.

Christoph told me the story: One night, during the worst period of the Plague, when thousands were dying, this man got very drunk and passed out in a ditch. In the morning, a cart came round to collect the dead. The driver saw the piper in the ditch, thought he was dead, and loaded him into the cart. They dumped him in a pit with the day's dead, a mass grave.

When the piper finally awoke, he did not know where he was. He was under something and couldn't move. When he realized the shapes around him were bodies, he struggled to get free. This was difficult because he was deep down among the dead. Finally he climbed out of the pit and ran, kept running, until he came to a lake. He stripped off his clothes and dove. He stayed in the water for a long time, then walked, naked, back to town. People laughed when they saw him, but he didn't care. He went straight to his house, where his wife and children were waiting. They thought he had abandoned them, or died. They had even looked for his body in the pit. He told them what had happened and vowed never to drink again.

From that day on, the story went, the piper played music in the main square. People said it was a miracle he never caught the Plague. Years later, after the piper had died, they erected a statue in his honor.

Christoph and I stood before the statue for a moment, then walked on. I thought again how strange it was that this was the only statue I had seen in Nuremberg, this survivor escaped from the death pit.

WE FOUND SEATS in a sun-shadowed beer garden near the main square. There were long tables set under vined trellises, rows of happy people leaning back and coming close again in laughter. For a moment I stopped wondering what Christoph was thinking, how much he cared about me, what would happen next. All those dizzying questions that had been on my mind all day, loosening gravity, they all vanished. I was suddenly seized by the urge to describe him as he was, sitting there in the shade, his head tilted, his brown eyes roaming the crowd in search of a waitress. The way a shaft of sunlight hit his face, his neck, seemed important. I thought this is what artists must feel, this need to secure the moment. It mattered that we were here in a shaded beer garden, tired, a little sunburned, that this was the culmination of the day, the city, the things we had seen and not seen. I could hardly believe I was in Nuremberg with Christoph, that I had made this happen. It was a kind of awareness not unlike the moment, earlier in the day, when I had felt for the first time beautiful.

He ordered us two weissbiers and watched carefully as I tilted my glass and poured. When I finished, he smiled and gave me a thumbs-up, then poured his own. Around us there was the low murmur of conversation and laughter.

He lifted his glass.

Prost, he said.

Prost, I said.

We drank and set our glasses down.

Shit, he said, we forgot to send Josh a postcard.

We can get one on the way back.

Remind me.

For some reason, just then, I didn't want to send Josh a postcard.

You Germans like your beer, I said.

Yes we do. Especially here, in the south.

But you grew up in Hamburg. In the north.

I remembered this, from our time in Cambridge. Christoph and I had spent so much time talking about history that I barely knew his own story.

Yes, he said.

Tell me about your family.

He shrugged. My father works in finance, my mother raised us.

Tell me more about your grandfather, the one who joined the resistance. What was he like?

Christoph shrugged again. He laughed a lot. I think he enjoyed life, despite what he had been through. Or maybe because of it.

Is he still alive?

Opa Hans? No, he died a few years ago. He only talked about the war in the last year of his life. He told us about his walk back to Germany through the east, after Stalingrad. The lake. The story I told you.

I remember. What about your mother's father?

He was fifteen when the war ended. He was forced to fight in the last days of the war. Luckily the Americans got to his village before he died for the Nazis. My mother said he made friends with the American soldiers. He was smart and spoke a little English. My mother said he was very good with languages. I don't really remember him. He died in a car accident when I was young.

What was his name?

Wilhelm.

So he was an innocent, Wilhelm.

Yes, he was an innocent. My mother told me that one of the American officers had a box of books that the army sent out, novels and poems by American writers. But the GIs weren't interested in them. They just wanted to read comic books. My grandfather couldn't believe what was in those boxes. He wanted to read everything. An officer told him to take whatever he liked, so he did. We still have some of these books.

What happened to him?

He became a professor. Philosophy. He wrote books about free will. He spent time in America, actually. Fellowships and things like that, before my mother was born. He translated some German philosophy into English. My mother said he had a great affection for America.

So it's in the genes, I said.

He laughed a little. Maybe. This was his watch, actually.

I reached over and turned Christoph's wrist in my hands, gently. I touched the dark leather band, the off-white face with bold, black numbers. I'd admired the watch's retro style but hadn't examined it closely until now.

It doesn't look fifty years old, I said.

I take care of it. Replace the parts. It's all I have from him.

I nodded. And your mother's mother?

She came from the east at the end of the war. They were refugees. My mother, she's . . . hinted about terrible things that happened to my grandmother on that walk. They were trying to escape the Red Army.

I understood what he was trying to tell me.

What about your grandfather? he asked. What did he end up doing after he captured the Eagle's Nest? Hard to come down from that, no?

He went back to Boston and met my grandmother, then started a business. Asphalt. You know, for roads. The business did okay but it was hard work. Loud and dirty. My father worked there too, with his brothers.

So he became a businessman, your grandfather?

Not the way you think. He had a hard time after the war. He drank . . . he had nightmares. Sometimes he locked himself in his room for days with a bottle of whiskey. I never saw that side of him, though. I just heard the stories. He was there but not there, I think.

Christoph nodded.

He quit drinking when he was older, I said. There were some good years when he was sober. He never went to college but he was always reading. He wanted to have these big discussions with me, about history. The Cold War, Vietnam. He gave me books. He was proud that I went to Harvard.

Of course.

He died last year. He started drinking again.

I'm sorry, Christoph said.

I wish I had gotten to know him better. I wish I had asked him more about the war.

I wish that too. By the time I was curious, it was too late.

Yes. Same.

What about your other grandfather?

He was in the navy, in the Pacific.

Christoph nodded. Sometimes I think we are the last ones who will remember the stories of our grandparents, he said. It will all be too distant for the next generation. Our children.

A little thrill ran through my body. What did he mean, *our children*?

Yes, I said. We're already forgetting that the world almost ended fifty years ago.

We sat in silence for a moment.

It was good to come here, wasn't it? he said.

I nodded. It's a beautiful city. Not as I expected.

He looked around.

Yes, he said. You would never even know about the war.

WE STAYED AT the beer garden as the sun sank lower in the sky. Others at our table came and went. The sound of our voices grew louder, and we realized it was almost seven o'clock.

Damn, the postcard, Christoph said. All the shops will be shut now.

We'll get one later.

All right. But we can't forget.

No, we won't.

He paid the bill and we walked down a quiet, tree-lined street away from the *Altstadt*. It was cooler now. The sun was dropping, the air losing its weight and density as the heat subsided. We walked slowly, slower than we had all day.

I want to show you something, he said. A place I know.

He led me farther down the quiet street, then turned left through an ornate iron gate. Suddenly we were in a large courtyard full of bright red poppies, bordered on four sides by a white stone building.

It's a convent, he said.

I stood, silent, transfixed by the flowers.

My mother spent summers in a small town in the Alps, he said. Sonthofen. Not a town you'd expect to be bombed. But it was. She heard the stories, growing up. There was a small munitions factory and one of Hitler's Nazi schools. They must have been the target. But the pilots missed, or maybe they had the coordinates wrong. The only things they hit were the church and the old priest's house. After the war everyone said it was punishment from God.

What did your mother think?

I don't know. I haven't asked.

Well, what do you think?

I think it's very simple. They missed.

We stayed silent for a while.

I like this place, he said. It's quiet.

Where are the nuns?

Praying, probably.

We stood still for another moment. Then we turned away from the garden and walked toward the gate.

4

We drove west, toward the setting sun, past trees the color of sage, the blue night deepening around us. We were quiet, tired from our day of sightseeing and the weissbier we had drunk late in the afternoon. The rush of talk, of alcohol, had subsided; we were floating, now, in its wake. I felt lightheaded, pleased by the irresponsibility of motion. The world outside the car windows lost its form as land receded into sky and trees sank into shadow. I imagined the black limbs closing in, the road disappearing behind us.

We came upon a small village crossroads. Tall streetlamps glowed next to wide-roofed chalets, their windows adorned with flower boxes full of white and blue and pink blossoms. Two men in lederhosen stood under a streetlamp, talking. They stared at us as we drove past.

This is Lichendorf, Christoph said. Where my grandparents lived. My father's parents.

I did not know if the village was on our way back or if Christoph had diverted our course to get here. But it seemed part of the natural progression of the day, that as darkness came, he would take me to the place where history had begun for him. Perhaps this was the village his grandfather had returned to after his long journey through the forests of the east. Perhaps he had walked across these streets in the uniform he had taken off near the lake, before he broke his reflection into pieces as he dove.

We turned onto a steep dirt road, then drove uphill toward a large chalet. It was white with a dark brown roof that stretched out on both sides in a wide, inverted V. Soft yellow light streamed out of windows laden with flowers.

Christoph pulled into a small parking lot and turned off the car.

Let's stop for the night, he said.

All right.

We got out of the car and walked toward the chalet in silence.

I think you'll like this place. My grandparents met here.

Really? This story was becoming important to me.

They knew each other from the village, he said, but hadn't talked much until the night they met. This was before the war. My grandmother was out with her friends, and my grandfather was drinking beer with his brother. There was a band. He asked her to dance.

We were standing on a large terrace with long wooden tables, lit by strings of white lights set against the dark sky. Below us was the valley, black and formless. I could barely make out the hills on the other side.

There's a nice view during the day, he said. We'll eat breakfast out here tomorrow.

He turned toward the door. Before I followed, I took a last look at the vista, searching for some light or landmark that would put the valley into perspective. But I saw nothing.

Inside, we rang a cowbell on the front desk. An older woman emerged from a room behind and, with a perfunctory manner, asked us to write our names and addresses in the guest book.

Massachusetts, she said, looking down at my address, then back at me. You are American?

Yes.

Ah.

She turned to Christoph, her face softening, and spoke to him in German. He smiled and nodded. They talked for a little while, then she handed him a clunky iron key. She waved after us as we walked up the stairs.

That's crazy, he said. I haven't been here in years and she still remembers me.

What was she smiling about?

She asked if you were my wife. I said yes.

What? I laughed, astonished.

People are more conservative here in the countryside. It's better to lie than to be stranded.

But . . . we don't have rings. I was giddy.

He smiled and shrugged.

We walked up another flight of stairs and found our room. He unlocked the door and stepped aside with a sweeping gesture.

After you, he said.

The room was large but cozy, with cream-colored walls and heavy green curtains framing the windows. There was a four-poster bed and a wooden rocking chair with carvings of hearts and flowers. I looked out the window and saw that more stars had appeared since we left the terrace. The moon illuminated the valley from above. Now it was easier to see where the hills met the sky. I could gauge distance again.

I turned around and saw Christoph stretched out on the bed. His eyes were closed. I sat down next to him, and he put his hand on my back. Outside, laughter floated up from the terrace and through the open window.

He traced a shape on my back with his fingers.

What is it? he whispered, his eyes still closed.

I don't know.

Try to guess.

I can't.

He stopped. The warm summer air drifted in through the window. He slid his hand under my shirt. For a moment I startled from the shock of his cold touch. Then I felt his fingertips on my back, warmer, tracing the same shape.

Now do you know what it is?

No.

A door slammed in the hallway. Voices trailed down the stairs.

Concentrate.

I felt his finger running along my skin, up and down, back and forth. What . . . what is it?

Do I have to tell you?

Yes.

He pulled me closer.

Nothing, he said. It's nothing.

THAT NIGHT I DREAMED of Kaspar Hauser. I was in the audience at a circus, listening as he said, *I want to be horseman like my father.* I approached the stage and touched Kaspar's hand. He looked at me without expression, then repeated the sentence again.

I woke up to Christoph's body stirring against mine. He put his arm around me. I did not know if he was awake or asleep. And suddenly, apropos of nothing, I wondered what the end of history would look like. It would not look like Dürer's woodcuts, a scene out of Revelation. It would look like a city that had been destroyed and rebuilt, a city with no memorials to the dead. A lovely old market square built on the ruins of a Jewish quarter. An empty church built on the foundations of a synagogue. Or the last thought of someone killed in the war.

THE NEXT MORNING we ate a late breakfast outside on the terrace. The air was warm and dry, and the view much clearer now. I could see the hills on the other side of the valley and the river down below, a silver vein pulsing through the green land.

You were awake last night, Christoph said, setting his white coffee cup back in its saucer.

I had a dream about Kaspar Hauser.

Oh God, I'm giving you nightmares.

No. It just woke me up, that's all. I didn't know you were awake too.

Only for a little while. I could feel you moving around.

I reached across the table and took his hand.

Christoph.

He looked at me and smiled. What?

There was so much I wanted to say to him. He held my hand in his, tightening his grip.

Thank you for all of this, I said. I'm happy.

Good. He smiled. Now eat your breakfast. We have a long drive back but I want to take you somewhere before we go.

Where?

You'll see.

All right.

Christoph?

Yes?

Were they sitting out here, your grandparents, when they met?

Yes, I think so. I remember my grandfather saying they danced outside on a warm summer night.

I looked around the terrace at the well-dressed German couples eating their breakfasts. I could not see his grandparents dancing there. Though I tried.

CHRISTOPH DROVE OUT of town, turned onto a dirt road, and parked at the edge of a clearing. We got out of the car and he pointed to a path through the woods. When I asked him where we were going, he said, simply, Come. I followed him down the half-hidden path until we came upon the ruins of what looked like a small castle.

I used to play here when I was a child, he said as he climbed up one of the crumbling walls. A robber baron lived here in the sixteenth century. There were many wars . . . well, not wars. Skirmishes, I think, is the word.

I marveled, as I always did, at his command of English.

Come, he said. There's a view.

I climbed up as he reached out his hand and pulled me to the top of the stone wall. I felt dizzy as I bent down to sit beside him. I lowered my head for a moment and closed my eyes.

Are you all right? he asked.

Yes, just vertigo.

It passed, as I knew it would. I opened my eyes and saw green hills to the south and shadows of leaves on the ground. A soft, warm wind blew around us. We were both wearing shorts, and our bare legs dangled, side by side, over the wall.

Have you read *The Sorrows of Young Werther?* he asked.

No, but I remember one of my professors talking about it. He kills himself, right?

Yes. He falls in love with a woman, Charlotte, but she's engaged to someone else. So he shoots himself. Young men started killing themselves, for love, after it was published. They wanted to be like Werther. Some countries banned the book.

It inspired the Romantic poets, right?

Probably. Goethe was part of Sturm und Drang. Do you know it?

No.

It means storm and stress. Big emotions. I always think about Goethe when I come here, the old Germany of castles and robber barons. Duels and Werther. *Innerlichkeit*. He looked out at the hills.

I'm glad you showed me, I said.

I wanted you to see it. I've never showed anybody.

To my surprise, he took my hand, brought it to his lips, and kissed it.

So this was your secret place? I said, delighted. When you came to visit your grandparents?

Yes, before they moved to Hamburg. My grandfather showed me where it was. He used to play here as a child too.

The two of us sat in silence. I watched the green leaves flutter in the slight wind, felt Christoph's leg next to mine.

We should get going, he said after a while. We have a long drive back.

All right.

He jumped down onto the ground and held up his arms to catch me. I could have climbed down the wall by myself. But I was with Christoph, in a forest, in the ruins of a German castle. And so I stumbled into his arms and laughed as he caught me. He held me for a moment, then took my hand in his.

As we walked back through the woods, all light and shadow, I saw a rectangular concrete structure half buried in the low slope of a hill.

What's that?

Christoph stopped walking, put his hand above his eyes, and gazed out to where I was pointing.

A bunker, he said.

A bunker?

Yes.

A World War Two bunker?

Yes, there are a lot of them around the countryside.

Really?

He nodded.

We looked at it for another moment, then he turned away and started walking. I followed him in silence.

ON THE WAY BACK to his university town I fell asleep in the car. When we arrived, it was raining. Someone had taken Christoph's usual space, and so we parked far away from his flat. The rain soaked us as we ran to his building.

Matthias smiled when we walked into the kitchen. I was happy to see him. He looked relaxed there at the table, drinking coffee, reading a newspaper.

Well, how was it? he asked.

The important thing, Christoph said, dropping his backpack, is that she has learned to pour weissbier.

That *is* important, Matthias said. So you spent some time in the biergartens.

Oh yes, Christoph said.

And you saw the Frauenkirche, the Schöner Brunnen?

We saw everything, Christoph said.

Except the Zeppelin Field, I said.

Don't worry, Matthias said. You didn't miss much.

We spent the night in Lichendorf, Christoph said as he opened the refrigerator. I was too tired to drive back.

Lichendorf is lovely, Matthias said. Very Bavarian.

Yes, I said. It is . . . or seemed like. I laughed nervously, and Matthias smiled at me.

Christoph set a block of cheese and some bread on the table. He turned to me.

Coffee?

Please.

I watched him scoop four large spoonfuls of coffee beans into the grinder.

I'm drenched, I said. I'll be back in a minute.

I walked into Christoph's room and changed into dry clothes. I could hear the electric whine of the coffee grinder through the wall, and their voices, speaking quietly in German.

When I walked back into the kitchen, both of them stopped speaking and looked up at me, startled.

Matthias smiled and said, *Hallo.*

Sit, Christoph said. He set a white mug in front of me and poured coffee out of the cafetiere. I was still getting used to that cafetiere.

Milk? he asked.

Please.

Christoph poured a little milk into my coffee, then poured himself a cup and sat down next to me.

So, Matthias said, it sounds like you enjoyed yourself.

Yes, I said. Very much.

Please. He pushed the plate of bread and cheese toward me.

Danke, I said. Matthias smiled at me as I cut myself a thick slice of Gouda.

I have to go out, Christoph said, just for a little while. We're initiating some new members at the *Verbindung.*

The *Verbindung?* I asked.

The fencing club I took you to. It's . . . like a fraternity.

Except with duels, Matthias said.

Don't listen to him, Christoph said, smiling. He stood up, poured the rest of his coffee into the sink, and placed the mug in the small dishwasher. Then he leaned over, kissed the top of my head, and walked out of the kitchen.

Matthias asked me more questions about the trip, but I could not concentrate. I wondered why Christoph had left so abruptly.

When I finished my coffee, I left the kitchen and walked into his
room. He was sitting at his desk, talking on the phone. He looked up at
me, then shifted his eyes back to his desk. He was speaking quietly, as he
had with Matthias, laughing a little. He talked for a few more minutes,
then said *Tschüss!* and hung up.

He turned to face me.

When you go back to America will you send me a Yankees cap?

Sure.

I had one but I lost it.

He got up then and said, I'll be in the shower.

He grabbed a towel from his closet and left the room. I heard him turn
on the water, shut the bathroom door. I sat down in his chair, looked at
some notes he had written on scraps of paper. I opened the top drawer
of his desk and saw pens, pencils, paper clips, a pack of condoms. I suddenly wondered who else had slept with him in the bed behind me, how
many other girls had woken up in this room, how many mornings they
had taken showers in his bathroom and shared breakfast with him. It
upset me to think that they had spoken German with him, that I had
not, could not. The idea of them speaking the same language, with no
need for explanations or sightseeing, made me very jealous. There was
no need to talk about history because it was not something you talked
about. He said I was the only person he talked with like that. I had been
happy to hear him say it but now his words made me feel foolish. Who
spoke about the war with their lover, a war that had ended fifty years
ago?

I imagined him waking up with a girl in the bed behind me, saying
something to her in German. I imagined her laughing.

I shut the drawer and looked out the window. It was growing darker
but the lights of the surrounding buildings gave the evening a soft, somber glow.

Christoph opened the door and came back inside the room, a white
towel wrapped around his waist. I watched as he unwrapped the towel
and used it to dry off his body. I had never seen him or any man standing naked like this in the light. My gaze moved up his strong legs to
his thighs, his taut stomach, the faint outline of his abdomen, farther

up to his muscular arms and rounded shoulders and the line where his shoulders met his chest. I had run my finger along that line many times in Cambridge and had come to think of it as my own. I almost had to look away—he was so beautiful, and I didn't want him to see me staring. But he caught my eye, smiled, and whipped me playfully with the damp towel.

You'll wait up for me? he said.

His blond hair was still wet, uncombed. Water dripped over his eyelashes, down his cheeks.

You bet.

He whipped me again with the towel but this time I grabbed it and pulled him close. He kissed me and I leaned into him and wrapped my hands around his biceps. I wanted to feel his strength. I liked that he let me do this, that he was not embarrassed by his nakedness as he stood there, holding me. It was because he was European, I thought. And it was him and only him as the sky darkened outside his window and he placed his hand under my shirt and touched my lower back, lightly, with his fingertips, and I closed my eyes and thought that he could do anything to me, that I would not try to understand him but that this would be enough, if I could just have this, his fingers on my lower back, my hands on his bare arms, the two of us holding each other in the fading light, that if I could just have this I would give up everything, I would surrender whatever I was or was to be just to be his, his.

He pulled away from me and smiled.

Later, he said.

And then he was busy opening drawers, getting dressed. Dark gray trousers, crisp white oxford. He pulled his sleeves down and pressed two silver cuff links through his buttonholes. I watched him look in the mirror, lift his chin, flick his collar up, and knot a green tie around his neck. His movements were deft, assured, and I could tell he dressed like this often. He took a thin red-and-green sash out of a drawer and draped it across his chest, then combed his hair and slid his arms into his suit jacket.

Shit, I'm late, he said, as he strapped on his grandfather's watch. He sat down on the bed, tied his black dress shoes, stood up, grabbed his wallet from his desk, and slipped it into his back pocket. He turned to face me as he pulled his cuffs down over his wrists. The elegant, tailored suit lent him an unfamiliar gravitas. He looked closer to thirty than twenty, and I let my eyes linger, again, on his tall, lean frame. I went to him and adjusted his tie, ran my fingers down the length of his shirt. He caught my hand for a moment. I wanted to go with him. I wanted to be the woman who walked into rooms on this man's arm.

Well? he asked, turning to face me.

Smashing.

He smiled. I'll see you in a few hours, he said, and blew me a kiss. Be good.

The door shut with a gentle click. He said something to Matthias in German on his way out, then I heard the apartment door, opening and closing.

I fell onto Christoph's bed and looked out the window at the dark shape of the cathedral blackening against the night sky. Christ almighty. This was a force I had never known, not truly, and I immediately understood the destruction it would wreak. This was the force that had launched the thousand ships. Now I knew, and the knowledge was like a great wind rushing through my body. I had to brace myself, protect myself, but at the same time it propelled me and lifted me and I moved in its currents and it was hard to breathe and I wanted more of it, more of him. I was losing myself and I knew it and I didn't care. I didn't care.

AN HOUR PASSED. I rummaged through my backpack and found the book Christoph had bought me, the one by the American psychiatrist at Nuremberg. I began reading, though I could not concentrate on the words.

I heard a soft knock on the door.

Yes?

Matthias opened the door a crack and peered in.

Hallo? he said quietly.

Hi there.

Christoph won't be back until later so I thought I would take you to dinner, if you like? Just a small café around the corner.

That sounds nice.

He brought me my fleece jacket—I had left it on a chair in the kitchen—and we walked outside. There was a slight chill in the air. I turned my jacket collar up and I noticed he did the same.

The café was nearby, on a street parallel to Christoph's. We sat inside and Matthias said, A beer, yes? I nodded and he ordered, and soon the waitress brought us two weissbiers.

Shall I explain the menu? he asked.

Is there . . . salad?

Yes, but not what you think. I'm afraid it's potatoes and beetroot here. What about schnitzel? Have you tried it yet?

No.

Well then, he said, I suggest the schnitzel. It's very German.

Schnitzel it is.

He ordered and gave the menus back to the waitress.

So. He smiled. Christoph tells me you like Germany.

I do.

Good. There's not too much to see, but some things are interesting. Did he take you to Heidelberg yet?

No.

Oh you must tell him to take you. Heidelberg is lovely. There's a famous castle that overlooks the city, and a river. It's very nice in summer. They have a ball there . . . it's quite romantic.

I'd like to go.

Christoph doesn't like Heidelberg much, but he should take you. Matthias leaned in a little closer. And if he doesn't, I will.

I smiled at him.

Christoph is happy you're here, he said, leaning back. I know he can be . . . funny sometimes. But, he's glad.

When I met him in Cambridge he was very serious. Quiet.

Sometimes he can be serious, but usually, no. Christoph enjoys life too much to be serious.

So I shouldn't take him too seriously?

He gave me a small smile. I think he likes you very much.

I don't know.

He lifted his glass. Enjoy Germany. Drink lots of weissbier. Prost.

Prost, I said. We clinked our glasses.

I told him not to take you to Nuremberg. Heidelberg would have been better. But he insisted.

It was a lovely city, but—

The war.

It was everywhere.

And nowhere, he said.

I nodded. Don't you think it's strange there are so few museums there?

Museums are difficult in Germany. They want to open a museum about the war in Berlin, but nobody knows how to present National Socialism. And so, no museum.

Isn't there some kind of memorial in Nuremberg?

Yes. It's near the Zeppelin Field. It was made from dismantled weapons.

There's only one?

I think so, yes. He was quiet for a moment, then said, Maybe Christoph told you . . . I used to have a Jewish girlfriend. I met her in England, when I was studying there. But she refused to come to Germany.

Because of the war?

Yes.

I have a friend who's the same.

Yes, Christoph told me.

He did?

Yes. He knows I went through something like that. Not the same thing, of course. But he asked me about it.

And what did you tell him?

Not to let it come between you.

I nodded.

Now I'm with Saskia, who you met before.

I understood he was changing the subject.

Yes, I said, I met her at the field party, or whatever that was. In America we'd call that a tailgate.

It was a football party. Soccer, as you say. Christoph plays.

Oh. He didn't tell me.

There's not much to tell. It's just a local team. But he's good.

What else does Christoph do that I don't know about? I teased.

Well, he drives an ambulance.

An ambulance?

For his military service. You can do something like that instead of joining the army. The *Bundeswehr*. We all have to serve. The men, I mean. But you can choose, military or civilian.

I didn't think Germany had a real army, since the war.

You'll have to blame NATO.

Right, I said. And what did you choose?

I take care of a disabled boy. I help him get to school in the mornings. He's good fun, Stefan. Maybe you could meet him sometime. I doubt he's ever met an American.

I'd like that.

We were quiet for a moment.

So what did you mean about a duel, at Christoph's fencing club? I asked.

Oh, it's an old initiation rite. *Mensur,* they call it. It's a kind of sword fight. They all end up with scars on their face.

Scars?

Yes, small ones. Nowadays the duels are mostly ceremonial. But before the war the scars were important. They symbolized courage. Honor. Some students even let the wounds fester so the scars would be bigger. Nasty business, really. It was all very Prussian.

And you don't belong to the . . .

Verbindung. No.

He said nothing more. Just then the waitress came with our food and we ate for a while in companionable silence. I wanted to ask him more about his old girlfriend, and Christoph's *Verbindung,* but I didn't. Instead I asked him about his studies, and he told me he was finishing a degree in engineering. But let's not talk about that, he said. I want to hear about you. He had never been to America, and he asked me about Boston and New York. I told him about Cape Cod, where I spent summers at my grandparents' cottage on Stone Harbor, bunking with my cousins, waitressing at seaside restaurants, sailing Beetle Cats. Idyllic days. But as I spoke to Matthias of summer and all the things I had thought were the best parts of my life, they suddenly seemed formless. I wondered how I could go back to that easy happiness, those slow, meandering sails to the lighthouse, now that I knew.

When we left the café, it was raining.

I should have brought an umbrella for you, Matthias said.

It's okay.

He held his coat above me as we ran to the flat in the rain.

IT WAS PAST MIDNIGHT when Christoph returned. I was reading in his bed.

You're still up, he said.

I put the book down and smiled.

Just following orders, I said.

He looked at me with something like contempt.

Don't say that, he said.

Shit, I didn't . . .

Don't ever say that to me again. His voice had a sternness I had never heard.

No, I won't. I'm sorry.

He turned away from me, undressed, and hung his suit in the closet. He sat down on the edge of the bed. I put my hand on his bare back.

I'm sorry, I said. I'm an idiot.

You're hardly an idiot.

I wasn't thinking. It's just that you told me to wait up for you.

He moved closer.

What are you reading?

The book you bought me yesterday.

Ah, *Nuremberg Diary*. A German classic. A bit heavy, no?

Well, you left me here all alone. I whacked him gently on his shoulder with the book. What's a girl supposed to do?

I asked Matthias to take you to dinner.

He did.

Good.

Matthias is sweet.

He nodded.

How long have you two been friends?

Oh, years. We know each other from Hamburg.

We were quiet for a moment.

I'm interested in your history, I said.

It's your history too.

In a way. But not really.

He looked at his watch, yawned, and said, It's late.

How was the initiation?

He waved his hands. Oh, the usual. Lots of drinking and—how do you say?—male bonding. You wouldn't have enjoyed it.

Well, I learned a lot about you tonight.

Is that so?

Matthias told me about the duels.

Ach, they're not real duels.

And he said you drive an ambulance.

Yes. Otherwise I'd be in the Balkans.

Fighting?

Peacekeeping. But the Serbs don't like the Germans much.

He yawned again, stood up, shut off the light, and got under the duvet.

Good night, he said, and turned away from me.

I smelled perfume and cigarette smoke in his hair.

WHEN I AWOKE the next morning Christoph was already up, making breakfast. I took a shower, dressed, and got my things together in his bedroom. I walked into the kitchen. He was standing by the small counter in his white robe, pouring coffee into two mugs.

Good morning, he said brightly. You're dressed.

Yes. I have to go.

He stopped pouring the coffee and looked at me. Go where?

To Switzerland.

Why do you have to go to Switzerland?

I'm teaching English at a summer camp there. It starts soon. I told you.

You never told me that.

Yes, I did. Before I came, I told you. On the phone. And we talked about it in Nuremberg.

We did?

Yes.

I don't remember.

Well I told you. That's why I was able to come here, to see you. Did you think I flew all the way from America to spend three days with you?

He looked away from me and finished pouring the coffee. Then he placed the two white mugs on the table and sat down. I stayed standing.

You're angry with me, he said.

No.

Yes, you are.

It's not like it was in Cambridge.

He said nothing.

I shouldn't have come, I said, and to my immense embarrassment, I began to cry.

He stood up and held me.

I shouldn't have come, I said again.

In a low, quiet voice, he said, Of course you should have. I'm so happy you did.

It's not working. It was different in Cambridge and I don't know why.

Well, we've had fun. We've had some good conversations. I like talking with you more than any other girl. Being with you.

I wiped my eyes and backed away from him. The morning sun was shining through the window, and I could see shades of gold and copper in his hair.

Will you come back, after you finish at the camp? he asked.

I don't know, Christoph. I don't know if I should.

It felt like the most honest thing I had ever said.

Please come back, he said. I'll have more time for you in August. For us.

I closed my eyes and leaned into him. He held me tighter and rested his chin on the top of my head. We stayed like that for a long time until I said, All right, all right.

5

Wilhelm, April 1945

He heard the plane before he saw it, a terrifying drone from above. He was walking on the road to his post. The Mustang descended and came straight at him, firing as he launched his body into the trees. The strafing bullets hit the dirt road, a staccato blast. The plane banked left, and then it was quiet.

He sat up, dazed. The Mustang was gone. Slowly he crept back to the road. When he emerged from the woods, up the small embankment, he began to laugh, then shout. He ran back to his village, exhilarated to be alive, as if he had survived a battle. For he was a soldier now.

He had put on the uniform a month before. They would have shot him if he hadn't. He and his school friends were stationed ten miles outside the village in different positions. They were supposed to stop the Americans and the Russians, he and his school friends. He had just turned fifteen and knew what they were asking him to do was wrong. He knew the days of the Reich were numbered. Everyone knew the Americans and the Russians were closing in. It was a matter of who would get there first. He had hidden his civilian clothes in the woods for when the Americans came, or the Russians. He would be shot as a deserter if a German soldier saw him in civilian clothes, shot as an enemy if the Russians saw him in uniform. Everyone said the Americans did not shoot on sight. They all hoped it would be the Americans.

A WEEK AFTER the Mustang, he felt the earth trembling under his feet and knew it was a tank. He abandoned his post on the edge of the village and ran into the woods, to the spot where he had buried his civilian clothes. He dug them up, changed, and buried his uniform.

He stayed in the woods all night and listened to the procession of tanks and trucks rumbling down the road. He heard echoes of their laughter, their speech. Americans. He was relieved but he did not want to return to the village out of uniform. Not while there might be German soldiers there.

At daybreak, he started walking along the road. Trucks sped by him. The Americans seemed to be in a hurry. None of them stopped. He knew then that he looked like a boy.

Closer to the village, there were paper flyers spread out along the dirt road, fluttering in the light wind. He picked one up and read it.

The Werwolf Group of Upper Bavaria warns in advance all those who want to help the enemy, or threaten or deceive Germans and their families who remain loyal to Adolf Hitler. We warn you!

Traitors and criminals against the people will pay with their lives and the lives of their whole clan. Village communities who sin against the life of our people or show the white flag will suffer a devastating retribution sooner or later. Our revenge is deadly!

He knew about the Werwolf Oberbayern from the radio. They were all supposed to fight to the death now. He dropped the flyer on the ground and kept walking.

Back in the village, he stayed off the main road and took the side streets to his house. He saw no one. The door to his house was locked. He was terrified the Americans had taken his mother. His father and older brother were both in the army, in the east. He and his mother had not heard from them in almost two years. He knocked on the window, softly, then again, and saw his mother's face peer at him from behind the curtain. She ran to the door and opened it and embraced him. She did not let go for a long time.

Two American soldiers came to the house that day and asked them to surrender any weapons. He knew some English, and so he translated. His mother told them she had no weapons, which was true. We have no guns, he told the men in dark green uniforms. Both of them smiled when they heard him. Kid speaks English, one said to the other. Hey, kid, where'ja learn English? He told them he had learned a little in school. In school? they said. Here? He nodded. They looked surprised, but it was true. The Nazis had replaced French with English at all the schools. Where's your dad? they asked. He told the soldiers he hadn't seen his father in two years. The men nodded and looked at his mother, staring at the floor. They were quiet for a moment, then thanked her. One of them offered him a thin bar wrapped in metal foil. It's chocolate, the soldier said. Wilhelm took it. The soldiers smiled, gratified by their benevolence, and left.

After, he sat at the table with his mother. They unwrapped the chocolate bar, carefully, and broke off two pieces. They ate the chocolate in silence, then smiled at each other.

The soldiers did not come back. But his mother kept looking out the window, afraid to leave the house. He was not afraid. He had survived the Mustang, and he knew some English. The soldiers had not harmed them. They had tried to make peace with the chocolate bar.

In the late afternoon he ventured out to the village square. The Americans had made a bonfire near the old fountain. They were walking around with beer, laughing. Some were lying on the ground in front of the fire. Their uniforms were wrinkled and dirty. No one noticed him. He ventured closer and saw that several of them were reading thin books that looked like they were for children. They had small pictures inside, with cartoon characters. One of the soldiers looked up and saw him staring. The soldier smiled and handed him the book.

Bet you haven't seen one of these in a while, the soldier said.

Wilhelm took the book. On the cover, he saw Superman holding Hitler by the collar, dangling him in the air. He dropped the book to his side and looked around, but it was only American soldiers in the square. He raised the book back up and stared at the silly cartoon of Hitler, half the size of Superman. He looked around again to see if anyone was watching.

What is this? Wilhelm asked the soldier.

The soldier looked at him, surprised. You speak English?

A little.

It's a comic book, the soldier said. Don't you know Superman?

Wilhelm shrugged.

Shit, the soldier said. Keep it, kid.

Hey, Jack, the soldier yelled across the fountain. This kid speaks English. And get this—he's never seen a comic book.

A tall young soldier with light red hair and blue eyes walked over to Wilhelm.

You speak English?

A little.

The soldier reached out his hand. Wilhelm hesitated, then shook it.

I'm Jack. What's your name?

Wilhelm.

He nodded. Okay, Billy, we need an interpreter. Come with me.

Wilhelm followed the American into the town hall. It was the biggest building in the village. The mayor and the police and the civil servants had gone. No one had been in charge in weeks. Now there was an older American soldier in a crisp, clean uniform sitting behind the *Bürgermeister*'s desk.

Sir, Jack said, saluting him.

O'Brien.

Sir. This kid speaks English.

That right? We could use an interpreter, the officer said to Wilhelm. We lost our only German speaker.

I can help, Wilhelm said, surprising himself. He would later wonder where this confidence had come from.

Good, the officer said. He extended his hand. I'm Captain Wilson.

Wilhelm shook his hand.

I am Wilhelm.

Well, Wilhelm, I appreciate your help. We're not here to cause any trouble. We need you to explain that to your neighbors. We just need to make sure everyone surrenders their weapons and then we'll be on our way.

Wilhelm nodded.

Here, the Captain said. He leaned down behind his desk, then handed Wilhelm a box wrapped in thick brown paper. For your help, he said. Wilhelm took it.

Come by tomorrow morning, the Captain said. And, O'Brien.

Yes, sir.

You go with him. That's all.

Yes, sir.

Jack saluted, looked at Wilhelm, and nodded for him to follow.

Outside, in the thin spring sunlight, Jack said, Go ahead, open it.

Wilhelm looked at the package in his hands.

Here?

They were standing in front of the town hall. Wilhelm worried, suddenly, that the package was booby-trapped, some kind of bomb. But then Jack took out his pocketknife, cut the twine, and gave the package back to Wilhelm. He opened it slowly. The first thing he noticed was a can with a picture of a pineapple. He picked it up in disbelief.

Ever had one of those? Jack asked.

Wilhelm shook his head and put the can back in the package. There was sugar, coffee, powdered milk, aspirin, a handkerchief, antibiotic ointment, cigarettes, chocolate, canned meat, matches, toilet paper, cookies, and something he didn't recognize. He picked up the small box and read the label. Prophylactics.

Jack laughed. In case you get lucky.

Wilhelm had no idea what he meant or why he laughed.

There's more where that came from, Jack said. But we need your help, okay?

Wilhelm nodded. The two stood in silence for a moment. It was dusk, usually a quiet time in the square. The time, before the war, when fathers headed home from their day's work and mothers began preparing supper. But Wilhelm didn't want to go back to his quiet fatherless house, his lonely mother. He wanted to stay with Jack.

Well, Jack said. Guess I'll see you tomorrow. Come to the square at eight in the morning.

But . . . Wilhelm pointed to the clock on the town hall, stuck at the wrong time.

Jack unstrapped his watch.

Here. Use this. I can ask my buddies for the time.

Wilhelm took the watch carefully in his palm, felt the weight of it.

It's okay?

Yeah, just don't lose it.

I will not.

Jack looked at him again.

How old are you, Billy?

Sixteen.

Sure about that?

Wilhelm nodded.

And you never saw a comic book before?

Wilhelm shrugged.

Jack shook his head. Fucking Nazis. I'm surprised they didn't force you all into uniforms, throw you to the wolves.

Wilhelm said nothing.

Well, we won't be here too long, Jack said. I guess it's been hard.

Wilhelm looked down at his feet, his beat-up leather shoes.

They're living like savages in Cologne, Jack said. Living on rat meat. It seems better here. In the countryside. He looked around. Where is everyone?

In their houses.

Jack nodded. I understand. But we're not the bad guys. Your people started this thing.

They wanted us to fight, Wilhelm said.

Jack nodded, a little coldly.

They shoot us . . . if we do not fight.

Doesn't exactly inspire morale, that tactic, Jack said.

They are gone now.

Jack nodded. You grew up here?

Yes.

I'm from Boston, in Massachusetts. You know it?

Yes, he lied.

Jack looked around the quiet square. This place isn't so bad. Compared to Cologne. Holy shit. At least you still have houses, places to eat. They don't have any of that there.

Wilhelm did not want to hear about Cologne.

Say, Billy, when's the last time you had a beer?

Beer?

Come on.

Wilhelm followed Jack across the square and into the village's small café. The place was full of American soldiers getting drunk. Wilhelm knew the woman working behind the bar. Not well, but he knew her. She eyed him when he walked in.

Jack asked for two beers and gave her some German marks. Wilhelm knew the marks were almost worthless. He wondered why Jack bothered to give her anything. The Americans could take whatever they wanted.

Jack placed two glasses of beer on a small table in the back, away from the louder soldiers. They sat down and Jack pushed a beer toward Wilhelm.

Sláinte, Jack said, raising his glass.

Wilhelm raised his glass, warily, and drank. The beer was tart and refreshing.

This is the good stuff, right? Jack said, raising his glass again. It was all wine in France.

Jack took a long drink, then set down his beer. Wilhelm thought that the woman behind the bar would know, now, that he was working for the Americans. But he didn't care. The past months had been loneliness and fear and obeying orders from men who were ready to kill him. That was over. The Americans had ended it. The Americans had given him beer and chocolate and pineapples. A watch, even. He would work for the Americans.

A dark-haired soldier approached their table.

O'Brien, he said. Who's this?

Our new interpreter.

The soldier nodded and clinked his glass against Wilhelm's.

Hey, kid, can you point us to the Fräuleins? the soldier said.

Wilhelm went cold.

Jack laughed. You're such a gentleman, Riley.

Asking for a friend, the soldier said. And hey, maybe your buddy here can point us to the Nazis. 'Cause, see, nobody around here knows anything about Nazis. Or slave camps. He looked at Wilhelm. I don't suppose you're a Nazi.

Easy, Riley, Jack said.

The soldier gave them both a dark look, then walked back to the bar. The men were growing louder now. Wilhelm understood that the mood in the small, hot room was shifting.

Jack took a cigarette out of his pack and offered one to Wilhelm.

Thank you, but I need to go home.

Jack nodded. Mothers worry.

Yes.

See you tomorrow morning, then. Don't be late. Jack pointed his cigarette at him. Eight a.m. sharp.

Wilhelm nodded, then stood up. On his way out, the woman behind the bar leaned over and whispered something to him, but he couldn't hear. He leaned in closer, and she spat in his face.

He looked around. Nobody had noticed.

WHEN HE GOT HOME, he told his mother about everything that had happened to him that afternoon. He had figured out what the condoms were and hid them in his pocket before he showed her the package. Together they opened the tin of pineapples and ate the fragrant yellow rings with their hands as the sticky juice ran down their fingers, their wrists. They knew they were lucky the Americans had come and not the Russians. But the feeling of luck did not last long. His father and brother were still in the east.

.   .   .

THE NEXT MORNING Wilhelm arrived at the square five minutes before eight o'clock. He took Jack to the small, well-kept houses along the dirt roads at the edge of the village. Always the same conversation: Please surrender your weapons. The Americans are not here to hurt you, but you must surrender your weapons. Wilhelm knew many of these women and old men. Some were the mothers and grandfathers of his friends. They smiled when they saw him but tensed when they realized he was interpreting for the Americans. He didn't care. He was more afraid of German soldiers now than he was of the Americans.

He and Jack walked back to the square after they had checked all the houses on the village's perimeter and those a few miles beyond. Jack sat down with his back against the dry fountain and lit a cigarette. He offered one to Wilhelm and this time he took it. They heard birdsong in the gathering dusk.

Wilhelm slumped down next to Jack, knees to chest. Jack leaned over and lit his cigarette. Wilhelm coughed as he inhaled.

Nothing like the first, Jack said.

Wilhelm nodded, still coughing.

Jack looked straight ahead and took a long drag from his cigarette.

You won't be very popular around here when we leave, he said. You should come with us.

Come?

We need an interpreter. He took another drag. We'll pay you.

My mother . . . I can't leave her. But Wilhelm felt a surge of excitement. The same feeling he'd had after the Mustang.

Your mother will be okay. The war's almost over.

I will think about it.

Well, don't take too long. We head out tomorrow.

Where?

Farther south.

Wilhelm nodded, took another drag of the cigarette, and coughed.

Easy there, Jack said, stretching his legs out in front of him. Wilhelm tried again, and this time he breathed the smoke out slowly, like Jack. They sat in the cool air, smoking, as the light fell.

It's beautiful here, Jack said. Like a fairy tale. The hills and fields. Birds. Even the way you're dressed, all traditional. It's like the war just passed this place by. Christ, you should see Cologne. The whole city . . . just . . . rubble. He looked at Wilhelm. You're lucky, Billy.

There was that word again, Wilhelm thought.

When we took the city hall in Cologne, we found these . . . bodies. A family. All in their Sunday best, you know, sitting on a big leather couch. They were leaning on each other. We thought they were sleeping at first. But they were dead. Even the kids. They killed themselves. Jack took a drag of his cigarette. Must have taken something. Poison.

Many are afraid, Wilhelm said. The Nazis, they say we cannot surrender. They say the Americans will kill us.

Jack nodded. We figured that. But we haven't seen much resistance since we crossed the Danube. All your men are on the run.

Wilhelm thought about his father and his brother, in the east.

I must go home now, he said.

Yep, about that time. But hold on a minute. Jack reached into his green rucksack and pulled out a camera. He shouted at a passing soldier.

Hey, O'Donnell, do me a favor?

The soldier approached as Jack stood up and passed him the camera.

This is our new interpreter. Billy.

A little young, isn't he? the soldier said.

Nah, he's older than he looks. Right? Jack smiled at Wilhelm as he dropped his cigarette on the ground and stepped on it. Wilhelm stood up and did the same.

They turned to face the camera as Jack draped his arm lightly around Wilhelm's shoulders. Wilhelm knew people were watching through windows, but he didn't care.

Tits out, the soldier said.

Just take the picture, you dirty mick.

Takes one to know one, the soldier said, clicking the shutter. He smiled and gave the camera back to Jack.

Actually, I was looking for you. Captain got a box of books delivered. He told me to tell you.

Books? Jack said.

Yeah, from back home. He said you're the only one who'll read 'em.

Jack turned to Wilhelm. You like books, Billy?

Yes.

I figured. Let's go.

The two of them walked to the town hall, back into the old *Bürger-meister*'s office. Captain Wilson sat behind the desk. Jack stood at attention and saluted.

At ease, O'Brien.

Sir. O'Donnell said you wanted to see me.

Yes. Captain Wilson looked at Wilhelm.

This is our interpreter, sir, if you remember. He was very helpful today. I thought, maybe, he could join us.

Join us?

We need an interpreter, sir.

Wilson nodded, then gestured to a large open box in the corner of the room. Supply unit dropped this off, he said. We're supposed to distribute them, win hearts and minds. Thought I'd give you first dibs seeing as you're the only man in the company who can read. Wilson chuckled softly to himself.

Jack walked over to the box, knelt down, and peered inside. Wilhelm stayed where he was until Wilson said, Go on, son, have a look.

Wilhelm sorted through the titles. There were books by Ernest Hemingway, F. Scott Fitzgerald, William Faulkner, Henry David Thoreau, Ralph Waldo Emerson, John Steinbeck, Jack London, T. S. Eliot, Wallace Stevens, Robert Frost, and others. There were books in German too, by Thomas Mann and Franz Kafka. Wilhelm had never read these writers. He suspected the Nazis had banned them all, like the American comic books.

Jack whistled. What is this, Captain?

Like I said, hearts and minds.

Jack laughed. Through Wallace Stevens?

Wilson shrugged. Jack picked up *The Poetry of Robert Frost*.

Take them all, Wilson said.

I would if I could carry them.

Give them to the boy.

Jack lifted the box and handed it to Wilhelm.

Here, take this home, Jack said.

Yes?

Yes. They're yours now.

The box was heavy, its weight uneven. Wilhelm struggled with it for a moment.

Hold on, Jack said, adjusting the box in Wilhelm's arms. There, that's better.

Thank you, Wilhelm said.

You're welcome. We leave at sunup.

WILHELM AWOKE BEFORE sunrise and walked quickly to the village square. He heard birdsong as the darkness yielded to new spring light. The air was mild. Winter was turning. Soon he and his friends would play football in the fields, near the place where he had slept in the woods, hiding from tanks and soldiers. That already seemed like a long time ago.

When he reached the square, he saw the Americans packing gear into trucks, getting ready to head out. There was a briskness and an efficiency about them, but an easiness too. Some of the men whistled. One wrote *Kilroy was here* in black paint on the side of the fountain.

Jack was polishing his gun. He smiled when he saw Wilhelm.

You joining us? he asked.

Wilhelm shook his head. No. My mother . . . she does not want me to go. The war is not over.

It will be soon.

Wilhelm thought Jack was right. But so was his mother. It wasn't too late to die in the war.

You'll be safe here? Jack said. When we head out?

Yes. My mother will say you made me work for you. If I go with you, it is dangerous for her.

Jack nodded. You're a good son, Billy.

Wilhelm kicked the ground with his foot.

I wish to go with you.

It's okay. Keep your mom safe.

I wish to go to America, he said.

Jack smiled, surprised. Yeah? Look me up when you get to Boston. He took a small notebook and pencil out of his front pocket, wrote something down, then ripped out the page and gave it to Wilhelm.

Here. It's my address. I'll introduce you to some nice American girls.

Wilhelm folded the paper into a square and put it in his pocket. Then he unstrapped Jack's watch and handed it to him.

Keep it, Jack said.

No, Wilhelm said, shaking his head. It is too much.

You need it. Yours isn't working. Jack pointed to the stopped clock on the town hall.

Yes? You are sure?

I'm sure. And stay safe, okay? Don't do anything stupid. The war's almost over. Another week or two, they're saying. Your men have all given up. There's a rumor about a renegade army down in Berchtes-gaden. Der Führer's last stand. That's where we're headed.

Okay.

And don't run off with the Volkssturm. I wouldn't want to kill you.

Wilhelm stayed quiet.

I'm kidding, Billy. Jesus! Jack laughed.

Just then Captain Wilson drove into the square and stood up in his jeep. All right, boys, he said, rapping the windshield, let's kick the shit out of some Nazis so we can all go *home*! The GIs cheered.

I gotta go, Jack said as he put on his helmet and ammo belt and slung his rifle over his shoulder. Thanks for your help, with the interpreting. And be careful.

I will.

See you in Boston?

Okay, Wilhelm said, nodding. Yes.

Look me up when you get there. I'll show you around this time.

Jack lifted his rucksack, then tapped a cigarette out of his pack of Old Golds. He offered it to Wilhelm, who shook his head.

Smart man, Jack said. He lit the cigarette and took a long drag.

Thank you . . . for the books.

You better read them, Jack said, walking backward, pointing his cigarette at Wilhelm.

I will.

Jack gave a mock salute, then turned around and headed for the assembling men. They were marching to Munich.

I hope you are lucky, Wilhelm called out to Jack.

I hope so too, Jack shouted over his shoulder. And then, to himself, as he fell into line, I hope so too.

6

It was the most expensive boarding school in the world, the place where American rock stars and Middle Eastern sheikhs and Russian oligarchs sent their children to polish themselves with a European gloss. In summer it became the most expensive camp in the world. I did not know any of this when I found the address in a book of European summer camps and sent off my résumé. I had never heard of the school. Later, the other teachers told me that there was a lot of dirty money floating around, so much, they whispered, it could make you uncomfortable. They said I would laugh when the parents came to pick up their children on the last day, that the women would be wearing garish designer blouses and dripping with gold.

The school was on the shores of Lake Geneva, in the shadow of the Alps. The first time I saw the grounds I experienced the same feeling of alignment I had in Nuremberg when I came upon the main square—that what I found was exactly what I had set out to find. It was uncanny to see my vision of Switzerland so confirmed: the blue-white Alps rising above the lake's reflection, long white cumulus clouds floating ethereally over mountains and water. Everything seemed iridescent, ablaze, diamonds and crushed ice.

In the mornings I taught English to a class of twelve teenagers. They came from Spain, Turkey, Russia, Saudi Arabia, Brazil, Mexico, France. The students were, for the most part, spoiled. It was not uncommon to interrupt the class eight or nine times in an hour to stop them from talking or listening to their Walkmans. They made it clear this was supposed to be a summer camp, not a school, and so all but a few rebelled against the formality of their lessons. Their logic was irresistible. I was barely out of college, trying to see the world, so why should I strive for rigor when this was, after all, a summer camp? Perhaps I was simply a bad teacher. I called Jess and Susie, who had both worked at camps, but they didn't have much advice. I had no experience working with teenagers, and I am sure this fact contributed to my frustration and, finally, my indifference.

I quickly befriended a few of the other counselors: Otto, a German; Hannah, a Swede; Johann, Swiss; and Tristan, a Brit. At night, after we put the campers to bed, we met down by the lake. We'd light a bonfire, pass around beers. Sometimes we stayed out all night. We were capable of it. We'd go home at dawn, sleep for a couple of hours, then wake up to teach our English classes, bleary-eyed and groggy. Sometimes it was clear the teenagers had also been up all night. We did not ask them what they had been up to. Complicity kept us allied.

I became close to the other counselors. We partied together, spent our days off in Lausanne, piled into the school van and drove to the summer music festival in Nyon. Tristan was a sailor who captained the school's forty-foot yacht. He brought the campers on sailing trips to Geneva. At night, he took us sailing on the lake, though this was against the rules. He was English, as I've already mentioned, a few years older than me, with deep-set blue eyes and wavy, shoulder-length blond hair. We did not have much in common other than sailing, our love for the ocean. For me, this was enough. So when he sat down next to me on the bow of his boat one night and offered me a beer, I took it. When he kissed me a few moments later, I lay back on the teak deck and brought his full weight down upon my body. The wind was light. I looked up and saw the sail luffing lazily back and forth above our heads.

It was like that almost every night, sometimes on the deck of the boat, sometimes in the small cabin below, or sometimes in my room on the top floor of the dormitory. By that time I had the confidence to make such things happen. Once we woke up very early to the sound of thunder.

My windows were open and I could smell the summer rain, the freshly cut grass, and the wet earth. Tristan told stories about the sea, voyages around the Cape of Good Hope, where the waves were high as houses. He sailed rich people's yachts for them, brought them from port to port. Once, on watch off the coast of South Africa, he tied himself to the mast so he wouldn't fall overboard. When they landed in Cape Town, he blew his paycheck on champagne and drank until dawn, then sailed for Mauritius. He had a flat, he said, in Antibes. I didn't know if any of it was true. But he did not tell me about men locked in cellars, men who awoke in a pit of dead bodies.

When the camp ended, he said, he would leave for the Caribbean. He told me he had a girlfriend in the Dominican Republic. She was American and taught windsurfing at Cabarete Beach. He said I reminded him of her. He told me all of this on the boat during our last night. He thought we were friends, and he wanted to tell me the truth. But I had been sleeping with him for two weeks and I did not want to hear about his girlfriend who taught windsurfing at Cabarete Beach. I raised my voice at him, angry words that echoed across the lake. How hypocritical I was. I too was on my way to someone else, and I too had treated our time together as a lark. I had used him to distance myself from Christoph. Now I realized I had let myself go under, just a little. He said he was sorry, he thought we were having fun. He hadn't meant to hurt me. It was just summer. I stepped off the boat, onto the dock, and walked away.

When I looked back, he was standing on the deck, holding on to a halyard, watching me walk away from him.

THE NEXT DAY I said goodbye to the others and left for Gstaad. I wanted to go hiking. Also, Christoph was expecting me and I was determined to make him wait. He had called me only once at the camp. He talked about sunny weather and parties, his perpetual hangover and lack of sleep. The easiness of his voice concerned me. I heard nothing that suggested longing. There were no deep pauses, no questions. He said to call him when I arrived and he would pick me up at the station. We did not talk about how long I would stay. Before I hung up he asked me if I had met any nice Swiss men. I said no, but I'd met a lovely Englishman. He laughed and said, See you soon.

All I wanted to do was walk for as long and far as I could.

In Gstaad, I checked into a youth hostel in an old chalet. They gave me a small room with two bunk beds and a balcony overlooking the Alps. By some small miracle—it was late July—I had the room to myself. It seemed like a sign, like this was the right place to have come. The middle-aged woman who worked at the reception was friendly. A few young hikers came and went. No one asked me why I was there or where I was from. I was anonymous, as I wanted to be.

I stayed in Gstaad for a week. Every morning I walked to the mountain's base and ascended to the summit on the chair lift. I took a map and walked for miles through alpine meadows, fields of soft green grass and pink and yellow wildflowers. I was Julie Andrews, high above and far away from everyone and everything that I knew. Nobody could reach me. Nobody knew where I was. I thought that if I walked far enough I would stop hearing the sounds of the halyards clinking against Tristan's mast, or the cathedral bells outside Christoph's window.

But Tristan was gone, and Christoph was waiting for me at the end of a train ride. I pictured myself hurtling toward him, down a dark tunnel, under mountains. It all returned, the dull fear, the heady anticipation, the loss of breath. I wasn't sure it was a good idea to return to him. But I knew I would.

I walked during the day and ate at night in small restaurants. One evening I was the only patron in an Italian trattoria. The waiter was older, in his sixties, and spoke a little English. He smiled as he set my plate down in front of me and whispered, I too like to eat alone.

7

When I alighted from the train, it was night. I walked to the end of the platform and there was Christoph, holding a bouquet of red roses. I was astonished and confused. We had barely spoken for a month.

He smiled, took my hand, and gave me the roses.

For you, he said.

I tried to hide my shock. Thank you, I said, and kissed his cheek. They're beautiful.

He slung my backpack over his shoulder and held my hand as we walked down the busy platform.

So, how was it? he said.

Good.

I didn't want to say too much. I was afraid of shattering whatever spell had compelled him to meet me at the train station with roses.

He brushed my arm with his fingers. Wow, you're *really* tan.

I went hiking in Gstaad.

Gstaad is beautiful. Quiet.

Yes. I loved it.

We walked in silence.

I called you last week, I said, but you must have been out.

Why didn't you leave a message?

I don't know. I should have.

He said nothing but gripped my hand tighter. I knew then that I had been foolish to think I could forget him in Switzerland. Nothing else mattered but the pressure of his hand in mine.

Switzerland is very clean, he said. But boring.

That's not true. It's lovely and the people are kind.

And the teaching?

It was fine.

I didn't care anymore. I wanted him to know.

But I missed you, I said.

He put his arm around my waist and said, I missed you too.

I stopped walking and wrapped my arms around his neck, quickly and tightly, and buried my face in his shoulder. For a moment he stood still, surprised, but then he embraced me and leaned down and touched his head to mine. We stood like that for a few minutes as travelers walked around us. His body was warm and smelled faintly of cologne. I stroked the hair on the back of his head. My time with Tristan had made me bolder. The nights on his boat, his strong sailor's body. I had delighted in his attention, in an attachment that came without the threat of ruination and self-abandonment. I began to fear the specter of all that again as Christoph let go. But when I looked up at him, he was smiling.

We drove a short way to his flat. He carried my backpack inside and held open the door to his bedroom. It was a simple gesture, but it moved me. I wasn't barging into his life like I had in June. This time, he had asked me to come. He wanted me in his room, in his bed.

He set my backpack gently on the floor, then took my face in his hands and kissed me, urgently. I reached under his shirt and touched the cool skin of his chest. He put his arms around me and lowered me onto his bed with its blue duvet and I gripped the backs of his shoulders and pressed my forehead to his. We looked into each other's eyes and smiled. We had come back to each other. I was happy, perhaps happier than I had ever been. He pulled my shirt over my head as I loosened his belt. I leaned back on his pillow. My heart rose to him. He was all of me.

.　.　.

WE AWOKE THE NEXT MORNING to the sound of cathedral bells. It was already hot, and I was sweating. Christoph got up and opened the window. The sound grew louder.

Damn bells, he said.

I think they're beautiful.

He got back into bed and wrapped his arms around me.

You would, he teased. I was happy he had come back to bed.

So you missed me, I said.

I did, he said, stroking my arm. It was as if we were back in Cambridge. That sense of easy affection, maybe even love, had returned. He was the same boy who had waited up for me in my room those nights, reading Schopenhauer, while I finished studying at the library.

Ach, du, I said, touching his blond hair.

He smiled at me.

It's from a poem, I said.

A German poem?

No, a poem by Sylvia Plath.

I don't know it.

It's about her conflicted feelings for her father, who might have been a Nazi.

Hmm. He ran his fingers up and down my arm, lightly.

She says every woman adores a fascist, I said.

That's not true.

I know, but it's a great line.

I like that you read poetry, he said.

Do you? Read poetry?

A little. Not enough.

Who do you like?

Rilke. He pointed to a book on his bookshelf. *Briefe an einen jungen Dichter,* he said.

I startled at his German words. Even the title of Rilke's book sounded cold and hard and lonely in that language. Christoph, too, sounded different, like someone I didn't know at all.

Letters to a Young Poet?

Yes.

I didn't want him to say another word to me in German.

What about that one, I asked, pointing to the book next to Rilke. *Montauk*.

It's a novel, by Max Frisch. He's from Zurich.

Montauk? That's south of the Cape, where I go in the summer.

Yes. It's about a love affair he had with an American girl when he was visiting New York. It only lasted a weekend.

The whole book is about one weekend?

Yes. But it was important for him, this love affair.

What was she like?

He doesn't say much about her. It's mostly about him. His life, his regrets.

So she's just a prism he looks through, to see himself better.

Christoph considered this idea. More like a mirror, he said. But it's a good book.

I wondered if there were any books like that written by a woman, about a man. All I could think of was *The Awakening*, which we had read in American literature that year. The heroine fell in love with a younger man one summer while vacationing on an island off New Orleans. He loved her, but abandoned her in the end. She drowned herself in the sea.

Christoph propped himself up on his elbow and took a strand of my hair in his fingers.

Where shall I take you today? he said.

I smiled and shrugged. I was so very happy.

Maybe we should go somewhere literary, he said, like Jena. We had enough of the war in Nuremberg, yes?

I like history, I said.

I *know*. He smiled. My American girl and her history.

I was amused by the way he pronounced *American,* with four distinct, clipped syllables.

I almost studied history, he said. At university.

Why didn't you?

My father thought I should study something more practical. He's right. I can read history on my own. And anyway, architecture is a kind of history here.

I like talking about it, I said, with you.

About history?

Yes.

I smiled, and he kissed my forehead.

How far is Munich? I asked.

Munich isn't very literary.

I've heard it's beautiful.

It is. Good beer too.

Berlin?

He moved his head back and forth, considering it. You would like Berlin, but it's far. We'll save that for next time, yes?

All right. I smiled at him. Something had shifted while I was away in Switzerland. I hadn't been wrong to come back.

Where's the Black Forest? I asked.

Hmm. He thought about it. It's not so far, and the weather is good. Matthias thinks I should take you to Heidelberg, to see the castle. I suppose it's very romantic.

But?

The Nazis, they twisted all that.

Well, I vote for the Black Forest.

Then we'll go to the Black Forest, he said, and kissed me.

I'm glad I came back, I said.

Me too. He kissed me again, slower this time. No one had ever kissed me like Christoph, with such intent. I closed my eyes, felt his stubble on my cheek. I pressed my body to his.

You make me happy, I said, before I could stop myself.

He looked at me and smiled. Who was the English guy?

No one.

He held me tighter.

Good, he said.

I noticed a fine white line, barely visible, on his left temple. I ran my finger along it.

Is that from the duel?

He gave a small nod. I ran my finger along it again.

Suddenly the phone on his desk rang. I heard Matthias answer the other phone, on the same line, in the hallway.

Christoph? Matthias shouted through the closed door, then something else in German.

Nein, sag ihr dass ich nicht hier bin, Christoph said.

I understood *nicht hier*. I thought that *ihr* meant "her."

WE DROVE SOUTH on the Autobahn, his hand on my thigh, my eyes on his forearm as he shifted. I had brought my small flip book of CDs and pressed Radiohead's *The Bends* into the player. He turned it up.

Christoph drove very fast, accelerating, weaving in and out of lanes. Driving in this country was almost sensual, so different from the stop-and-go traffic on the Boston expressway. I was glad for him to take control of the car, the route. I would do whatever he said, go wherever he took me. I closed my eyes.

We were off the Autobahn in less than an hour. It was August, high summer. The sun shone through the green-leaf canopy of trees and made dappled shadows on the road. We climbed higher into the hills as the forest grew thicker, darker.

I can see why it's called the Black Forest, I said.

Well, the name comes from the mystery of it, he said. The things that happened inside it.

Witches and gingerbread.

He glanced at me and smiled. Yes.

We arrived in Freiburg, a smaller version of Nuremberg with its Gothic cathedral and pretty cobbled squares. Christoph wanted to take me to Schauinsland, a local mountain with a cable car to the top and good hiking trails. He said there was a tower at the summit where you could see all the way to Mont Blanc. This vista appealed to me—I remembered Shelley—and I told him I wanted to hike up and take the cable car down. We parked the car and got out.

I thought you might want to do it the other way round, he said. But okay.

I'm a rower, I said, and flexed my bicep.

He smiled and wrapped his hand around my upper arm. Not bad! he said.

I hadn't touched an oar in two months but my body was still fit. I didn't miss rowing. I was glad to be free of it, the endless hours on the water, the pain I leaned into each day. It was a kind of atonement, a way to subdue myself and my wild desires. Beating myself into exhaustion, quieting my grandiose thoughts. Now I was free of that intimate punishment, and I felt almost lightheaded. It was a luxury to spend my days walking in the Swiss Alps, or here, in the Black Forest, in the company of a man whose touch made me shiver. I never wanted to see the inside of a rowing shell again.

Christoph consulted an ordnance map, then folded it and put it in his backpack. We set off on a wide gravel path that grew steeper as we ascended above grassy velvet fields dotted by dark swaths of evergreens. Here, the hillsides sloped gently but the forest was dense. A forest one could get lost in. As we walked higher, the path narrowed, bordered on both sides by tall evergreens. It was still early, the air still cool. We saw no one.

About halfway up, we sat on a large rock that offered a sweeping view of the countryside. I leaned against Christoph as he put his arm around me. Before us were miles of light green meadows and rolling hills, dotted by farmhouses. I heard cowbells in the distance.

Gorgeous, I said.

Ja.

We sat for a long time, quiet in the wind. I felt protected with him there. The urge to punish myself, through rowing or casual sex or a thousand other ways, fell away. I knew I shouldn't need a man to make me feel whole, but I did. I needed Christoph. I let the unfamiliar feelings of peace and happiness wash over me as I sat with him on that rock looking out over the ancient hills of his country. I pulled him toward me and kissed him. He reached under my shirt.

Wait, I said. What if—

He took my hand then, and led me into the forest, away from the path. Do you know where you're going? I said. Yes, he said, pulling me quickly through the dark maze of trees. When we had gone some distance, he stopped and kissed me against the trunk of a towering evergreen, pressing his body into mine. I could feel the rough bark on my back as he placed his hand under my thigh and lifted it, slowly, against his hip. I reached under his shirt and touched his chest, encircled him with my arms, and pulled him close, so close I could hardly breathe. My back was hurting, pressed up against the bark, and I knew there would be bruises. We sank down together onto the forest floor.

But, I said.

Shh, he said. No one will see.

AFTER, WE LAY on the ground. I was still breathing heavily. I took Christoph's hand and put it on my chest and looked up at the dark trees that formed a spire overhead.

He laughed a little.

This is very German, he said, looking up at the sky.

What is?

Goethe. *Waldeinsamkeit*. He paused. It means "forest loneliness."

But we're not lonely.

Lonely in a good way. It's a feeling of . . . freedom. That your soul is free.

I was thinking more Hansel and Gretel, I said, touching his hair. Witches and gingerbread.

That too.

I hope we can find our way back.

Oh yes, he said. We will.

I gripped his hand tighter.

Christoph, I said.

Hmm?

I turned to him. He looked at me.

What? he said.

I smiled.

What? he said again.

I raised my eyebrows.

You mean . . .

It never happened before.

Really?

I nodded.

He kissed me and smiled, a little smugly. This makes me very happy, he said.

Me too.

So none of those American guys . . .

I laughed. No.

He stroked my cheek with the back of his finger.

Mein Schatz.

Forest loneliness. Freedom of soul. I looked up at the trees and felt that nothing would be the same for me again.

We should get going, he said, sitting up.

He drank from his water bottle, then handed it to me. I drank, dazed, and passed it back to him. I didn't want to go. I wanted to stay there on that mossy ground looking up into the high canopy, Christoph's hand on my heart. I already knew I would remember this day for the rest of my life.

How many of us mistake oblivion for transcendence?

AT THE SUMMIT, we ate brunch at a busy restaurant—ham and cheese and smoked salmon and muesli and pumpernickel. There were three different kinds of jam, butter I could spread with a knife, and strong coffee. We didn't say much to each other, but Christoph looked at me often and smiled. He asked me if I liked the food, told me the restaurant was famous for its Black Forest brunch. Everyone around us spoke German.

When we finished, we left and walked up a rocky trail, then up the eighty-five steps of the Schauinslandturm, a tower that offered a panoramic view of the countryside. I thought it looked like a guard tower, the kind that kept watch over a prison. But I said none of this to Christoph. I pretended to enjoy the view even though it was hazy. I couldn't see Mont Blanc.

We took the cable car down the mountain and saw several hikers, in miniature, walking up the winding path below.

It's good we came early, he said, and gave me a knowing smile.

I reached for his hand. Maybe he, too, would remember this day.

Look there, he said.

He pointed to something on a distant ledge, two stone pillars with a slab across the top.

What is it?

A monument, he said. There was a group of English schoolboys who lost their way here in the 1930s. They set out from Freiburg in shorts and sandals. People told their teacher bad weather was coming, but he didn't listen. He could barely read a map and he didn't know the countryside. They hit a snowstorm as they were ascending Schauinsland and lost their way. Some of the boys froze to death. A group went for help, to Hofsgrund, a little village over there. Christoph pointed to the east. The villagers rescued them, but five of the boys died.

Five?

Yes. It was the teacher's fault. He kept telling them to have courage, be manly. They were only about thirteen years old.

God.

And then Hitler, he saw an opportunity. He had some boys from the Hitler Youth escort the bodies back to Freiburg. Later they built that monument to them.

But England and Germany were enemies.

This was before Hitler annexed the Sudetenland. He turned the whole thing into . . . propaganda.

I thought about the English boys, shivering in the cold, freezing to death in their shorts and sandals. And I thought, too, about the German boys, commandeered by Hitler.

What happened to the teacher?

Nothing. They gave him a hero's welcome back in London.

I looked out at the heart-stopping vistas that seemed to hold us aloft. Then I looked back at the squat, ugly monument.

That, too, was very German.

·   ·   ·

LYING IN BED that night, the windows open, Christoph said, You should come back in December, when I'm off for the long vacation. I'll take you to the Christmas market.

Really?

You've never had glühwein, correct?

Never.

Well then. It's settled.

We were quiet for a moment. I was not surprised he had asked me to come back, not after what had happened in the forest.

He looked down at the strand of my hair in his fingers.

Actually, I'd like to take you to Hamburg, at Christmas. To meet my parents.

Okay, I said, my compass spinning. Do they speak English?

Of course.

Do they . . . know about me?

Yes.

We were lying on our sides, facing each other. I leaned into him and kissed his neck. He kissed my shoulder, wrapped his hands around my arms, and pulled me to him. Close, closer. I was above him now, my palms flat on his chest. In the moonlight I could see his brown eyes. They were completely focused on me. I spread my fingers wide across his skin and moved my hands down his torso. He breathed in sharply. Birds' wings flapped outside.

HE DROVE ME to the airport a few days later. He carried my backpack, walked me to the security gate as announcements in German and English echoed through the vast hall.

We'll see each other in December, he said.

That seems far away, I said, holding back tears.

It will go by fast.

You'll call?

Yes.

Why did you only call me once in Switzerland?

It's different now.

I reached for him and closed my eyes and held him tightly.

You should go, he said. You don't want to miss your flight.

I can't believe I won't see you for four months.

It will go by fast, he said again. I'll do all my studying so I have lots of time for you at the vacation. We'll see the Christmas market and you can meet my parents. They'll like you, he said, smiling.

I wish you could come to Massachusetts before then.

I can't, *Schatz*. I have exams.

I know.

He didn't ask me what I planned to do that fall, the dead time between my visits to Germany. I didn't know myself.

Goodbye, *Schatz*.

He kissed me, then stepped back and began to walk away. I held his hand until the last moment, until he let go.

8

Those four months did not pass quickly. I only wanted to go back to Germany, back to Christoph.

I lived on Cape Cod, rent-free, in my grandparents' cottage on Stone Harbor. They had bought it in the early 1950s, when the Cape was quiet and remote and beautifully desolate. It still felt that way in the winter. I had spent my teenage summers in that cottage, sleeping in basement bunk beds, sailing, partying with my cousins. It had been a kind of paradise for us, and we always retreated there in the cold weather when we were unhappy or broke. It was where I'd had some of my best talks with my grandfather before he died. The two of us often woke early and sat together at the dining room table overlooking the harbor. He never spoke of the war. He talked around it. Politics and power. JFK, FDR. Northern Ireland, the Catholic Church, Boston mayors, Chappaquiddick. He talked, I listened. I was content to listen. He sensed that I cared, and I did.

I got a job waitressing at a waterfront restaurant in Woods Hole, one of the few places in town open year-round. It was an easy, uncomplicated option. I'd worked there the summer before I graduated, and knew the table numbers and menu by heart. The restaurant sat on pilings next to a drawbridge that connected Eel Pond with Vineyard Sound. The drawbridge went up and down several times a day as sailboats motored out for late-season cruises to Hadley's Harbor and Martha's Vineyard.

I took on double shifts. Work distracted me. I was good at waitressing, and I enjoyed the banter with the cooks and the dishwashers. The
manager wasn't around much in the offseason, and we had the place to
ourselves. I ate all my meals there and busied myself with side work
when it got quiet. Regulars scared off by the summer crowds returned.
Some came in every morning for breakfast, and by October I was greet-
ing them by name. I tried to enjoy the season. I had always loved fall on
the Cape, how the light shifts, becomes thinner. The color of the water
changes to metallic blue, the beaches empty, and a quietness descends.
I wondered if I would still be there when the weather turned and ice
formed around the edges of the jetties.

Most of the people who ate at the restaurant worked at the Woods
Hole Oceanographic Institution. Engineers and marine biologists. Men.
They were kind and tipped well. I envied them their science and their
fixed paths. I wondered if I should become a marine biologist. Maybe
I could live in Woods Hole and smile kindly at waitresses as I planned
my next research trip on the *Knorr*. That was the boat that had found
the *Titanic*. It belonged to the Oceanographic Institution and was usually docked by the small park near the aquarium. Maybe I would work
on the *Knorr* and meet another marine biologist and we would do our
research together and marry and raise our children in a house by the
water in Woods Hole. But whenever I thought of Christoph, this fantasy dissolved. That fall I didn't even try to meet the gaze of a young
scientist who came to the restaurant often and smiled at me and tried to
make conversation. He wore flannel shirts and John Lennon glasses and
was, as I would have said then, cute. But I kept my eyes on the horizon.

In the mornings, before work, I sat on the deck and drank my coffee
with a blanket around my shoulders. I stared out at the empty harbor,
watched the wind ripple on the water, and I thought about this man
across the ocean that I tried not to love. I still had no idea what I meant
to Christoph. I wanted to ask him what was happening between us, what
we were, but I didn't. It was better, maybe, not to know. There was a
kind of defiance about me then, trying to forget Christoph but at the
same time not trying at all, lingering in the memory of him, the way he
would sometimes kiss me at a bar, then lean back and smile like it was

nothing, like he hadn't just parted the waters. Did he know what he meant to me? Did I want him to know? Sometimes he seemed to cherish me, but not the way I cherished him. He was a man, after all. I thought I would teach him tenderness.

This time he did call, once a week. On the phone he was quiet, serious. We talked about what was happening in the world, the books he was reading, the books I was reading. Sometimes we talked about the war. Once he said to me, that fall, You can't leave your house here without finding something that shocks you. I told him I had started to feel the same way in Germany, but I thought he was used to it. No, he said, I will never get used to it.

I began to wonder what I was doing as the days passed and it grew colder. Friends from Harvard were interning for literary magazines, but those internships were unpaid. I couldn't afford to live in New York or Boston without a salary. I knew I should have figured out a better plan during my senior year. I had been so busy with rowing, my thesis, the band. My parents, bewildered as I was about my future, had suggested law school. But I had no interest in the law. I had vague ideas of "writing," but I hadn't thought any of it through. He had come to me the week I was supposed to be studying.

All I knew was that I wanted to get back to Europe. The easiest way was graduate school. A professor had encouraged me to think about doing a PhD after my thesis won the English department's prize. She assured me there were scholarships. I had been ambivalent about the idea—I had grown bored of literary analysis—but now I felt a sudden sense of purpose. I wrote polite letters to my former professors and asked them for recommendations. They agreed, and I applied to Oxford.

When I told Christoph, tentatively, about my application, he said it was a good idea. He didn't say that studying at Oxford would bridge the distance between us. I never mentioned this fact either. But I was waiting for Christoph to decide my future. I would go to graduate school in England if it meant being closer to him. It was as good a plan as any, and I began to fantasize about spending weekends with him at Oxford. We'd go punting on the Isis, spend hours in bookstores, walk across misty meadows to country pubs.

At night I met up with friends at the Landfall or the Leeside. We sat at the bar and drank vodka tonics with lime. We knew everyone. Men hit on me but they mostly backed off when I told them to. I could hardly blame them for trying. I just wanted to drink and laugh and bask in the warmth of the bar. To prove my fidelity to an absent man who was content to let me go.

I woke up with hangovers more often than I should have. I worried I was drinking too much. Alcoholism ran in my family. And so I tried to be more careful. I went on long runs every day. Penance. My route stretched up through Alden's Neck to the Point, then back down to Stone Harbor. Boats were out of the water now, the air chillier each day. The late-season heat of September had dissipated. The light was changing too, losing its density as the coast tilted farther away from the sun. I wanted to show it all to Christoph, the long jetties and the rippled sandbars, the driftwood and sea grass and small, broken shells. The sandpipers dodging the waves as the tide came in, their tiny legs moving fast as hummingbird wings. I wanted to take him sailing, to the lighthouse.

Sometimes I ran all the way to Massaquoit, past the beach where I had sex for the first time, one drunken night I barely remembered. Warm beer and a bonfire and a summer boy. We'd hooked up a few times before that night and I thought he was my boyfriend. But nothing came of it, and he ignored me for the rest of that summer, and the summers after. A girl's story.

If I could run for an hour every day, I would be all right.

ONE NIGHT I RAN into Mike. I knew I'd see him eventually. We'd met the summer I turned nineteen and had been sleeping together, on and off, ever since. If I went to a party with friends and he was there, I always left with him. If I ended up at the Forecastle, where he tended bar, I'd order a drink and he'd ask me to wait until his shift ended. I knew he slept with other girls. But I was lonely and he was tall and good-looking with short dark hair and blue eyes and a wicked sense of humor. We laughed a lot in bed, often at someone else's expense. Sometimes he pretended to love me, but we both knew it wasn't true.

When I was a junior, I invited Mike to the spring formal at Harvard. He showed up looking smart in a rented tux, and downed Jell-O shots with us in our common room. He flirted with my roommates, who were charmed and intrigued by my summer romance. Mike had never come to see me at Harvard even though he was working as a bartender in Boston that year and taking classes at UMass. He was busy, he said. And so I was grateful he came to the spring formal as my date, my actual date, and thought maybe it was the beginning of something real. I had bought a little black dress that I hoped was sexy enough to hold his attention through the night. But when we got to the dance, he stood in a corner of the dark ballroom, silent and sullen, drinking Jack and Coke. In the morning he saw that his car had been towed, and we spent most of the day in Somerville trying to find it. He never visited me at Harvard again.

Now it was late October and a bunch of us were at my friend Jenn's house, on Herring Cove, playing Beirut at the Ping-Pong table she had set up in the living room. The house was perched on a ledge and had a sweeping view of the bay. But it was dark and all we could see were the red and green lights of the buoys offshore, and, farther away, the lighthouse beacon, circling and disappearing.

I saw Mike's black pickup truck pull up to the house, and braced myself.

Miiiike, the guys cheered as he entered the living room. He was wearing a baseball cap backward and already had a beer in hand. He walked right past me, and Jenn threw me a look.

I went into the kitchen to get a beer. I knew I should leave, but I had a buzz on and I was having fun with friends I hadn't seen in a while. I wasn't going to let Mike ruin my night. I took a Rolling Rock out of the refrigerator and looked around for a bottle opener. Suddenly I felt Mike's weight behind me, pushing me, slightly, against the counter. He reached up under my shirt and put his cold hand on my breast. Someone came into the kitchen, saw us, then abruptly turned around.

Stop it, I whispered over my shoulder.

What?

I'm with someone.

Yeah? Where is he?

Germany.

Germany? He laughed. What, some Harvard guy?

No.

I managed to turn around, but he put his hands on the counter, pinning me between his arms. He leaned into me, harder.

Stop it. I told you, I have a boyfriend.

He smirked, stepped back, and took a beer out of the refrigerator.

Like I'm your boyfriend? he said, and walked away.

MY HARVARD ROOMMATES, Jess and Susie, had been asking me to come to New York all fall. I didn't know New York City well. I had visited a couple of times and couldn't understand why everyone wanted to live there. I had grown up in Massachusetts, in a family with Boston roots, and so I had my suspicions about New York. It seemed loud and dirty and expensive. But I needed a break from the restaurant and the cold house on the harbor. Winters on the Cape were long. Mike would find out I was living at the cottage, start dropping by. I could see how it would all play out and I didn't like it. I knew Mike wasn't good for me. I didn't understand why I kept that door open. Jess, Susie, and New York City seemed to hold an answer to this problem of loneliness, the wrong man.

I took the Fung Wah bus from Boston and met them in Chinatown the weekend before Thanksgiving. Anna! You're here! Jess said as she hugged me. Susie hugged me too. Both of them were pretty and petite with long brown hair—Jess's lighter and straight, Susie's dark and wavy. Jess was wearing low-waisted jeans with a silky blue tank and ballet flats; Susie wore cutoffs, a tight black tee, and espadrilles. They always looked put together. They were not afraid of flaunting their figures, as I was. No heavy flannel shirts for them. I admired their physical confidence and their intellectual chutzpah. They were smart and industrious, and always spoke up boldly in class. They hadn't been afraid to debate the prep-school boys who dominated our seminar discussions. I had lived with Jess and Susie for four years, and they knew all my secrets, my bad habits. I trusted them. They could survey the landscape from a distance and see things I couldn't, whereas I always got too close.

As I hugged them, my black thoughts about Christoph and what would happen between us—boring, repetitive thoughts—ebbed away. I realized I should have come to see my friends sooner, much sooner. And yet I was troubled by the way they had treated Christoph.

We took the subway to their place in the East Village, a one-bedroom in a town house with hardwood floors and tall, wide windows. Susie and I flopped down on the maroon couch they'd picked up for free on a corner. Jess made screwdrivers. We talked about work—Jess was doing a master's in psychology at Columbia; Susie was interning at an environmental nonprofit—and the guys they were dating. There seemed to be an inexhaustible supply of good-looking, professional Jewish men in the city, and Jess and Susie were having the time of their lives. They informed me we would be meeting some of these men later that night at a bar in the West Village.

We'll hook you up! Susie said.

I shook my head.

Come on, Jess said. This thing with Christoph is going nowhere.

Not true, I said. I'm flying over there next month. He wants me to meet his parents.

His parents? Jess said. But you barely know him.

I shrugged. It feels serious.

Okay, Jess said. But wasn't he kind of a dick to you? That's what you said when we talked to you in Switzerland. He was all hot and cold and then he barely called you at that camp you were working at.

It's complicated.

What's complicated about being a dick? Jess said.

Well he was, a little bit. At first. But things got better when I came back from Switzerland.

They looked at me, skeptical.

We got closer, I said. It's hard to explain.

We're just trying to bring you into the fold, Jess said. Protect you from your own worst instincts.

It's weird you're dating a German guy, Susie said, sitting cross-legged on the couch. And now you're all flying to Germany to meet his German parents.

I know, I said. It's a little weird for me too.

What's it like there? Susie asked. In Germany?

I bet you don't meet a lot of Jews, Jess said.

I looked from Jess to Susie.

What was he doing over here again? Susie asked, ignoring Jess.

He went to Bradfield for a year and lived with Josh's family. Remember, he was visiting Josh in May?

Oh yeah, Susie said. He came to one of your gigs.

And then he moved into your room for a week, Jess said.

I shrugged and smiled. The memory of that week with Christoph still filled me with delight.

He's not an asshole, I said.

They both nodded seriously, then cracked up.

He's hot, Susie said, swirling the ice in her drink. I'll give you that.

For an Aryan, Jess said.

For a member of the master race, Susie chimed in.

They laughed again and I laughed a little too, but then I said, Come on, guys.

Seriously? Jess said. He's two generations from Auschwitz.

Christoph isn't anti-Semitic, I said.

Well, good for him, Jess said. Have you asked him what his grandfathers did in the war? Because I can guarantee it involved killing Jews, directly or indirectly.

I did ask. One of them was too young to join the army, and the other joined the resistance.

The White Rose? Jess said. That was only students.

I'm not sure.

Nazis didn't leave Hitler's army to join the White Rose, she said.

Maybe there was another group, I said. I don't know the whole story. Christoph said he was in the Wehrmacht, before he joined the resistance. That it was different from the Nazis.

Jess gave Susie a frustrated look, then turned back to me.

They were all the same, Jess said. Have you read *Hitler's Willing Executioners*? It just came out. Daniel Goldhagen. You should read it.

I will.

We sat in silence for a minute. Silence was unusual for us.

So there's no way we can hook you up tonight? Susie said.

No.

Why not? Jess said. Has Christoph committed to you?

Sort of.

That means no, she said flatly.

So all bets are off, Susie said. Come on, let's have fun tonight.

No. I don't want to be with anyone else.

Okay, I'll say it, Jess said, leaning forward. I don't have a good feeling about Christoph. And I'm usually right about these things. Let's face it, you have shitty judgment when it comes to men. I mean, Mike?

I know. But Christoph is different.

We'll see, she said. I'm not trying to be a bitch. I just don't want you to get hurt.

I know.

My bitchiness comes from a place of love. Plus he's too good-looking. I don't trust guys that handsome.

He's not arrogant.

Well, like I said, you barely know him.

I do know him.

You've spent a grand total of, what, two weeks together?

Yes, but they were . . . intense. Maybe the most intense of my life.

And he spent half that time being a dick, according to you.

Can we talk about something else? I laughed, trying to lighten the mood. Susie, help me out here.

Sorry, but I never thought you'd get involved with a German guy. It's messing with my head.

You two weren't very nice to him the week he stayed, I said.

Why should we be, Jess said. He's German.

I was nice, Susie said.

Not that nice, I said.

Well, I tried to be, Susie said. I mean, I know it's not his fault. That he's German.

Of course it's not his *fault*, Jess said, her voice rising. That's not what I'm saying. I'm talking about history. I'm talking about genocide.

I get that, Susie said, her voice low. You know practically my whole family died at Treblinka.

I know, Jess said, quieter.

I just think . . . Susie said.

What? Forgive and forget? That's what they want, the Germans.

You know that's not what I mean, Susie said.

Actually, I don't think that's true, I said. About the Germans. And forgetting.

They both turned to me.

Look, Jess said, Christoph made us uncomfortable. She glanced back at Susie, who stayed quiet.

I'm sorry, I said. I should have checked in with you guys about it.

Maybe you should have, Jess said. Just hearing his accent—

I get it.

No, you don't. You don't.

I'm sorry, I said again. Honestly, I am. But Christoph's not going anywhere.

It doesn't matter, Susie said. Come on, let's all chill out.

It does matter, I said, because I think I'm in love with him.

Jess sighed. Seriously? How can you know that? You hardly ever see him.

I just know.

I assume you haven't divulged this dark secret to Christoph.

No. Not yet.

Didn't think so.

Hold on, Susie said. Why are you flying back to Germany? Isn't it his turn to come here?

Yes, but he wants me to see the Christmas markets and meet his parents.

But it's his turn, Susie said again.

Don't you think it's a little strange he wants you to meet his parents, at Christmas? Jess said.

Why?

Because you barely know him.

But I do know him.

Just . . . be careful, Jess said. You have a pattern of letting guys walk all over you. We know of what we speak.

Christoph is different.

They looked at each other, dubious.

We'll see, Jess said again.

WHEN I GOT BACK to the Cape, I called Josh. He was living in Central Square, taking premed classes at Harvard. I hadn't spoken to him since graduation, and I missed him. I missed playing music with him.

He recognized my voice when he answered the phone. We talked about his classes, the humidity in Cambridge. I invited him to Falmouth. He said he might come. It wasn't as easy to talk to him as it had been during those afternoons when I was hanging out in his room, playing my guitar. Before I met Christoph.

I went to Germany, I said.

I heard. You should have sent me a postcard.

Sorry. We will next time.

You're going back?

Yeah, in December. Christoph didn't tell you?

Nope.

Huh.

Come to Cambridge, he said. We'll play some music.

I can't. I'm waitressing.

Why are you waitressing?

Because I need money.

Right, but . . . what's the plan? The real plan?

I applied to grad school. Oxford. I hear back in March.

You'll get in.

I don't know.

Get up here. We'll do a gig.

It's hard with my schedule at the restaurant.

Yada yada.

I'm serious. I do a ton of doubles.

I've been working on some new Evan Dando songs. Wanna listen?

Sure.

He set the phone down and played "Into Your Arms" perfectly.

That was awesome, I said.

Your turn.

Nah, I'm rusty.

Come on.

No, seriously, I'll sound like shit.

You better not stop playing.

Why would I stop playing?

You know why.

I don't.

Girls stop playing if their boyfriends don't play.

What? That's ridiculous. And anyway I don't even know if Christoph's . . . my boyfriend.

I told you before, you need to be careful.

So you said. Please elaborate.

It means what you think it means.

We talked a little longer but the easiness I usually felt with him had vanished. I said I had to go. I knew I would not go up to Cambridge to see him, to play music together. Nor would he come to see me. And I knew, too, that my guitar would stay in its case.

9

When I walked into the arrivals hall at Frankfurt Airport, I didn't see Christoph. I looked around, scanning the crowds, and began to grow angry. Then I felt his hands on my waist and I turned and it was him and he was smiling that wide, white smile and he put his arms around me and held me tight.

You're here, he said, not letting go.

I'm here, I said, my face in his neck. He held me and kissed me and then took my backpack. We left the busy terminal and walked out to his car. Walking next to him, his hand in mine, I felt that I had been rewarded for my fidelity. I had stayed true to my vision of myself as his and now the vision was real. It was not like after Switzerland, when I had come to him in the wake of Tristan, angry and unsure. This time I had kept myself pure for him, and I was glad. It meant so much to me, my fidelity.

In his car we sat quietly for a few minutes as he held my hand. I leaned my head back against the headrest. I had taken a night flight from Boston and hadn't slept. Somehow, it was morning.

Are you tired? he said.

A little.

You can sleep when we get to the flat.

Okay.

Thank you for coming.

Finally, I said, and squeezed his hand. But our time together was already dwindling. In a week he would drive me back to this airport and I would say goodbye again.

I wish you could stay longer, he said. I wish we could spend Christmas together.

So he felt it too, this vertiginous loneliness.

Next year, I said.

He smiled at me, a little sadly, then started the car and drove onto the Autobahn.

HALLO! MATTHIAS SAID when we walked into the flat. He gave me a small hug as Christoph put my backpack in his room. When he returned, Christoph pulled out a chair for me at the kitchen table and said, Let's get you some coffee. Matthias sat down as Christoph scooped coffee grounds into the cafetiere and filled the kettle, then rummaged in the refrigerator.

To think that you were in Boston yesterday, Matthias said.

I know, it's wild.

Something to eat? he said.

No thanks, I'm not hungry, I said.

Christoph set a plate with gouda and half a baguette on the table. Eat, he said.

Well, all right. Thanks.

They asked me about Cape Cod, the restaurant, the Oceanographic Institution and its ties to the U.S. Navy. I asked them about their classes and exams. They were both enrolled in graduate courses now. The kettle clicked, and Christoph poured the boiling water into the cafetiere. He washed a bunch of red grapes, placed them in a white bowl and set it on the table, along with butter, jam, spoons, and knives. Matthias asked if I wanted milk or sugar for my coffee. Christoph said, She just takes milk. Matthias opened the refrigerator and poured some milk from a glass bottle into a tiny silver pitcher. He handed it to me as Christoph poured coffee into our mugs. I smiled at them and said, *Danke*.

After a little while Matthias excused himself. Have fun in Hamburg! he said as he left. Enjoy the Christmas market!

Goodbye, Matthias, I said. I was sorry to see him go.

About Hamburg, Christoph said. I've booked seats for us on the train later this morning.

This morning?

Yes. I hope that's okay.

It's fine. I just didn't realize.

I know it's a lot of traveling for you. Why don't you rest before we go.

All right.

We got up and went into his bedroom. I lay down on his bed, suddenly very tired. He lay down next to me.

Do you want to sleep for an hour? he said quietly. He took a strand of my hair in his fingers.

I smiled at him. Do you? I said.

Only if you do.

Maybe later?

Maybe later? he repeated, laughing, tickling me. I laughed too and then he stopped, and kissed me, hard. We moved toward each other, narrowing the distance until there was no space between us.

BEFORE WE LEFT for the station, we sat on his bed and exchanged Christmas presents. I gave him a Yankees cap, a Black Dog T-shirt from Martha's Vineyard, Yeats's *Collected Poems,* and a mixtape I'd spent hours arranging—R.E.M., the Pixies, Blur, Oasis, Radiohead, Sinéad O'Connor, U2, Nirvana, the Lemonheads, Hole, the Breeders, Smashing Pumpkins, Elastica, Tori Amos. I also gave him a poem I'd written, a love poem. I gave all of this to him in a box I'd wrapped in red-and-green paper. He smiled as he held up the T-shirt, put on the cap. He looked boyish and American with his blond hair poking out from under the deep blue. I had bought the cap for him in New York City.

I was nervous about the poem. I had never given anything like that to a man before. He took it out of the envelope, unfolded it, and scanned it quickly.

I'll read this later, yes? he said. I nodded, relieved.

These are for you, he said, handing me two boxes wrapped perfectly in gold paper and thin green ribbon.

Did you wrap these yourself?

He laughed. No.

I untied the ribbon and opened the small box first. It was a bottle of Chanel N°5. I didn't really wear perfume, but I was thrilled by the glamour and romance of his gift. I smiled and thanked him, then opened the bigger box. Underneath the delicate cream-colored tissue paper was a small Burberry purse, the kind I'd seen young German women wearing. I knew it was expensive, and suddenly I was embarrassed about the T-shirt and baseball cap, the poems and the mixtape.

Christoph, it's too much.

He waved my complaint away and took the purse out of the box.

Show me, he said.

I stood up, slung the elegant purse over my shoulder, and posed for him as if I were on a catwalk. I thought he would laugh, but he didn't. He stared at me, and I enjoyed his gaze. He took the perfume out of the box, reached for my wrist, and sprayed on the Chanel. I rubbed my wrists together and stretched my arm toward him. He brought my wrist to his face and breathed in the scent. He had never acted this way around me and yet his gestures did not surprise me. I knew what he wanted me to do, and I did it.

There's one more, he said.

No, this is already too much.

He waved the air again as he opened his desk drawer and pulled out a rectangular green box. I opened it carefully. Inside was a thin strand of pearls.

Christoph.

He took the necklace out of the box, stood up, and walked behind me. I felt his fingers clasp the strand round my neck as I touched the cool, smooth pearls. I had never owned a piece of jewelry like this. Normally I wore the same pair of earrings every day, gold studs I'd gotten for my sixteenth birthday, and a Cape Cod bracelet. In summer, I wore cutoff jean shorts and T-shirts; in winter, ripped jeans and flannels and heavy wool sweaters. I bought most of my clothes at thrift shops. I enjoyed rummaging through the racks, hunting for bargains. But standing there, before Christoph, I felt transformed by that necklace. I didn't want to wear secondhand clothes anymore. Not for him.

Do you have a dress for tonight? he asked.

I nodded and turned to face him. He had told me, over the phone, to bring a dress for dinner with his parents.

Good, he said.

I smiled as he hooked two fingers under the pearls and pulled me toward him.

LATER THAT MORNING we went to the *Bahnhof* and boarded a high-speed train to Hamburg. He had paid for my ticket over my protests. I had never been on such a train before. I was used to the lumbering, fetid commuter rail north of Boston. This was something else entirely. The compartment was light and modern, the smooth seats clean and comfortable, the passengers well-dressed and quiet. Even the children spoke softly. We pulled out of the station and the train began to accelerate. It barely made a sound.

It will take about four hours to Hamburg, Christoph said. I was happy about this, excited by the prospect of sitting with him for so long. I thought maybe he would tell me about his childhood, his family. But instead he took *The Economist* out of his leather satchel and began to read. I took Milan Kundera's *The Unbearable Lightness of Being* out of my canvas purse. I had started it on the plane, wondering if I was Sabina or Tereza. But now I couldn't focus on the words, not with Christoph so close to me, our shoulders almost touching. When he finished reading *The Economist,* he took a book out of his bag, something technical for one of his architecture courses. I fell asleep.

He woke me later, tapped me gently on the shoulder and told me he was going to the dining car. He brought back two coffees. I was in the aisle seat, and this time, when he sat down, he leaned against me so that he was facing the window slightly. I put my head on his shoulder. I wondered if he'd read my poem.

I've been reading Habermas, I said. I didn't know he was Adorno's research assistant.

Yes. Adorno was a big influence. What did you read?

The Past as Future.

He nodded.

I bought it in New York when I was visiting Jess and Susie.

Ah, Jess and Susie, he said. How are they?

They're fine.

Have they told you to break up with me yet?

Break up? I said. I wasn't sure he knew what those words meant, whether the phrase had been lost in translation. I wanted him to understand exactly what he was saying.

I had the feeling they don't want us to be together, he said. Because I'm German.

And are we . . . together?

He turned his head to look at me.

Yes, we're together.

I closed my eyes and reached my arm across his chest.

Of course we're together, he said again, his voice quieter. Relief and happiness washed over me.

After a little while, Christoph said, Adorno changed his mind, you know. About no poetry after Auschwitz.

He did?

Yes. Later he wrote that the world needed art even more, after.

When did he write that?

In the sixties, I think.

But . . . why does nobody know this?

Christoph shrugged. Some people know.

What do you think?

He shrugged again. Of course we need art. Otherwise there is only silence and forgetting.

Yes. I think that too. But I understand why he said it, the first time.

Ach, people took him too literally. He was making a bigger point about . . . rupture. About *before* as much as after. Does the music and art that came before look the same, sound the same, after? Do we know it differently? That's what he was asking, I think.

I nodded, moved, as I always was, by his seriousness, his vast intelligence. I had missed talking to him. I had missed this so much.

Do you? Know it differently?

Yes, he said. I think so. Some things.

Like?

He thought for a moment.

Kafka. Mahler. And you?

I don't know, Christoph. You've given me a lot to think about.

Have I? He smiled.

Yes. You always do.

I nestled into him, and he cupped his hand over mine.

Do you know about the *Historikerstreit*? he asked.

No. Tell me.

It was a debate about German history that went on for years. It started in the eighties, between the right and left. The right tried to make it all relative . . . Nazism, the Holocaust. They argued it was no worse than other totalitarian movements, other genocides. They compared the Allied bombings to Auschwitz. They said that if Germans were not allowed to take some pride in their history, if the past was lost, then we were lost as a nation. Habermas was against all that. He felt that the Nazis were different. That the Holocaust couldn't be compared to other genocides, or the horrors in the Soviet Union. He felt the war needed to be approached as a . . . moral issue. That it could not be rationalized . . . how do you say . . . relativized, yes?

I nodded.

The debate went on for years, he said, mostly in the newspapers.

And Habermas won?

Yes.

Christoph looked out the window. But they may have had a point, he said, about a lost past. There were two different versions of history then. It was . . . destabilizing for the new country.

But it's better now, right? You said you started learning about the Holocaust when you were a child. That Germany has faced up to it.

Yes, but for how long? How long until the other side's version of history wins?

We were quiet for a moment.

Hannah Arendt talked about the banality of evil, I said.

Yes, and she's right. Think about the people who ran the railways. They're just as guilty, in a way, as the camp guards.

I don't believe that. She downplayed Eichmann's responsibility.

You mean in *Eichmann in Jerusalem*?

Yes.

You've read it?

Yes. In a history class. The same one where we read Adorno.

He nodded.

The phrase suggested that the evil itself was banal, I said.

But that's not what she meant.

Maybe not. But she should have chosen her words more carefully. Because that's the phrase everyone remembers. And it downplays personal responsibility. It downplays the evil itself. To say that anything about Nazi Germany or the Holocaust was banal . . . she chose the wrong word.

She was *saying* that the evils of Nazism were unexceptional. That any one of us is capable of it. That's what she meant by *banal*. The bureaucracy, the people who kept the whole thing running, even down to the railway workers.

His tone was strident.

But is it fair to implicate railway workers in the same way as the Gestapo? I asked. Doesn't that relativize the Holocaust? Like you were just saying?

That was exactly Arendt's point. That we're not so different from the Gestapo. That we're deluding ourselves if we think we are, or that we would have acted differently. She's saying that this kind of evil *isn't* extraordinary. It's banal.

But there were people who resisted, I said.

In Germany, not so many. Imagine your neighbors just disappearing one day. And you move into their flat, their house. Ordinary Germans did this in every city and every town, for years. So I see Arendt's point.

Your grandfather resisted.

Yes, he said, a little hesitantly. But not until 1943.

When he left the Wehrmacht.

Yes.

We were silent for a few minutes.

I like that you think about history, I said. You don't try to forget it or explain it away.

Well, I can talk about these things with you.

Because I'm American?

Yes.

It all started in Cambridge, I said, brushing his cheek with my fingertips. The week I was supposed to be studying.

He leaned his head against mine.

You did all right, he said.

You *were* a distraction.

He smiled.

Do you remember our first conversation? I asked. Our first real one? About the wall?

I was surprised you knew so much about it, for an American.

I'd never met someone from Germany. I wanted to know what you thought. I still remember the day it came down.

You and me both.

I'd like to go to Berlin, actually.

We'll go, he said.

We will?

I'll take you. Next time.

You need to come back to Boston so I can show you around for a change.

I'll come. I have to win over Jess and Susie.

I smiled and squeezed his hand.

We should send Josh a postcard from Hamburg, I said.

Yes, we can't forget this time.

No, we won't.

We were quiet again.

Hannah Arendt had an affair with Martin Heidegger, he said after a while. He was a Nazi. She went back to him, after the war. After she had escaped from Germany, escaped from a prison camp in France, worked for Jewish causes.

I know. It's hard to understand.

Not really, he said. You can't police desire.

He looked out the window and closed his eyes as the train sped north. He slept the rest of the way to Hamburg, my head on his shoulder, as I replayed his words over and over in my mind. *Of course we're together, Of course we're together . . .*

WE TOOK A TAXI to his house in a quiet neighborhood north of the city center. The streets were lined with mature trees and stately older homes that looked like they had survived the Allied bombings, though I didn't know how that was possible. Much of the city, I knew, had been destroyed in the firestorms.

Christoph's white stone house was large and imposing—a mansion, I thought to myself, as the taxi pulled up—with a maroon slate roof folded down at each end in the German style I recognized but for which I had no name. I wished I could have seen his house in summer, under a canopy of green leaves, sun and shadow. That day, the tree branches were dark and skeletal against the gray sky.

Christoph's mother opened the door, smiled, and embraced him. I immediately noticed her bright, crystal-blue eyes, how they lit up in his presence. Christoph introduced me to her, somewhat formally, as she smiled and clasped my hand.

Welcome. It's nice to meet you, she said in a strong German accent. She was dressed elegantly in a white blouse, slacks, a floral silk scarf, diamond studs, and soft leather loafers. Her hair was straight, shoulder-length, frosted blond.

Christoph spoke to her in German as I walked behind them into a large, white foyer with abstract paintings on the walls. He slung my backpack over his shoulder and said, Come. We passed through an airy white living room decorated with mid-century modern furniture and more abstract art, then down a small staircase to a basement room with exposed brick walls and a double bed in a brass frame. A mirror hung on the brick wall next to what I now recognize, in my memory, as a Toulouse-Lautrec print. A vase of fresh flowers sat atop a wooden dresser. Christoph set my backpack down next to the bed and shrugged apologetically.

We're Catholic, he said.

Me too.

Really? I didn't know that.

But I don't . . .

No, me neither.

I thought he might take my hand or kiss me, but he walked back up the stairs. I followed.

His mother made us coffee in the spacious, white-tiled kitchen. The three of us sat at a long, dark wooden table with our steaming mugs. She had set the cafetiere in the center of the table alongside a small pitcher of milk shaped like a cow, and a plate of croissants. A radio sat on the sleek, gray granite countertop, set to a classical music station. She and Christoph spoke in German as I drank my coffee and smiled. I didn't want them to speak English for my sake, and yet I was uncomfortable. Christoph had told me that his mother's English was not as good as his. There would be no easy way out of this, I realized.

After they had talked for a little while, she turned to me and said, Anna! She asked about my flight from Boston, how long it had taken. She talked about Josh and his parents, whom she had met when Christoph lived in Boston. I latched onto this mutual acquaintance and spoke highly of Josh.

Yes, he's such a nice boy, she said, smiling.

Anna and Josh were in a band together, Christoph said.

She looked at me expectantly. Yes? A band? What instrument do you play?

Guitar.

And she sings, Christoph said.

Yes, this is true? His mother smiled.

Yes, I said. We met at a . . . show.

And you have graduated from Harvard, yes? she said.

Yes, in June.

And what are your plans? She smiled at me again, somewhat tightly.

Christoph had never asked me this question. I was hoping he might intervene and fill in the blanks, but he stayed quiet and drank his coffee.

Their kitchen was the biggest I'd ever seen.

Right now I'm waitressing.

She raised her eyebrows. In a restaurant?

Yes. I'm sort of . . . between things. But I'm applying to graduate school.

Ah, she said. In what subject? Her voice rose as she spoke.

English literature?

She nodded and smiled, softer this time. Good, that's good. Christoph tells me you are a *reader*.

Like you, he said to his mother. Show her.

Later, she said. Drink your coffee. Your father will be home for dinner.

I'm going to take Anna into the city, he said.

Yes, yes. She turned to me. Hamburg is a wonderful place. There is so much to see.

She spoke to Christoph in German, and he nodded, saying *Ja, ja, ich werde*.

All of a sudden his mother startled, pointed her finger in the air, and looked expectantly at Christoph. I heard tinny violins coming out of the radio. They both listened for a moment.

Shostakovich, he said. And then, after another minute, The Fourteenth Symphony.

She smiled and turned to me.

It's a game we play, she said.

Guess the composer, Christoph said.

I smiled, nodded.

Christoph stood up and pushed in his chair. Ready?

Yes.

I stood and thanked his mother for the coffee, then followed Christoph out of the kitchen, down a long white hallway, and back through the living room. This time I noticed the large windows that looked out onto a round brick patio and an expansive yard, covered in snow.

I have to get my purse before we leave, I said.

In a minute. Come.

He led me up a dark wooden staircase, the only part of the house I had yet seen that looked original. At the top of the stairs, he rounded a corner and opened a door into a small room with two tall windows overlooking the empty winter street. There was an antique wooden desk, a blue velvet love seat, and a brass floor lamp. The walls were lined with books on white shelves.

This is my mother's library, Christoph said. I wanted to show you.

I walked around the room, inspecting the titles, taking some books off the shelves. There were German writers and philosophers, Goethe, Schiller, Rilke, Wittgenstein, Wolf, Ledig, Grass, Sebald. There were books in French by de Beauvoir and Sartre, books in English by Toni Morrison and Joan Didion. And many others. Hundreds of books. I had never seen a personal library like this. I was proud of the fact that my parents owned books by Hemingway, Steinbeck, and Frost, but now I saw how paltry our single bookcase really was.

These are all your mother's?

Yes. Some of them were my grandfather's.

Is your mother a writer? I asked.

He laughed. No.

He took Faulkner's *Light in August* off the shelf.

I think this one is from the Americans, he said.

As he opened the book, a small paper square slipped out. I picked it up off the floor and unfolded it. There was an address, barely legible in faded pencil: 15 Church St., Charlestown, Massachusetts.

Look, I said.

Christoph peered over my shoulder.

Charlestown, I said. I think my grandfather lived there when he was a kid.

Really?

I'm not sure.

What if? Christoph smiled.

No, I said, shaking my head.

I don't know, that's a strange coincidence.

Not really. Lots of GIs came from places like Charlestown and Dorchester and South Boston. That's where all the Irish lived back then.

You should ask your grandmother.

I will, I said. But I knew I wouldn't. History didn't work that way. I folded the note, put it back in the book, and returned the book to the shelf.

I picked up Sebald's *Die Ausgewanderten* and held it up to Christoph.

The Emigrants, he said.

I brought the book over to the love seat and sat down. I had read the English translation after Christoph left Cambridge. Longing for him, I had spent an hour in the German section of the foreign-language bookstore in Harvard Square. Two copies of *The Emigrants* were on display, in German and English. I had never heard of W. G. Sebald, but I picked up the book and started reading. I didn't understand it then, but something in the writing, perhaps nothing more than the German names, made me think of Christoph, and I bought it. Now it occurred to me that Sebald's writing had begun to frame Christoph for me rather than the other way around.

He sat down on the love seat and leaned against me as I flipped through the pages, looking at the strange, illusory photographs.

I liked this book very much, he said.

You've read it?

Yes.

This surprised me. I knew he was well-read in history and philosophy, but I didn't know he read contemporary German novelists. It suddenly seemed like a tie that bound us together, another sign that I needed to hold tight to him.

And what did you think? he asked.

I've never read anything like it.

It's not an easy book.

No, I said. I liked the last part best, about Max Ferber.

Me too.

He writes about the war . . . without writing about it.

Maybe it's the only way, Christoph said. What he doesn't say is more important than what he says.

Yes, and what is not said casts a kind of . . . invisible shadow over the story.

That's right, he said, smiling at me. Maybe you should write your PhD on Sebald.

I don't speak German.

It doesn't matter. Everything he writes will be translated.

No, I don't know enough, I said. I just like reading him. He writes about the war in a way that feels honest. The way Adorno said.

Yes.

Actually, I started reading Sebald because of you.

He smiled.

I probably shouldn't tell you that, I said.

I'm glad, he said, brushing a strand of hair away from my face. I read Hemingway. *A Farewell to Arms.*

This admission thrilled me.

And?

I prefer Vonnegut. He shrugged. Sorry.

You're not alone. Hemingway isn't assigned anymore, to students. People think his books are sexist.

Do you?

Yes, but I love the way he writes and the things he writes about.

He's like Sebald, in a way. No . . . sentimentality.

I'd never have put them together that way, but yes.

We sat there in silence for a few minutes, turning over the pages, looking at the photographs. Then I stood up and put Sebald's book back on the shelf. I eyed the Faulkner, wondered, again, about the address from Charlestown.

Vámonos, Christoph said, slapping his hands on his thighs.

We walked out and closed the door behind us.

.　　.　　.

WE BUNDLED UP in our heavy coats and scarves—he wore a navy blue peacoat—and took a tram into the city center. We got off and walked to the Binnenalster, a large lake connected to the Elbe River. Christoph talked about the city's port history, the Hanseatic League that linked it to trading partners on the Baltic Sea. I admired the grand nineteenth-century stone buildings with their green copper roofs, and the river-boats docked nearby, German flags flying. A fountain in the middle of the lake threw a plume of white water high up into the air. The scene was civilized and elegant, and reminded me of the lakeside promenade in Geneva. I took a photo of Christoph on the waterfront, smiling, his blond hair falling over his brown eyes, his hands in the pockets of his dark peacoat. I still have it.

The air was raw and cold with the wind whipping off the Binnenalster, so we made our way to the *Altstadt*. As we walked, I noticed an enormous banner hanging on the side of an office building. It was a close-up of a young man's face that read *Gefühlsecht*. I asked Christoph about it, and he said it was for an art exhibition at the museum. Something to do with AIDS.

He brought me then to the St. Nikolai Church. Christoph told me it was bombed during the war and never rebuilt. It had once been a massive, sprawling cathedral but now only the high steeple and some outer walls remained. A banner across the spire read *HIROSHIMA*, along with some German words. I didn't ask Christoph what they meant.

We stood together in the open air where the altar and tabernacle had once been.

They called it Operation Gomorrah, Christoph said, facing the spire. The night they bombed Hamburg. This was July of '43. The English bombers hadn't been very successful till then, so they changed tactics. Instead of trying to hit the factories, they decided to kill the workers. Actually, they wanted to destroy the whole city. And don't kid yourself, the Nazis would have done the same to London if they could have.

They certainly tried.

The pilots said they could feel the heat from the fires below. When they landed back in England there was soot on their planes, from the smoke.

Did you . . . have family here, during the war?

No, not then.

We were quiet. A gust of wind hit my face and I smarted. It was growing colder.

Forty thousand people died that night, he said, his voice low. They brought in prisoners from the concentration camps to clean up the city. It took years. This wasn't like Guernica. This was something different. It was like . . . Nagasaki. People tried to escape the bomb cellars when the oxygen ran low and the walls got hot, but they got stuck in the melting asphalt outside. Or they died in the firestorm. It was a hurricane in the streets. Everything was burning. I don't know how anyone survived.

Christoph's German accent became more pronounced as he spoke. *They* became *zey; was* became *vuz*. I looked at the shell of the church before me.

A million people left Hamburg, he said. They went south. One of my great-aunts, she worked at a train station in Frankfurt during the war, helping with the refugees. She said that some of the women from Hamburg had corpses of dead babies in their suitcases. They were crazy with grief.

I remembered what Christoph had told me, over the phone, that fall. That every time he left his flat he found something that shocked him.

Maybe we deserved it, he said.

Not the children.

No.

I held on to his arm and leaned my head against his shoulder. He kept his hands in his pockets.

But, he said, the bombing helped turn the war. Psychologically. We Germans were terrified after Hamburg. It was like the end of days.

His voice became familiar again, his accent more American.

The Allies bombed other cities after, he said. Cologne. Dresden, of course. Half a million people died in those bombings. Germans still don't like to talk about it. There is . . . shame.

Is that why there's no museum?

Probably. Maybe they will build one someday.

I looked up at the enormous steeple with its arches and bells and stone carvings. It was beautiful, even in its ruined state. I remembered lines from *The Waste Land*.

> *There is the empty chapel, only the wind's home.*
> *It has no windows, and the door swings,*
> *Dry bones can harm no one.*

Let's go, he said flatly.

I followed him out of the destroyed nave.

WE ATE A LATE LUNCH at a crowded Jungfernstieg café he knew. He looked at the menu and ordered a local beer, not the weissbier we always drank in the south. The beer arrived in tall goblets.

Prost, he said.

Prost, I said.

We clinked our glasses and drank.

Thank you for taking me here, I said. To Hamburg.

You're very welcome. I wanted you to see it. There's more after lunch. And we'll go to the Christmas market tonight.

Glühwein, I said.

Yes, glühwein. He smiled. And maybe I'll show you the Reeperbahn as well. He raised his eyebrows.

The what?

The Reeperbahn. The red-light district, like the Combat Zone in Boston. Prostitution is legal in Hamburg, same as Amsterdam. It's all regulated.

I wasn't sure what to say. I didn't want him to take me there.

We ordered burgers and fries, in honor of me, he said. He told me he missed American food, especially pizza. I told him the beer here was okay, but I liked weissbier better. He agreed. For a few minutes, we ate in silence, half listening to the low hum of others' conversations. I was still thinking about the St. Nikolai Church and the firestorm. I had the odd sensation of wanting to protect Christoph from its danger even though the danger had long since passed.

Do you think you'll come back to Hamburg, I asked, after you finish your degree?

I don't know. I'd like to go to America, actually.

That can be arranged.

He smiled.

Come in the spring, I said, hopeful.

He leaned back in his chair and looked at me.

Yes, he said.

My heart leaped.

Maybe . . . in February? I asked.

New England is not so nice in February.

What about March or April? You can stay with me on the Cape.

In March I have exams. April might work. And we can see Josh. Let's send him a postcard today.

Yes, let's.

We can't forget.

No, we won't.

I said nothing more about the trip—I didn't dare in case he changed his mind—and he paid the bill. He was always paying for things. Whenever I offered, he would laugh off my attempt and tell me I was his guest. Maybe I would pay for his plane ticket to America. Yes, I decided as we stood up to leave, I would.

HE WANTED TO take me to a Herbert List exhibit at the Hamburger Kunsthalle. List was a German photographer who had known Robert Capa and Henri Cartier-Bresson, and worked for Magnum, Christoph said. I had never heard of List. I had never been to a photography exhibit before. But Christoph was at ease in that space, strolling among List's photos of couples on the beaches of Italy and Greece, pointing out details I hadn't noticed. I knew he was interested in photography. He had shown me some of his own black-and-white photographs back in his flat. He kept them in a drawer in his desk. Mostly buildings, angular and moody. I felt close to him in that sepulchral white room amid those languorous bodies lounging at the sea's edge. Humans looked like statues, statues like humans. There was one photo of a young man, eyes closed, leaning against a tall rock on an Italian beach. He had blond hair, a strong, defined jawline, and a muscular neck. The sun lit his face in a halo. I thought he looked a little like Christoph.

I wonder what he's thinking, I said, pointing to the photo.

Christoph bent down to read the placard.

Light and Shadow, 1936, he said. He studied the photo and said, He looks like a German tourist.

Yes, even the way he's dressed . . . that checkered shirt, the dark shorts and backpack. Like he's about to set off for the Alps.

He looks glad to be out of Germany, anyway.

I nodded. We stood before the photo for another minute. Christoph seemed stuck in a thought.

There's a poem with that same title, he said. Or poems. I can't remember. They were by a Polish poet. Borowski, I think his name was. He survived the war.

What were they about?

They were love poems. Set in Auschwitz. And Dachau.

Love poems?

Yes, if I'm remembering correctly.

Christoph looked at the photograph for another moment, then said, Ready? He put his hand on my back and steered me toward the gallery's exit. We emerged into the bright winter light and wrapped our scarves around our necks. It had begun to snow.

Look! he said, laughing, suddenly lighter. He took my hand as we walked to the tram.

Just for you, he said. A white Christmas.

WHEN WE RETURNED to the house, Christoph's mother was in the kitchen, wearing an apron, cooking. Christoph leaned against the counter and spoke to her in German—about our day, I assumed—as she opened and closed the oven, and stirred steaming pots that smelled of rosemary and cloves. I stayed standing. She smiled kindly at me as she wiped her hands on the tea towel draped over her shoulder and asked if I'd had a good day. Yes, I said, great! She seemed more relaxed than she had been earlier in the afternoon. Her manner was gentler now. I offered to help but she shooed us out.

Christoph suggested I change for dinner, so I went downstairs to my room. I had brought the black cocktail dress, black tights, and black leather heels that I always wore to Harvard formals. I put on the dress, reached behind my back, and pulled up the zipper. I stepped into my low black heels, clasped the pearl choker around my neck, and dabbed Chanel on my wrists. I brushed my long hair and put on some makeup, though not too much.

Hallo? I heard Christoph shout down the stairwell. I gave myself a last approving glance in the oval full-length mirror, then went up. He was waiting for me at the top of the stairs, clean-shaven and handsome in a white oxford and a navy blue blazer. He smiled and took my hands in his when I reached the landing, then leaned down and kissed me gently on the lips. I grazed the buttons of his blazer with my fingertips.

Come, he said, as he guided me through the long hallway, his hand on my lower back. We walked into the living room and there was his father, sitting in a gray suit on a stylish black leather sofa, his legs crossed, reading a newspaper. When he saw us, he put the newspaper down, stood up, and embraced his son. I could see how Christoph took after him, the same build, the same brown eyes.

And this must be Anna, he said, with barely an accent. He shook my hand and smiled. You've come a long way. Sit.

Christoph led me to the matching black leather sofa opposite his father. When we sat down, he laced his fingers through mine. I had wondered whether I was reading too much into this visit. But now, holding Christoph's hand, facing his father, I thought, yes, it meant something. I stayed quiet, lest I sound too American.

Christoph was different around his father. I noticed it as they spoke in German for a few minutes. There was an edge in his voice I had not heard when he was talking to his mother or Matthias. But of course, I didn't know what they were saying. I remembered that it was Christoph's paternal grandfather who had fought in the Wehrmacht.

I thought I heard Christoph say, in German, that they should speak English. Immediately his father turned to me and said, Tell me, Anna, how did you find Hamburg?

Oh, it was wonderful. Christoph took me all around.

Americans usually go to Heidelberg and Munich, he said, but there's so much to see here.

Yes! I nodded enthusiastically.

We went to the List exhibit, Christoph said.

How was it?

Good.

List was a bold choice for the Kunsthalle, his father said. He looked at me and said, List was gay. He looked back at Christoph. Was there. . . . much of that? I wondered how they would stage it.

Nein, Christoph said, then something in German.

His father looked at me again. His gaze was focused, as if he were taking me in. Something about that look reminded me of Christoph.

And where did you eat? he asked.

Christoph offered the name of the café, which I had forgotten.

Ah, good choice. He was silent for a moment, then said, So, Anna, Christoph tells me you're from Massachusetts. I spent a year at Dartmouth on an exchange in the sixties. One of the best years of my life. I wanted Christoph to have a similar experience. That's why we sent him to Bradfield.

We spoke then of Christoph's year at Bradfield, of Josh, of how I met Christoph, how I had enjoyed Harvard.

Is Alan Dershowitz still at the law school? he asked.

I think so. I was relieved I knew the name. Everyone at Harvard knew Alan Dershowitz.

He'll die at his desk, probably, he said.

I laughed.

And Greta tells me you plan to go to graduate school?

I hope so. I've applied to Oxford.

I'm going over to Boston in the spring, Christoph said. To visit Anna.

I looked at Christoph, surprised.

Yes? Well, that's wonderful, his father said, smiling. Your brother will be jealous. Christoph's older brother just started practicing law, he said, here in Hamburg.

Is he coming tonight? Christoph asked.

No. He got caught up. Work.

Christoph nodded.

Just then Christoph's mother called us into the dining room. She had changed into a sleeveless, dark blue dress cut just above her knees. She, too, was wearing a strand of small pearls.

The table was laid with a steaming roast, scalloped potatoes, green beans, sauces, bread rolls, and a bottle of French red wine. I was surprised a family would eat like this on a weekday, though I suspected it was all for Christoph. And maybe, I hoped, for me too.

I complimented his mother's cooking and worried about my table manners. We told her about our day, and Christoph's father talked for a long time about Bill Clinton. He asked me what I thought of Clinton's economic policies, and I said, lamely, that I agreed with them. I was terrified of appearing ignorant. I didn't read the newspaper every day then as I do now, and I didn't know exactly what Bill Clinton's economic policies were. There was a silence, and then his mother asked me which writers I planned to study in graduate school. I told her that I might write a PhD on Emily Brontë's poetry.

Her eyes brightened. I love the Brontës, she said.

Greta has read everything, Christoph's father said, his voice droll.

I never studied in America, she said to me, apologetically. But my father did.

Well, I never got a chance to study in Germany, I said, apologizing back. What women we were. Now I wish I had, I said. I turned and smiled at Christoph, sitting next to me.

Oh, you wouldn't want to spend a year at a German university when you're at Harvard! his father said.

Anna is interested in German history, Christoph said. Her grandfather fought in the war.

The table went quiet.

He captured the Kehlsteinhaus, in Berchtesgaden, Christoph said, fork in hand. At the end of the war.

His father raised his eyebrows at me and wiped his mouth with his linen napkin.

The Kehlsteinhaus?

Tell him, Christoph said to me.

I didn't want to talk about the war.

His unit got there just after the . . . the Nazis had left, I said. He could still smell perfume in the air.

He took Hitler's flag, Christoph said, helping himself to more potatoes. From that huge dining room, the one overlooking the mountains.

Mein Gott, his father said.

He was only nineteen, I said. I didn't want to talk about the flag.

That's very young, his father said. But—he shrugged—it was the end of the war.

Opa would have been in Bavaria around that time, right? Christoph asked. Spring of '45?

His father nodded.

Did you grow up in Boston, Anna? he asked.

No, a small town about an hour west.

She went to Groton, Christoph offered.

Really, he said, suddenly more interested. FDR's alma mater.

Yes.

One of your greatest presidents, though he turned away the Jews.

I knew about this. Our American history teacher had discussed Roosevelt's decision to send a ship of Jewish refugees back to Europe during the war. This teacher had questioned whether the school should honor him as it did.

And of course they perished when they were sent back, his father said.

No one spoke for a few minutes. Then Christoph's father turned to me and said, Groton is a wonderful school.

Yes, it is, I said.

We thought about sending Christoph there, he said, but they didn't have a program for foreign students like Bradfield did.

Christoph smiled at me and raised his eyebrows. If only, he said.

Where did you say you grew up? his father asked.

In Groton. I was a day student.

You grew up in the town?

Yes.

Ah. And what do your parents do?

This was a question only other people's parents asked me. Christoph and I hardly ever talked about our parents.

Construction and education, I said. I didn't say that my father worked in the family asphalt business, or that my mother taught middle school. Or that I'd gone to Groton on a scholarship for local students.

Christoph's father smiled politely and said nothing more.

The table fell quiet again, and his father offered to refill my wine. Christoph stopped him.

We're heading out. To the Christmas market.

Ah, yes. His father refilled his own glass.

We finished eating. Christoph and I helped his mother clear the table as his father stood up and excused himself. I offered to help with the dishes but she shooed us out of the kitchen again, saying, Go, have fun. As we put on our coats, Christoph's father emerged into the hallway, holding his glass of wine.

Christoph, why don't you play something for Anna before you go?

No, he said, we're on our way out.

Oh, come. His father turned to me. He plays piano beautifully, he said.

I didn't know, I said.

Oh yes, he plays extremely well.

Christoph sighed. All right. Just one.

We put our coats back on the hangers in the foyer closet and followed his father down a hallway into a spacious room I hadn't seen. The other rooms in the house were mostly white-walled and decorated with modern art, but this room looked like it had not changed since the nineteenth century. Romantic oil paintings of rivers and mountains hung on forest-green walls. Two enormous, intricately patterned Oriental rugs covered the floor. There was a jet-black grand piano; a tall, dark wooden hutch full of gold-rimmed porcelain plates; blue-and-white Chinese lamps atop two oval wooden tables; a rolltop desk; wingback chairs; and a fireplace with a faux medieval stone mantel. Large paned windows looked out onto the snow-covered backyard. Christoph's father sank into an overstuffed brown leather sofa, glass of wine in hand, and motioned for me to sit next to him.

Christoph sat down at the piano and pulled in the bench. He straightened his back, put his hands on the keys, and, after a moment, began to play—something I recognized but couldn't place. Debussy, his father whispered, leaning close to me, somehow aware of my ignorance. Christoph's mother hovered in the doorway. I watched Christoph's fingers move over the ivory keys, watched him lean forward, then back, his head bowed. All of it was softness and grace. The way he played the light, deliberate notes made me feel like I was floating, lambent, on water. My chest tightened in panic. I felt astonished and overwhelmed, afraid of the depths of my feeling.

When he finished playing, his father clapped, slowly. I joined him.

One more, his father said.

No, Christoph said, standing up. We have to get going.

Well, his father said. He stood up stiffly. I was relieved. I wanted to leave this room, this house. I needed air.

As the three of us walked into the hallway, I noticed a framed black-and-white photograph on a bookshelf. It was a young man in lederhosen on an alpine ridge, smiling. I stopped and looked at it closely. This man looked exactly like Christoph. I pointed at it, confused.

Is that you? I asked Christoph.

No, silly, that's Opa Hans. My grandfather.

Oh. I looked again. The similarity was unsettling.

His father stopped and looked at the photograph. Yes, you two do look alike, he said. That was before the war.

His father turned away from the photo.

Don't drink too much glühwein, Christoph. You're driving my car.

Don't worry, Christoph said.

Be good, his father said, handing Christoph his keys.

Christoph held my coat up for me as I slipped my arms into its sleeves.

.   .   .

HE DROVE HIS FATHER'S black Mercedes through the wintry streets into the city center. The snow had stopped, but it was much colder now than it had been that afternoon. Christoph parked and I put on the wool hat and mittens I had brought from home. We got out of the car and started walking, our heads bent against the wind.

Why didn't you tell me you play the piano? I asked him.

Ach, I don't play very well.

You do. You were amazing.

I don't play as much as I used to. And if you don't practice . . . He shrugged.

Isn't there somewhere you can play at your university?

Yes, but I don't have the time.

I wish you had told me.

Why? There was annoyance in his voice.

Because music is a part of you. To play like that, you must have spent years . . .

He said nothing.

I just want to know you, I said. All of you.

Everyone in my family plays much better. Honestly, I'm not that good.

But you are.

It's not some secret I kept from you.

I didn't mean it like that. It's just that . . . you're a musician. And I didn't know.

I'm hardly a *musician,* he scoffed.

I just meant . . . I didn't know we had that in common. I mean, the two of us. Remember the night we met?

Yes, he said, his tone lighter. He put his arm around my waist. You were very sexy with that guitar, you know.

I was playing for you.

He stopped walking, pulled me close, and kissed me. I put my arms around his neck. The winter wind had picked up, but I wasn't cold.

Come, he said, taking my hand, we're almost there.

When we turned the corner into the *Altstadt,* I gasped. I had never seen anything so charming. There were rows of wooden stalls festooned with white lights and spruce garlands, stands piled high with ornaments, handmade toys, stollen. Standing above it all was the *Rathaus,* lit up in a warm yellow glow. The night air smelled of evergreen.

We wandered through the cheerful crowds and Christmas trees until we came to a stall that sold glühwein. Christoph handed me a steaming cup, and I took a sip. It tasted like mulled cider, but spicier.

So? He smiled.

I took another sip. I could drink this all night!

Drink all you want, he said, amused.

I was full of exclamations and delight as we walked through the maze of stalls. Christoph pointed out German crafts and delicacies, and I could see now how many American Christmas traditions had come from Germany. I had never realized this. I drank another cup of glühwein, then another. The more Christoph spoke, the quieter I became. This urge toward silence was happening to me more often. I worried I had already shown him too much of myself, my obsession with history, the war. If I kept revealing myself like this, he would grow uneasy. I had seen it happen before with other men, though no one I cared about as much as Christoph. That night at the Christmas market, I said little. I smiled as much as I could. For how had I ended up here, in this garlanded place, with a man I adored? What had I done to deserve such happiness?

WHEN WE GOT HOME, the house was dark, quiet.

Shh, he said as he closed the heavy wooden front door. He motioned for me to go downstairs to the guest room and whispered, I'll come soon.

I heard his footsteps on the stairs a half hour later. He lifted the duvet and crawled into bed next to me. He was wearing a white T-shirt and baby blue boxers.

Is it okay? I asked.

They're sleeping.

I don't want them to think badly of me.

Ach, they don't care.

They might.

They're Catholic. They have to pretend.

My parents would be the same.

We were quiet as he stroked my arm.

I never sleep well in this house, he said.

Why not?

He looked up at the ceiling. You'll think I'm paranoid.

Tell me.

You saw all the old furniture and paintings in the music room, yes?

The room with the piano?

My father inherited those things, but his parents weren't that wealthy. It doesn't make sense, where it all came from.

Why? Where do you think it came from?

He kept his eyes on the ceiling.

Shiploads of antique art and furniture came to Hamburg and Bremen during the war, he said. From the flats of Dutch Jews.

Oh—no. Oh my God.

Every time I'm in that room, I wonder.

Is there some way to . . . find out?

I asked my father once. He said he had never asked his parents about it, that all of it was in his house growing up. He got angry with me.

Maybe it all belonged to some distant relative.

Maybe, Christoph said. Maybe not.

We were quiet again.

I'll sleep better with you here tonight, he said, turning to face me.

I hope so. I laid my palm on his chest, felt it move up and down as he breathed.

That boy in the photo today, I said.

The German tourist?

Yes, 1936. I wonder what happened to him.

Nothing good.

He was silent for a moment, then said, I'd like to think I would have resisted.

His words startled me. I propped myself up on my elbow and looked at him.

You would have, I said.

He stayed quiet and took a strand of my hair in his fingers.

You would have, I said again.

But suddenly I wondered too, and I felt it enter me, the cold shadow of his history.

I AWOKE LATER that night. He was still there, sleeping beside me. I looked at him. He wasn't a Nazi. He was a twenty-three-year-old German man wrestling with questions of evil and guilt and responsibility, questions that would probably haunt him all his life.

But I wanted to know what his grandfather had done in the war.

I ASKED CHRISTOPH on the train back to his university town.

Tell me about Hans, I said. The one in the photo, on the mountain.

Outside, the country sped by in a blur of white and brown.

I told you. He joined the resistance.

When?

After Stalingrad. Would have been . . . late '43.

So he went back to Lichendorf?

Yes. He married my grandmother after the war.

What did he do in the resistance?

Christoph shrugged. Forged documents, pamphlets, probably some spying. It was dangerous.

I'm sure. Did he ever talk about it?

Not much. Christoph turned away from me and looked out the window. If you have a grandfather who fought in the east, in the Wehrmacht, he said, you have a responsibility to find out whether he committed war crimes. Someday I will have to learn what happened, before Stalingrad.

But how?

There are records. In Israel and Berlin. Maybe in Lichendorf.

Is your grandmother still alive?

Yes, but she's not well. I can't ask her about the war. I'm sorry, Christoph.

I laced my fingers through his. I wanted to tell him about the scrapbook then. But I couldn't. I was afraid of those photographs—of what they revealed and what they prophesized, how they dishonored the dead. I didn't want to make Christoph's burden heavier by lightening my own. I loved him.

He leaned his head on my shoulder. Eventually he fell asleep. I looked at his face, the ginger stubble on his chin, his blond eyelashes. I kissed his forehead.

Surely he knew it was very easy to tell your son, and, later, your grandson, that you had joined the resistance during the war.

WE SPENT THE NEXT few days in his room, in his bed, leaving only for coffee, occasional meals. We knew we didn't have much time. We had agreed not to talk about it, this looming deadline. And so we were mostly quiet with each other. We had talked so much already, and we could talk later, on the phone. But soon there would be an ocean between us, and we could not touch.

The day before I left, I asked him to take me to the Rhine. I knew my grandfather had fought along its banks, closer to Cologne. But that wasn't why I wanted to see it. I was thinking about the Rhine Maidens, the Lorelei. I had always loved that story, the passion and the sacrifice.

The river wasn't far, but the air was frigid that day. We drove to a small park on the bank with a cobblestone landing. The sky was white, the grass dry and brown under a thin layer of snow. The trees on the opposite bank were straight and stiff, their branches bare. We held hands as we watched the dark water flow past, a quick-moving current.

There's a famous rock upriver, Christoph said. The Lorelei. It's where she jumped, in the legend. The rock echoes.

How does a rock echo?

I don't know. I've never been.

Where is it?

Far. A couple hours' drive.

Oh.

Heine wrote a famous poem about it. And then Wagner, of course.

Yes, I know the opera. Do you remember the poem?

Not really.

I'd like to hear it, I said. The poem. And the echo.

He looked out across the wide river, then back at me.

Next time, he said.

HE DROVE ME to the airport a few days before Christmas. I checked in for my flight to Boston and then we held each other for a long time.

You never played the Shostakovich for me, I said. The piece about Dresden.

I will, *Schatz*. He ran his hand up and down my back. I closed my eyes and held him tighter. We'll listen to the Thirteenth too, he said, quieter. We'll listen to them both.

I let go of him and looked out at the long line of people waiting to cross the sky. Beyond the security gate lay a wellspring of loneliness. I didn't know how I would get through the winter without him.

I turned back to him and touched his cheek, lightly, with my fingertips.

I'll see you in the spring, I finally said.

Yes, he said, holding my hand. This time I'm coming to you.

10

Jack, May 1945

They were billeted in Austria, not far from Berchtesgaden. Hitler was dead. The Germans had surrendered. All Jack wanted now was to lie alone in the long grass with the sun on his face.

The air was quiet. The sound of planes and explosions had disappeared. The war was over but he kept his gun close. He didn't believe in the peace. Not yet. He lifted his head up from the grass and looked out at the women with scythes in the field, their bodies moving back and forth in a steady, predictable rhythm. Children loaded the new hay onto a wagon. The horses stood motionless in the heat. The women sang, a low, soft hum. A German song he did not understand.

His war had been short, just forty-two days of combat. Time had collapsed for him during the firefights in the Ruhr pocket, at the gates of Dachau. But it had stretched out ahead of him, too, on the long marches between the Bavarian villages, twenty, thirty miles, when he had felt bored and impatient but also like he was skimming along the surface of some vast knowledge waiting to be tapped. He had learned not to sit during the short breaks between the marches because he would not be able to stand up again. He had learned to sleep as he marched. Once, while marching, he dreamed he was falling off a tank, and when he awoke he was at the bottom of a small hill. Another soldier had run after him, reached out his hand, and pulled him back on his feet. He had not known the soldier's name.

He remembered leaving Boston on the troop ship, reading *For Whom the Bell Tolls* on deck. He was too seasick to read down below in his cramped bunk. They crossed the Atlantic in a convoy, fifty ships that had grown more distant from each other until they were miles apart. Or so it felt three days out from Le Havre. He remembered the panic that night when the orders came over the ship's intercom: *Navy personnel, man your posts! This is not a drill!* He and the other infantry grunts were ordered to stay below in their dank bunks while the navy men clambered up ladders. They knew it was a German U-boat. They were all quiet; they didn't dare move or speak as they held tight to the pins that would fill their life jackets with air. A boy next to him—they were all boys—whispered that he didn't know how to swim. Jack told him he didn't know either, but that they'd be okay with their life jackets on, that another ship from the convoy would pick them up. But that was a lie. He knew they wouldn't survive more than ten minutes in the cold North Atlantic.

They sat and they sat in the quiet, airless berth and felt the ship veer to the left, then circle back, trying to outrun the U-boat. The terror of those minutes, all of them wondering if the U-boat had launched a torpedo, whether it would hit. Probably he would die soon. He said the Hail Mary over and over and tried to accept his fate. He would drown in the cold, black Atlantic. A terrible way to die. He had made his peace with dying in combat, but not this. Not death by water.

They heard depth bombs, three of them, deep below the hull. Fathoms below. They hoped they were depth bombs. None of them knew what depth bombs sounded like. Someone said it might have been a torpedo that missed the ship. They felt the hull shudder, a small earthquake in the stinking berth. They kept their hands on the pressure pins of their life jackets, ready to pull, and then the captain yelled the all clear. Sweet Jesus, he had never known such relief. Some men fell to their knees. Others shed their life jackets and ran up on deck. But then

the captain came back over the intercom and announced that U-boats
hunted in packs, that everyone should be ready to return to their posts.
The men who had fallen to their knees stood up quietly. Jack took out a
pack of cigarettes and offered it around. They smoked in silence. When
he finished his cigarette, he went up on deck. Men were already sitting
outside, playing cards. Looking for luck, and who could blame them.

He walked to the stern and he stood in the cold, clean air and he looked
out at the dark water for a piece of the submarine they had destroyed.
Nothing. He breathed and he breathed and he watched the ship's enormous wake recede into the blackness. Later he heard that the U-boat had
been following them for days.

The cold March winds at Camp Old Gold, the forty-and-eight box-
cars at Yvetot. Leftovers from the First World War, transporting them
to Maastricht. From there to bombed-out Aachen, and on to Cologne
in the trucks. The Rhine. They were billeted in an old mansion on the
western bank, near the Remagen bridge. It looked like a high-ranking
Nazi had lived there. They had torn down the swastika flags from nearly
every room and fought over who got to keep them. Souvenirs. There
was an enormous garden full of Greek and Roman statues, warriors
with swords in hand. A replica of *The Dying Gaul*. One night a drunk
soldier shot out at the statues. The soldier thought they were Germans
in the fog. They had all laughed until they cried, nearly, the men billeted
in that Nazi mansion. Laughter was rare on the western bank of the
Rhine. The ringing chorus of it, the relief. It made them braver for what
was ahead. Cologne. The rubble and the bodies and the rats. The Ruhr
pocket. The firefight in the forest. The young, dead Germans. Nearly
twenty dead. He did not know whether he had killed one of them but he
suspected he had. His friends were cheering and boasting but he did not
want to know. And the two bodies, Americans, lying not far from him,
both shot through the head. His nightmares that night, sleeping under
pine boughs, trying to keep warm, and the shell that had come without
warning, an 88 exploding over the trees, killing the medic and wounding
five men.

He remembered the German sniper in one of the village churches.
There were always snipers in the church spires. He had dived for cover

into a ditch and found a young boy in a Wehrmacht uniform that didn't fit. The boy was hiding, terrified. He could have killed the boy but he didn't. The boy was too young. He took the boy's gun and ammunition and said, *Get out!* The boy just stayed there, frozen, shaking his head. *Bitte, bitte.* Jack used his hands to make the boy understand: *Leave! Shoo!* Finally the boy climbed out. Slowly. When the boy stood up and put his hands over his head, the Nazi sniper shot him and he fell back into the ditch, dead. Goddamn it, why did they have to shoot their own like that. For surrendering. The boy had just wanted to live. He should have let the boy stay with him. He should have known.

Some of the men thought the war would be over soon, but Captain Wilson said it could go on for another year if the Germans had a redoubt in the mountains. And so they marched south.

They thought they were in the Black Forest but nobody knew for sure. No one knew the names of the towns. The names didn't matter. He had read *A Farewell to Arms* at the army training camp in San Luis Obispo and he remembered the part about how the names of the towns held more dignity than words like *honor* and *glory* and *courage*. But now he knew that was not true. No one cared about the names of the places where the firefights raged, where German snipers shot German boys. They just went where they were told and did what they were told. But they cared about words like *courage* and *honor*. They cared very much. That was what kept them marching, even when they were freezing and hungry and afraid. He didn't know if they were in the Black Forest but someone said they were, and the trees were dark and there was snow on the ground and it was cold and foggy. Maybe it was the Black Forest. There was something romantic about it, he could imagine witches and gingerbread. It was beautiful there in the snow among the evergreens, a fantasy of Christmas though it was closer to Easter. Captain Wilson told them that the Germans had laid mines and so they were careful and slow as they walked, and he thought he might die then, in the Black Forest, looking for Germans to kill.

They heard them at dawn, pots and plates and tin cups banging in the distance. Echoes of a language he did not understand. Laughter. He watched his steps, barely breathing as he made his way through the cold fog. A bird startled him, a robin flying up from the ground, so close he could almost touch it. He hadn't seen a bird up close like that in a long time. When he looked down in the snow he saw that there was a nest with eggs and under the nest was a patch of black metal. He reached down and picked up the nest and saw the outline of a round mine, an upside-down frying pan, underneath. He placed the nest back down, lifted his hand high in the air, and walked backward. The men behind him did the same. They backtracked and took a different route to the line. The Germans were drinking coffee from tin cups and laughing when he started shooting.

The slave labor camp. He had not known the name of it then. They had expected a firefight, but the SS guards were gone when they arrived. They found Polish women, all Christians, inside. They were wearing the clothes of their dead Jewish friends, they said, the ones who had been taken away and killed. The women were crying, touching his sleeves, falling on their knees and grasping his legs. That night he and a few other men invited some of the women to an empty gymnasium with a piano inside. He could play, not well, but well enough. Mostly Tin Pan Alley songs everyone knew. A little Chopin. Women sat next to him on the piano bench, moving closer. It was hard to play with the women next to him, but he tried. He was happy the women were free now but he did not want anything to do with them. They were like ghosts, wearing the dead Jews' clothes. One woman stood over him and watched his hands, only his hands. Her eyes were hungry for the keys. He offered her the bench, but she shook her head and backed away. He offered again, and the other women cheered her on. One of them spoke English and told him that this woman was a piano teacher. They had been arrested in a mass roundup in Warsaw three years ago, and no one had heard any music since then. Music was forbidden. For three years they had not heard music.

He took the piano teacher's hand in his and sat her on the bench. He suggested she play a Chopin étude, but she shook her head, no, and said something in Polish. He thought he understood—too much time had passed. Finally she hit a single note, then another, and then a chord. Then she truly began, running her hands over the keys. Slowly at first, then more forcefully. The other women gathered round and began weeping and singing. He thought it must be the Polish national anthem. The women raised their heads and wept and sang. There had been no songs, no music at all, for three years.

Dachau. The bodies in the train cars. Bodies from Buchenwald. He didn't know what Buchenwald was, not then. But now he did. Now they all did. Nobody had told them about the death camps. Nobody had warned them about what they might find a few miles outside Munich. They had seen a couple of the prisoners on the road, fleeing. He had not understood why they were dressed like that, in stripes, like the prisoners in the chain gangs down south. Those men had looked at him with fear in their eyes and run. He hadn't understood who they were or what they were running from. When he reached Dachau, he knew.

He was furious at the SS and Wehrmacht soldiers who had killed and tortured with such vicious abandon, and he was furious at the civilians outside Dachau who had let it all happen. They had known. They had all known. Nothing would convince him otherwise. The Americans had forced the residents of the town to come and walk through the crematorium and look at the bodies. To see what had happened there. But most of the Germans had looked away, covered their eyes with their hands. He had not looked away. He had seen the bodies on the train, on the ground, in the room next to the crematorium. Thousands of bodies. And after Munich, Jews, he now knew, groups of them, shot and beaten to death, dried blood, lying on the road. The SS had forced them to leave Dachau. They hadn't survived the march. He hoped some had survived, escaped into the woods, but there were too many bodies. Bodies at Dachau, bodies along the road.

He had marched south toward Austria trying not to think about anything except putting one foot in front of the other. The old cliché, and yet it had helped. They were all quiet, the men, after Dachau. Nothing in their lives had prepared them for that. But now he knew what humans could do to each other. That was all. The veil had been lifted. Bodies in the train cars. Bodies on the ground. Bodies in the crematorium. Bodies on the road. Now he knew and he wished he didn't. He would have to stop thinking about the things he had seen at Dachau, seen along the road to Berchtesgaden. He would not develop the photographs he had taken. He would never look at them. He was ashamed now for taking them. As if it were some kind of spectacle. He would never develop those photographs.

They had raided Hitler's Eagle's Nest, in the Alps, and his friends took pictures, but he could not let himself touch the camera again. He could not press the shutter. He could not let the photos of the bodies stand next to the photos of the maroon-marbled fireplace, or the view over the Obersalzberg, or the sun terrace that seemed to float aloft in the sky. He had taken a Nazi flag from the wall of the great room, and a lamp. He had carved his name into the fireplace. He could have taken more but he didn't. The French had moved all the wine out by then. They had taken it down the mountain on stretchers. He had laughed as he watched the French soldiers take hundreds of bottles of wine down that mountain to ambulances waiting at the bottom. The ambulances were taking it all back to France, Hitler's looted French wine. How ridiculous, he thought, as he watched the French soldiers. He had laughed, softly at first, and then very hard, at the care they took with those bottles. As if the liquid within were sentient. As if the bottles were religious relics. Surely there were people who needed the stretchers more. The prisoners at Dachau had needed them more. He remembered that. And now here were the French, taking wine bottles down a mountain on stretchers. The generals took more care with the wine than they did with their soldiers. But that didn't surprise him, not in this war.

There was still a little snow on the ground, even in May. They were already high, a few thousand feet, and it wasn't easy, getting all the way up to the Eagle's Nest. They moved slowly over the ground, afraid of traps. But they had not encountered many on their march through Bavaria. The SS men had left their posts quickly. His division had expected more fighting but in the end there was silence. Resignation hung cloudlike over the land.

The tunnel to the Eagle's Nest had been filled with wine but the French had cleared it. On stretchers. Ambulances. At the end of the tunnel there was an elevator, all gilt edges and mirrors. The kind of elevator that might ferry guests between floors at the Ritz. Though he had never been to the Ritz or any such hotel. The French told them the Nazis had sabotaged the elevator and so the men backed away, wary of setting foot inside. The war was all but over and none of them wanted to die in Hitler's elevator. They left the tunnel and emerged back onto the cul-de-sac where the SS cars had dropped off SS men. Together they climbed the rocky hill to the top.

When they caught their breath and stood to their full height, they saw that the view was long and wide and surrounded them on all sides. They were from the East Coast or the Midwest, and none had ever been atop a mountain like this. The surrounding slopes were covered by grass and evergreens, but the summits were gray and daggered and capped in snow. The view was the most beautiful thing he had ever seen. The closest he had come was skiing in New Hampshire, but that was nothing like this. He felt faint for a moment, standing there, so far from where he had come.

Hitler's stone chalet sat at the end of a promontory that jutted out from the side of the mountain. An alpine peninsula. They walked in slowly, quietly, but the place was empty. There was still beer and brandy, and the kitchen was stocked with bread and cheese and meat. They moved around the great room in silence, picking things up, putting them back down again—crystal ashtrays, black-and-silver steins. None of them spoke for a long time.

To the victor go the spoils. He had taken the flag and the lamp. Something to prove he was there, that he had been one of the first. They had gotten drunk on the sun terrace and looked out at the mountains and said very little. Everyone was tired. He had sat among them with a bottle of cognac. He wondered if he would tell his children about this day, the day he had stormed the Eagle's Nest. Only they hadn't stormed it, not really. The French had already taken it. The French general had nearly stopped them. This general didn't want the Americans anywhere near Hitler's chalet. The French wanted all the glory for themselves. In the end the general let them through after shouts and threats and so he was one of the first. But not the very first, and that was all that mattered. They were not the first. Still, he let a friend take a photo of the four of them, sitting outside on the terrace, holding their bottles and smiling. He didn't ask anyone to take a photo with his camera. He didn't want anyone else touching his camera's shutter, taking another photograph after what was on the reel. But he let O'Donnell take his picture. He posed and he smiled and he raised his bottle. He imagined telling his children about the smoke that was still in the air at Berchtesgaden the day he had stormed the Eagle's Nest. They weren't there long. By the time they left, other GIs were coming in, a long trail of them from another division. Maybe those GIs would say they were the first. Maybe they would tell their children stories of smoke in the air, perfume in the air. This was something he could tell his children about. But not Dachau. He did not want to think about Dachau, ever, but he knew he would. He knew he always would.

He sat in the long grass and listened to the women singing and he thought about the books he had given the German boy, Wilhelm. He hoped the boy would read them. That was before Dachau. Jack had wanted to read those books then, but he didn't anymore.

He knew he was lucky. They had lost men. Not many but enough to make him pray in the firefights. He knew the longer the war went on, the greater his chance of dying. He had lived with uncertainty since he joined the army a year ago and started his training at San Luis Obispo. Whether he would fight in Europe or the Pacific, whether he would live or die. Now he was going home. He had not known anything definite like that in a long time. But the uncertainty was still there, lodged deep within him. Ruth had stopped writing.

He knew the things he had seen had changed him, would change him, but he did not want to think about change as he lay there in the long grass with the mild May heat dissipating all around him and the sun dropping low on the horizon. They would have three days off in Heidelberg before they boarded the forty-and-eight cars at Mannheim that would take them back to France. They hadn't bombed Heidelberg. It was, maybe, the last city left. He wanted to see the famous rose-colored castle, and he wanted, very badly, to get drunk. He hoped he would never again have to feel the things he had felt in this war. The fear, the aching promises to God, the horror and the grief. It had been too much to bear and yet he had borne it. They all had, the men in his division.

He hoped they would keep close to one another when they returned to America, but he knew they would not. He did not want to be alone anymore. His war had lasted little more than a month but he knew that time would hover, shadowlike, around the perimeters of his life. The knowledge made him fearful about the years ahead. He wondered where he would go from here, who he would love. That seemed the most important question. Who to love.

11

As the winter weeks passed in the cold house on the harbor, Christoph became harder to reach. Whenever I called, Matthias answered the phone. After a brief, pleasant conversation, he would tell me Christoph was out but that he would be sure to tell him I called. *Tschüss!* Another week would go by. I took on as many double shifts at the restaurant as I could.

When I finally talked to Christoph in late January and asked him what was going on, he said he had to study for his exams. He apologized and promised he would have more time to talk when his exams were over. For now, he said, he had to focus. Fair enough, I thought, but he had come to me the week I was supposed to be studying.

I bundled up and ran my usual route through Alden's Neck, around Stone Harbor, sometimes all the way down to Massaquoit. In the fall I had told myself I was running toward Christoph. I could almost feel my body lifting off the ground, propelled by the memory of him, the prospect of seeing him again. There was elation in my stride then. Now, with every week that passed, with every phone call unreturned, I was running away from him. Toward what, I didn't know. But I ran just as quickly.

IN FEBRUARY, I had an abortion. We'd been careless a few times that December, and I hadn't stopped him. I could have, but I didn't. I romanticized this risk I was willing to take for him.

I didn't tell Christoph. He was so far away, and I knew the knowledge would weigh on him. Besides, the decision was mine and I made it without hesitating. I had applied to Oxford to be closer to him, but I was becoming excited about the years of research and writing that I hoped lay ahead. I wasn't ready for a baby. Neither was he.

I think of it now more often than I did then. I wonder if it is why Christoph stayed so stubbornly, for so long, in my memory.

A MONTH AFTER the abortion, he told me he wasn't coming to Massachusetts. He said he had bought me a ticket to Germany in May, an early birthday present. He said all of this in a jovial tone, as if I should be glad. He never explained why he wasn't coming. The reasons didn't matter. I was furious but said nothing. I was still waitressing, drinking too much, fending off men in bars. Fending off Mike, who thought he owned me.

He's not coming, I told Jess over the phone. I hadn't told her about the abortion. I didn't want to get into it with her, how I could have taken such a stupid risk, and what about AIDS, and how I should have known better.

I'm absolutely shocked, she said, deadpan.

He has to study for exams, I lied. I was too embarrassed to tell her he hadn't given me a reason for backing out, that I hadn't had the courage to ask.

That's funny, she said, because I seem to remember you were also studying for exams the week he never left your bedroom.

I know. But he bought me a ticket to Germany. As a birthday present.

Don't go. Blow him off.

I can't.

Yes, you can. You do know what the Germans did to the Jews?

Jesus, Jess. I told you, Christoph isn't anti-Semitic. He's going to search the German war records to find out what happened with his grandfather.

You mean to find out if his grandfather killed Jews.

Yes. I'm sorry.

Poor Christoph. What a heavy historical burden he's carrying.

He's trying, Jess. He thinks about it all the time. How to be . . . a good German.

It sounds like he comes from a wealthy family. You said he lives in a big house in Hamburg.

Yes.

That wealth came off the backs of murdered Jews.

But is that true? His father works in finance. It's not like they owned Siemens.

Yes, it's true. How do you think Hitler kept the Germans happy during the war? Think about everything they stole from us. Houses, art, furniture, money, cars, all of it. Everything that could be plundered was sent back to Germany. They even took the fucking light bulbs. I've seen photos. The Germans never went hungry during the war. They went hungry afterward.

I remembered, chillingly, the antique furniture in Christoph's house.

I don't know what to say, Jess. He's trying to work through this stuff.

This stuff, she said, angry. You mean the Holocaust. Stop speaking in euphemisms because you're in love with a German.

I'm sorry, I said again, ashamed, knowing she was right.

There was silence on the line.

I'm sorry too, she said. This is hard for me.

I know.

She sighed. Anna, there are so many great guys in New York. Nice, smart Jewish guys. Susie and I are dating like crazy. It's not like Harvard, full of waspy finals club pricks. We can hook you up. Seriously, it's a whole different world. Why do you have to go for this random German dude across the ocean who won't commit to you, who won't even come to see you? I'm sorry but this is just one long transatlantic booty call.

It's not.

Well I'm sure he *likes* you, but it's not serious for him. And it's not serious for you either. He's hot and you're infatuated. This is simpler than you think.

It's not about that.

Right.

It's not.

At least you knew where you stood with Mike and those rowing guys.

Those guys were assholes. Fucking Mike, I never want to hear his name again.

Christoph isn't so different. He's just smoother.

He's not. Honestly, Jess, he's different.

Look, I don't know Christoph. All I know is what I remember from senior spring and the stuff you told me about your visits to Germany. And none of that is great. I'm sorry, but I think he's playing you. He's like the guy in Kierkegaard, the seducer.

What seducer?

The Seducer's Diary.

Since when do you read German philosophy?

Danish. We read it in Existentialism. Whatever. I'm just saying, you're blind to his faults. He's dicking you around, Anna. Just end it. Tell him you won't come to see him. Tell him it's his turn. I'm not saying this just because he's German. He doesn't treat you well. He never makes an effort except when it's easy for *him*. He just pays for stuff, like you're his mistress. The situation is fucked-up. He probably has a girlfriend.

I'm his girlfriend.

Are you?

Yes.

All I know is that you're the one who always goes to him. You're at his beck and call.

I had thought the same thing myself, of course.

He doesn't need to have a long-distance relationship, I said.

I wouldn't be so sure of that. Maybe those German chicks are on to him. And anyway, it's more fun to summon an American girl across the Atlantic, right? I'm sure his friends are impressed. We have a reputation in Europe, you know.

No, his roommate is sweet.

Banana, listen to me, I can see where this is going.

You think he's out of my league.

No, I think you're out of his. But you can't see that. I know you don't want to hear this, but you need to get real about Christoph. What's the endgame anyway? You marry him and move to Germany? See your family once a year at Christmas? Raise German kids? I mean, what the fuck.

I didn't know what to say. I was ashamed and embarrassed. Nothing about Christoph felt within my control. Was I just a novelty to him? An American girl he showed off to his friends? Or maybe he really was busy with exams that would determine his future. Maybe Jess didn't know what she was talking about.

Just try to be more . . . self-aware with him, okay? she said. Don't trust Christoph with your heart.

But it was far too late for that.

IN MARCH THE LETTER CAME from Oxford telling me I had been accepted into their PhD program with a full scholarship from the British government. I called Christoph, willing him to pick up, and he did.

Congratulations, *Schatz*! I'm so proud of you!

We'll be so much closer now! I was breathless, surprised and happy he had picked up. I hadn't expected to hear his voice.

It's a short flight from London to Frankfurt, right? I asked.

Right. When do you start?

In September.

Okay. He paused, then said, I'm really happy for you, *Schatz*.

The connection was bad. His voice was fading in and out.

I can't hear you very well, I said.

I said I'm happy for you. It's where you belong.

That's nice of you.

It's true. You're wasting your mind in that restaurant. We'll celebrate when I see you in May, on your birthday.

May seems so far away.

It's not so long, really.

We'll see each other more, when I start at Oxford. Right?

Right, he said. That will be an improvement. He yawned. Well my little scholar, I need to get some sleep.

Okay, I know it's late there.

We'll talk soon, *ja?*

Mmm-hmm.

I was holding back tears. He'd been so hard to reach all winter, and I didn't know when I would hear his voice again, that slight, familiar accent, whether it would be a week or a month. I wasn't ready to let him go.

I miss you so much, Christoph.

I miss you too, *Schatz.*

He was silent for a moment.

I wish you were lying next to me, he said.

I wish that too.

I wish I could touch you.

I wish you could touch me too. My voice cracked a little.

A fiery silence hung between us.

Damn, he said, then let out a long sigh. This is terrible.

I know.

He sighed again. I have to get up early.

Imagine I'm lying next to you tonight as you fall asleep, I said.

I will.

Promise me.

I will, he said, softer. You know I will.

Fall asleep in my arms.

I will. And when you come in May you'll fall asleep in mine.

It was the tenderest thing he had ever said to me.

I will, I said. Always.

Goodbye, *Schatz.*

Goodbye, Christoph.

I LANDED IN FRANKFURT on my twenty-third birthday. He was waiting for me in the arrivals hall, holding roses. I wanted to run to him, but I didn't. Nearly half a year had passed since we had seen each other. I reminded myself to be careful, to pretend I hadn't thought of him constantly for the past few months. I walked toward him, slowly, and put my arms around him, lingering in the feeling of his body against mine, finally. We kissed, then smiled at each other.

Happy birthday, *Schatz*. He handed me the roses.

I hugged him tightly, my cheek on his chest. He was wearing a navy blue polo shirt, the collar turned up, and I could smell his cologne, tobacco and clove and leather, the same one he always wore. I breathed him in, deeply, and in that moment the world seemed to right itself. I felt I was where I was supposed to be, that my life had rediscovered its proper course. I had no interest in a future that did not include him.

We kissed for a long time in his car, but then he stopped and said, Let's get home, and I thought, yes, take me home. The joy of driving back to his flat, hurrying into his room, crashing onto his bed. Touching his chest, bringing him close to me, as close as I could, my arms round his neck. We were always quiet like this in his bed and that was how I wanted it. I may have said his name. He never said mine. The only sound I wanted to hear was the cathedral bells, ringing outside his window. But I didn't listen for them.

THE NEXT MORNING we drove to Heidelberg with Matthias and his girlfriend, Saskia. Christoph reminded me I had met her once before, my first night in Germany, at the field party. We picked her up a few blocks away, and when I saw her emerge from her building I was struck by her beauty. She was thin and toned, with wavy brown shoulder-length hair, pearl earrings, and just the right amount of makeup. She wore shorts and sandals, an ivory tee, and a pretty pink-and-orange floral cotton scarf. I remembered the conversation I'd had with Matthias about his Jewish girlfriend. I wondered if Saskia knew about her.

She opened the door and ducked into the back seat, next to Matthias, who kissed her cheek. I was sitting in the front and offered, awkwardly, to switch places with her, but she smiled and said, Don't be silly. She had a stronger accent than Christoph and Matthias. I wanted her to like me. I knew I needed to make girlfriends, and I suspected it would not be easy.

As we drove away from Saskia's building, they all began speaking German. There was a lot of laughter and what sounded like teasing. I looked straight ahead, unsure how to react. I wanted to turn around and smile at them, to somehow participate, but I would look like a fool. I felt inadequate, staring out the windshield as we drove onto the Autobahn. I thought Christoph would tell them to speak English, or translate for me, but he didn't. I had never heard him speak his own language for so long, and his voice was strange and confusing. I had no idea what he was saying. I felt disoriented, like I didn't know him at all.

I pretended to sleep until we arrived in Heidelberg a half hour later. We got out of the car and Christoph took my hand. Matthias took Saskia's.

What were you talking about? I asked Christoph.

Oh, just a party, people you don't know. He put his arm around my waist. You need to learn German.

Christoph had never broached the subject of our future together and he was rarely sentimental. I often found myself translating his words into deeper emotional truths I assumed he was uncomfortable articulating because he was a man. But now he was telling me he wanted me to learn German. That meant, in my translation, a future that included me.

I want to learn, I said. I didn't before, but now I do.

Good, he said, and pulled me closer. You'll learn quickly, especially if we stop speaking English around you.

But not yet, I said.

Why not? It's the best way.

Christoph, I don't understand.

You know more than you think, probably.

No, I don't. I can barely count to ten.

You just need to make an effort.

I will. I'll take German classes at Oxford.

Good, and when you come to visit, you can practice with us.

I didn't like the casual way he said *Come to visit*. Maybe he had meant *Come to stay*. Maybe it was just his English.

I don't mind when you speak German with your friends, I lied.

We'll try to remember, he said. But Saskia's English isn't so good.

It's better than my German.

Don't worry, *Schatz,* he said, as he ran his hand up the length of my arm. I saw him glance down at my canvas purse, hanging over my shoulder.

I left the one you bought me at home, I said. I didn't want to mess it up.

He gave me a mocking frown.

I thought you liked it, he said.

I do. It's just . . . really nice.

But I like to see you in nice things.

I know. I'll bring it next time. I'm sorry.

Okay, he said, drawing the word out. I leaned my head against his shoulder.

We walked arm in arm behind Matthias and Saskia across an enchanting medieval bridge flanked on one side by two white towers with fanciful spires, like something out of a fairy tale. When we reached the middle of the bridge, the four of us leaned against the stone ledge and looked down into the brown river flowing beneath us.

Heidelberg was barely bombed during the war, Christoph said. This bridge was destroyed, but most of the city survived.

I looked across the river to the red-roofed, half-timbered buildings, the leafy green trees on the bank, and the famous rose-colored castle sitting high above the city. A German flag flew from its turret.

It's lovely, I said.

Yes, the most romantic city in Germany, Christoph said, his voice heavy with sarcasm.

Matthias poked his head forward and looked at me. I've been telling him to take you to Heidelberg since last year, he said.

Ach, too many tourists, Christoph said.

The four of us began walking again, slower this time. Saskia dropped back as Christoph and Matthias walked ahead together.

Matthias says you are studying at Oxford? She spoke with the same halting, upward lilt as Christoph's mother.

Yes, I start in September.

Oxford is very prestigious, yes? She smiled at me.

Well, yes. I'm lucky.

She smiled again. And what are you studying there?

English literature.

Shakespeare?

No, more . . . modern writers.

I love F. Scott Fitzgerald. We read *The Great Gatsby* in our English class.

That's a good book.

Do you live in New York City?

No, closer to Boston. Christoph went to a school there for a year.

Yes, I know.

I was in a band with a friend of his. That's how we met.

Yes, he told us.

I nodded. I was starting to feel the limitations of this conversation.

I'm sorry I don't speak German, I said.

That's okay. We all speak English.

Americans are terrible with languages. They don't teach us. It's not like here, where you start in kindergarten.

Well, we know we have to learn.

And what are you studying?

Dance, she said. I'm a dancer.

Ballet? I had never met a dancer before.

All kinds, but yes, mostly ballet. Then she said, her voice lower, Christoph speaks very highly of you.

He does?

Oh yes, she said, her voice still low. He talks about you.

What does he say? I couldn't help myself.

All good things. He misses you when you are in America.

I smiled. I miss him too.

Maybe now you will come more often? From Oxford?

Yes, I will.

I think he would like that.

I hope so, I said. Christoph and I had not spoken about the fall, whether I would come to Germany or he would come to England. His silence worried me.

I must be honest with you, she said. At first I did not like you. I am close to Christoph's girlfriend, Katya.

His girlfriend?

Sorry, excuse me, I mean his old girlfriend. How do you say it?

Ex-girlfriend.

Yes.

We crossed the bridge and emerged into the *Altstadt*. I was sweating.

Christoph likes American girls, she said.

He does?

Oh yes. None of us were surprised. By you, I mean.

I nodded.

There are a lot of you here in Heidelberg, she said. Studying at the university.

Uh-huh.

But you are different. For him.

How's that?

He likes you. And you keep coming back.

He asks me to come back.

That is what I mean.

Has Christoph had . . . a lot of girlfriends?

She laughed and put her hand on my shoulder, as if we were old friends. You don't want to know.

That many? I pretended to laugh too.

Don't worry, you have made a new man of him.

I have?

He is different lately. More serious.

And what about . . . Katya?

Oh, she doesn't care about Christoph anymore. She has someone else now.

Right. Okay.

We walked in silence. I knew I was vulnerable here in Germany, at the mercy of a man who, as Jess liked to point out, had never once called me his girlfriend. Sometimes he called me his American girl, but what did that mean, really?

Christoph, I said loudly.

He turned around.

Can we stop? I need some water.

Before I could say anything more, he ducked into a nearby shop. I waited outside with Matthias and Saskia. I hadn't meant for him to get the water. It was something I could have done myself.

Anna was telling me about Oxford, Saskia said to Matthias.

Yes, he said, I haven't congratulated you properly. Well done!

Thanks.

Which college are you at?

Corpus Christi.

I went to Oxford once, he said. Just a day trip from London. It was beautiful. The dreaming spires. Isn't that what they say?

I've never been.

Really? he said.

No. I just . . .

I stopped myself. I didn't want them to know how much Christoph had weighed upon my decision to study in England.

Just then Christoph emerged from the shop with bottles of water. He stepped out, looked around, and met my gaze. His face lit up in a wide, white smile. His hair was very blond in the sun. I forgot about the conversation with Saskia.

He passed around the water and Matthias said, Let's go see the castle. Christoph let out a small groan.

Come on, Christoph, Matthias said, she's never been.

Do you want to see the castle? Christoph asked me.

Of course I want to see the castle, I said. I smiled at Matthias, who smiled back. Saskia gave me a look and took Matthias's hand.

All right, Christoph said, raising his hands in surrender. We'll see the castle.

The four of us walked down a narrow cobblestone street past white and pink and light blue buildings with window boxes full of flowers. We started up the hill. It was a long walk, but I was glad we chose the pathway rather than the funicular with the tourists. There was little shade, and the sun was strong. By the time we reached the castle terrace I was hot and tired. But the view over the moat toward the red roofs of the *Altstadt* and the Neckar River was extraordinary, exactly what was promised in the German guidebook I had read that winter. Even

Christoph seemed impressed, standing there in the sun, his hands resting on the stone ledge. Matthias offered to take my picture, so I gave
him my camera and turned to face him with a smile. He said something
to Christoph in German, and then Christoph turned and put his arm
around me. Smile! Matthias said. I was grateful. I wanted a picture with
Christoph but I refused to ask him for one. And he had never offered.

Even in its ruined state, the castle was majestic. The round tower
had been destroyed by an invading French army in the sixteenth century, Matthias said, and had never been rebuilt. We stopped to admire
a Renaissance façade, with its statues of Bavarian dukes. Christoph let
out another groan and I laughed. I was enchanted by the charming log-
gias and Gothic windows, the crumbling walls and fountains. This was,
I thought, a very romantic place to visit with the person you loved.

She needs to see the wine barrel, Matthias said to Christoph.

Christoph nodded but said nothing as we followed Matthias down
into a cool cellar amid a crowd of tourists. Inside, there was an enormous wooden cask, so big you had to walk up a staircase to reach the top
of it.

It's the biggest wine barrel in the world, Matthias said. It was built in
the eighteenth century, but then it started to leak. That floor up there, on
the top of the barrel? It was made for dances.

Dances? I said. Down here?

He shrugged and smiled and then read a wall plaque, out loud,
informing us that the cask held eighteen thousand bottles of wine.

Such decadence, Christoph said, but he was smiling now too.

Our ancestors, Matthias said, smiling, pointing at the giant cask.
Saskia was silent beside him.

We emerged back outside onto a different terrace and took in another
wide view of the *Altstadt*. Behind us a bride and groom posed for photographs in front of the rose-colored castle wall. I tried not to stare at
the bride in her white tulle gown and long veil, her bouquet of red roses.

What now? Matthias asked. Shall we do the Philosopher's Walk?

Let's relax, Christoph said. Have some wine. What do you think? he
asked me and Saskia.

That sounds nice, I said. Saskia said something in German.

Okay, *vámonos,* Christoph said.

We walked down the hill to the *Altstadt.* Saskia started speaking German with Christoph and Matthias, and soon they were all laughing. I looked out at the view. I didn't mind. I understood now that Christoph wasn't shutting me out when he spoke his own language. He was letting me in.

We walked back over the bridge to the other side of the river, returned to the car, and drove up a series of winding, wooded streets. I didn't know where we were going and I didn't ask. Christoph parked the car, and we walked up a dirt-and-gravel path that led to an enormous amphitheater. The stone benches and stage were covered by grass and moss and dandelions. The entire structure seemed to be sinking into the ground. And yet there were children playing, couples stretched out on blankets with picnic hampers, groups of mothers laughing and cradling their infants.

Christoph and Matthias spread two blankets on the grassy stage, and the four of us sat down. They took bread, cheese, salami, and two bottles of wine out of their backpacks. I hadn't realized they'd packed a picnic for us, these men, and I was delighted. It all seemed very European. Saskia stayed quiet as I thanked them. The energy had changed between us, and it was she now who seemed wary of me.

We drank the wine, ate the bread and cheese. They spoke English at first, then Saskia began speaking to Matthias in German. The two of them lay back on their blanket and Christoph and I lay down on ours. We closed our eyes and held hands, sleepy after the wine. I felt the sun warm my arms and legs. After a while, Christoph opened his eyes and leaned toward me.

Come here, he said quietly.

I'm here.

Closer.

I moved toward him, and he leaned down to kiss me.

You're beautiful, he said.

What? I laughed. No one had ever said this to me before.

You're beautiful, he said again. He moved a strand of hair away from my face.

So are you, I said. I had wanted to tell him this for a long time.

He smiled and kissed me again and then we both lay back down on the blanket, our faces to the sky, my hand in his. He rubbed the back of my hand with his thumb. I was so very happy.

After a while, I propped myself up on my elbows and looked around. What is this place? I asked.

An old Nazi amphitheater, he said, his eyes still closed.

What?

Goebbels opened it. He got his PhD from the university here, in Heidelberg, in the twenties.

Goebbels had a PhD?

Yes. Christoph sat up and drank some water. In Romantic literature. There are powerful connections between German Romanticism and the Nazi movement. Surely you know this.

Wagner.

Yes, and others. That's why I don't like Heidelberg. Look at this place, it's dripping with Romanticism. When they held the Nazi rallies here, there would have been torchlights up and down this hill, twenty thousand people. All this stone was supposed to symbolize the endurance of National Socialism.

Then why do people still come here?

Ach, the city doesn't know what to do with it. Do you turn these old Nazi sites into museums, or do you let people reclaim them, transform them? Well, this place has been reclaimed. There are music shows here in the summer, families come for picnics. Tourists don't know about it. But the city won't keep it up. They don't know what to do with it. So it's in this . . . limbo.

I nodded. I had assumed any site with a Nazi past, however tenuous, would be metaphorically radioactive, like Christoph had said. Apparently not. It struck me as odd that so many people came here to relax in the summer sun. I felt uncomfortable lounging there with Christoph, knowing what it had once been. Joseph Goebbels had stood on the stage where I was now sitting.

You're okay with this place? I said.

Yes. We've taken it back.

I nodded. Who was I to say. But I thought of Jess, of what she would think if she saw me lounging in a Nazi amphitheater.

Christoph, I don't like this place.

Do you want to go?

Maybe.

He looked over at Matthias and Saskia, and said something to them in German. Okay, Matthias said. He began to get up, but Saskia grabbed his hand and pulled him back down, laughing.

Christoph turned to me and shrugged. It wasn't my country, my history. But I couldn't shake it off, that dark, lingering presence.

WE DROVE BACK to his university town, mostly in silence. Christoph parked the car and Saskia returned to the flat with us. I wondered why she had never stayed over before when I was visiting. I asked Christoph about it that night in bed.

Usually he stays at her place when you're here, he said.

Why?

He shrugged. To give us privacy.

That's nice of him.

Yes.

But tonight she came.

Maybe her roommate has someone over.

I think we got off on the wrong foot.

You and Saskia?

Maybe I was too friendly with Matthias. I don't know.

It's not that. Saskia's difficult, and she doesn't like me.

Oh. Why not?

She's friends with someone I used to go with.

Katya?

Yes.

She called her your girlfriend.

He gave me a confused look. I don't know why she said that.

Okay. Just making sure.

He sighed, suddenly exasperated. This is a stupid conversation. I don't know why Saskia brought her up.

Don't get mad. I just want to make sure I'm not missing something.

You're not.

All right.

He sighed again. The air around him was charged. I didn't like it.

Why are you upset? I asked.

I'm not.

You are, I can tell. What's going on?

Nothing. He laughed. Come.

He put his arms around me and kissed me and said, Did you have a nice day today?

Of course I did. Because I was with you.

He smiled.

So let's not fight about stupid things. Forget Saskia. She's just jealous of you. You're American, you're smart, you're beautiful. Any girl would be jealous of you.

I wanted her to like me, I said, my head on his chest.

I know.

Maybe you could introduce me to some of your other friends.

You didn't like it when I tried that before.

At the field party?

Yes. You got angry with me.

Things were different then.

I know.

It would help me learn German, if I made friends with other girls.

I'll make it happen.

You'll set me up on some dates? I said, tracing circles on his shoulder.

Yes. I have a lot of friends. I just haven't taken you around to meet them. I didn't want to make you angry again.

I don't want to meet Katya, though, I teased.

No. And she doesn't want to meet you either.

She told you?

No, but . . . I've heard.

When I thought about Christoph with Katya, I felt ill.

She was there that night, at the football party, he said. In the car with us. She was in the back seat with Matthias and Saskia.

She was?

Yes. So you've already met.

I don't remember her.

Well, you were jet-lagged and cranky.

Why was Katya in the car?

We're still friends.

Oh.

I try to stay friends.

I nodded, willing myself to look casual.

Have you had a lot of them? I asked. Girlfriends?

A few. And you?

I wanted, in that moment, to tell him what he meant to me. That he was the first man who didn't leave my bed at dawn. That he was the first man who made me breakfast, poured me coffee, gave me roses. That he was the first man who didn't fear my intelligence. Who played Debussy for me, who took me to museums, castles, mountaintops. That he was the first man who told me I was beautiful. Who cared about my pleasure. Who listened.

Same, I said. A few.

He nodded.

And what would they make of me, do you think? he asked.

I thought of Mike, how jealous he would be of Christoph, his sophistication, his worldliness.

Maybe I'll introduce you someday, I said.

Or maybe not, he said, holding me closer.

I had a few run-ins with one this winter.

He tensed. Who?

This guy Mike . . . We've known each other for a while. He wouldn't leave me alone. He thought he was still . . . with me . . . even after I told him about you.

Asshole, he said.

Yeah. Well, you never came.

I will come, *Schatz*, I promise. I knew you were angry. But I needed to study. Exams are more important here. They determine everything.

I know. It's okay.

I wanted to tell him about the abortion then, and how lonely I had been all winter. How lonely I would be when I returned to Massachusetts without him.

Matthias was right, I said. Heidelberg is lovely.

Tomorrow we're going to Munich.

We are?

Yes. I thought I could take you to Berchtesgaden too. So you can see where your grandfather went, in '45.

Really?

Yes. It's beautiful up in the Alps.

I was moved by this gesture, that he had remembered. It made me feel closer to him. Maybe all this sightseeing was Christoph's way of showing love. He was returning me to my own history, and I wanted to meet his generosity. He had shared so much with me, things he hadn't told anyone. It was my turn, now, to trust him.

There's something I haven't told you, I said.

He looked at me. What?

I don't know if I should.

Tell me, he said. It's all right.

My grandfather was at Dachau. His unit was one of the first to get there.

He looked up at the ceiling. My God.

I don't think he actually liberated it. I think another unit had already done that. He didn't talk much about it. But his unit was the next one to arrive. He saw everything. All of it.

Christoph was quiet for a moment, then turned back to me.

Do you want to go? he asked.

Yes, I think so.

I'll take you.

Have you been?

Yes. He shook his head. Whatever I say won't be . . . You'll see. You want me to come, yes?

Yes. But you don't have to.

I'll come. But why didn't you tell me, before?

I wanted to. I just . . . couldn't.

He nodded. Do your roommates know this, about your grandfather?

No.

You should tell them.

I don't know why I haven't. It's not a secret.

I understand, he said, and held me tighter.

You always understand me.

Always? He smiled.

Always.

We were quiet again.

You should see it, he said.

You'll come with me?

Of course I'll come with you.

I don't want to go alone.

I'll be with you.

You'd do that for me?

Of course.

I'm worried it's too much to ask.

It's not.

But I felt a vague sense of warning, that I shouldn't ask this of him. That we should spend what little time we had left together strolling around the places I had read about in my Munich guidebook, like the English Garden or Marienplatz. I suddenly wished I had not brought it up. I wanted to take the story back. And that desire, to sail calmly on, made me ashamed. I needed to tell him everything.

He took pictures, I said.

Your grandfather?

Yes. At Dachau.

He was silent for a moment.

You've seen them?

Yes. His sister put them in a scrapbook she made for him when he got back from the Pacific. After Hiroshima.

Are they . . .

Horrific.

He nodded. They should be in a museum.

I know. The scrapbook is in my grandmother's attic.

With the flag?

Yes.

Listen, it's good that your grandfather took those pictures. Maybe he wanted to document it in case the Nazis said it never happened. Those photos are evidence of war crimes.

I know. But it's hard for me to imagine him standing there, taking them. Having the composure.

Did he ever tell you why he took them?

No. And now I'll never know.

This has upset you, he said, stroking my hair.

The photos, Christoph. The bodies, stacked in the train cars. It was car after car after car of bodies. From Buchenwald, he said. And piles on the ground . . . *hills* of bodies. Emaciated, naked. Worse than any of the photos I've ever seen in school, in books, anywhere. And my own grandfather took them. Why? Why did he take them? Were they some kind of . . . souvenir? Like the flag?

Schatz, he said.

I wish I had never seen them. I wish I had never looked. I don't know how he could stand it. I don't know how you live a normal life after witnessing something like that. After I saw those photos in his scrapbook, I knew. It's why he drank.

Shhh, he said, holding me tighter.

I don't want to speak when we go there, I said.

No, we won't.

It's not my history. I'm not Jewish. I'm not German. But I feel this terrible connection to that place. Because of him. I hesitated. And because of you.

Shhh, he whispered again. You don't have to explain.

His words were kind, but I thought I heard something else in his voice, a distant, rueful note. And then I realized that the word I was looking for was a word Sebald often used.

Disquiet.

12

Christoph and I stayed at a small hotel near Munich's *Hauptbahnhof*. After we checked in, I pushed the button for the elevator, but Christoph shook his head and gestured for me to follow him through a service door and up the concrete stairs. He was carrying my backpack. I had felt such satisfaction the night before as I watched him place his folded clothes into that backpack, thinking, We are going away together.

I followed him up three flights of stairs and then we turned right, down a long, dark hallway. Our room was at the end. Christoph unlocked the door and set the backpack gently on the floor. The room was small and clean, the walls navy blue. There was a queen-size bed with a white duvet in the middle and, to its right, a large, wide window that overlooked bustling Bahnhofplatz. Christoph lay down on the bed, smiled at me, and stretched his arm across the mattress.

Come, he said.

I dropped my purse on the floor and went to him. He curled his arm around me as I lay on my side and pressed my body to his. He kissed the top of my head, and I closed my eyes. We stayed like that for a while, listening to the sirens outside and the bells of the trams as they ran smoothly and quietly along their flat city tracks. What was happening between us felt, finally, aligned with my vision of what I wanted to happen, what was supposed to happen. And yet I didn't trust that vision. It had the hazy, shimmering quality of a mirage.

Shall we wander? he said.

We got up and left the hotel. Christoph led me through the wide, busy streets to a small, quiet square with trees and outdoor cafés. We emerged onto Marienplatz and stood among the crowds before the famous Gothic *Rathaus* with its glockenspiel that danced twice a day. Christoph told me this was where the Americans had set up their headquarters, after the war. I wanted to linger, to watch the royal figures in the clock tower turn, but he seemed impatient and said we could come back later. He walked quickly as I followed him through a large archway and down a busy street lined with souvenir shops selling Bavarian kitsch—teddy bears in lederhosen, cowbells, a hundred different steins.

He led me into the Hofbräuhaus, past long wooden tables full of loud, drunk Americans until we found seats. There was a mural on the arched ceiling of vegetables and pigs' heads and Bavarian flags. Ornate glass lanterns hung low. I saw a painting on the wall of a blond woman cradling two beer steins in her bodice. Waitresses in dirndls roamed the echoing hall with baskets of enormous pretzels. It was all ridiculous, and I laughed as a waiter set down huge beers in heavy glass steins before us. Christoph lifted his stein and smiled. I lifted mine with both hands.

Prost, he said.

Prost.

You have to look someone in the eye when you do this, he said.

I always look you in the eye.

Well if you *don't*, it's seven years of bad sex.

That's not the answer I was expecting, but okay.

He laughed. I should have told you before.

Germans are weird, I said, and he laughed harder into his beer. I loved to make him laugh. It didn't happen often.

Just then the oompah band on the small stage behind me started to play. I moved to the other side of the table, next to Christoph, so I could see the bright brass instruments and the musicians decked out in lederhosen and feathered green caps, but mostly just to feel the heat of him, the touch of his arm, his leg next to mine, his hand on my thigh. I remembered, again, that I would be leaving in a few days. The knowledge pierced through me, the opposite of waking after a bad dream. I willed it away. We sat and we drank out of those heavy glass steins and we listened to music that reminded me of crisp Oktoberfests on New England village greens. Maples blazing crimson, cloudless blue skies, the days still warm.

Ready? Christoph said when we finished our beers. I nodded and followed him outside to the sunny street. I was already feeling the alcohol.

We walked back the way we came. He turned a corner, a few steps ahead of me, into a small square and there, suddenly, was the Frauenkirche with its Gothic brick façade, copper-green domes, and red-orange roof. I recognized the church from photographs. The domes looked vaguely Russian. The church was closed to visitors for restoration, so we walked into the adjacent square, protected from the bustle of Marienplatz. Christoph said there was a good restaurant there, an Augustiner that served traditional Bavarian food. We sat down at an outdoor table, under a blue-and-white checkered awning, with a view of the Frauenkirche. Everyone around us spoke German, quietly.

A pretty waitress in a dirndl came over, and Christoph ordered. I noticed that the waitress smiled at him longer than she should have. And that he smiled back.

So what did you think of the mother ship? he said after she took our order.

Sorry?

The Hofbräuhaus. It's the most famous beer hall in the world.

It was fun. But I like it better here.

I thought you might.

He looked up and pointed to the twin towers of the Frauenkirche.

The Allied pilots used those spires as reference points when they bombed the city, he said.

Did it survive?

No. In the end they bombed it too. They bombed everything.

But not Heidelberg, I said.

No, not Heidelberg. They left Heidelberg alone. It was too beautiful to destroy. They had plans to make it a headquarters after the war. But Munich, they destroyed. Munich was the beginning of everything. You know all this, yes? About the Beer Hall Putsch?

In the Hofbräuhaus?

No, a few miles from here. Hitler and some of his followers stayed up all night drinking, then marched into the city. This was 1923. The police stopped them near Marienplatz. They fired, killed some of them. Hitler was arrested and went to jail. That's where he wrote *Mein Kampf*. Everything began in Munich.

I nodded, drank my weissbier.

How do you say Munich in German? I asked.

München.

Moonshen, I said, my mouth wrapping round the odd-shaped syllables.

He smiled. Good enough.

I have a good teacher.

You do.

When we finished eating—schnitzel and cabbage and potato dumplings—he paid the bill and stood up. Come, he said. I followed him through the crowded streets until he stopped in front of a stolid, stately stone building.

This is where Chamberlain met with Hitler in 1938. Where he annexed the Sudetenland.

Peace for our time.

Yes. I thought this place would interest you.

It does.

I searched the building for a sign of what had happened inside it. But the façade bore no trace of its history.

People think Chamberlain was naive, Christoph said. But he was just buying time. The British weren't ready for war in 1938. Look what happened at Dunkirk. Their army had to be rescued by fishing boats.

I nodded, though I didn't know about Dunkirk then.

Chamberlain was just buying time, he said again. He knew what he was doing.

We stood before the building for a few minutes, and then Christoph began walking. I followed in silence. Twice he pulled me back as speeding bicycles came within inches of me. They were everywhere, and yet I couldn't see them coming.

You seem to have a death wish, he said, the second time he grabbed my arm. You need to watch where you're going.

But these bikes are coming from all directions, I said. I can't tell the difference between the bike lanes and the sidewalks. And the trams are so quiet.

Well, the bike lanes are, you know, the lanes with *bikes*.

I thought he was joking, but his face was expressionless.

Sorry, I said.

He half nodded and started walking again, faster this time. I followed him until we came to a grand arched monument with statues of lions and imperial soldiers. It looked like something from before the war. He stopped alongside it.

This is the Feldherrnhalle, he said. See? He pointed to some bullet holes, barely visible in the stone wall. He seemed impatient again. These are from the Beer Hall Putsch. What I was telling you about before.

I touched the bullet holes.

When Hitler came to power, Christoph said, lowering his voice, he turned this place into a shrine. Everyone had to *heil* Hitler when they walked by.

What if you refused?

They'd send you to Dachau.

I nodded.

Some people went through a passageway, nearby, he said, but the Gestapo watched them. There was no way around.

Christoph looked at the bullet holes for another moment.

Heil Hitler or go to Dachau, he said.

I wasn't sure if he was asking me. I didn't answer.

We walked back to the hotel in silence.

IN BED THAT NIGHT I kept forgetting to breathe. As if my breath could make him disappear. The way he touched my arms, my shoulders, my back. Lightly, so lightly I barely felt his fingertips. I looked down at him and touched his chest and he rose to me and then I was beyond him, my hands behind my head, his fingers laced through mine. We had forgotten to close the curtains and I could see the stoplights of Munich flashing green, yellow, red, and the drunks stumbling along empty sidewalks on Bahnhofplatz.

The sun woke me at dawn. I stood up to close the curtains. But when I looked at Christoph sleeping, his arms round his pillow, the white duvet halfway down his bare back, I opened them again. I watched him turn gold in the new morning light.

THE NEXT DAY we drove down the Autobahn to Berchtesgaden, past green meadows and Swiss-style chalets and glimmers of the Alps, still snowcapped in May. I played Blur and Radiohead, a little Hole. The ride was long, and by the time Christoph parked at the bottom of the mountain, I was ready to walk. But he said the walk would be steep and we weren't wearing the right shoes, so we took the bus up the winding road to the Kehlsteinhaus. The Eagle's Nest. My grandfather had called it Hitler's summer house, but the bus driver announced, in German and English, that the Nazis had built it for Hitler's fiftieth birthday and that Hitler hadn't spent much time there. Bullshit, Christoph said under his breath, looking out the window.

I wasn't paying attention. I was entranced by the view of the forest and the Alps as we drove up the mountain. The scene reminded me of Switzerland, of my time in Gstaad the previous summer, when I had walked and walked and tried to forget Christoph. Now I was glad I had returned to him, after Switzerland. I had made the right decision.

We were practically in Austria, the bus driver said. The road and the house were marvels of engineering at the time, he said. My ears popped as we ascended.

The bus stopped at a small parking lot high up the mountain. I knew this was where the black Gestapo cars had dropped off Hitler's henchmen, small swastika flags flying on the cars' hoods. Christoph took my hand and together we walked through an arched entryway into a long, dank tunnel, deep into the mountain's core. Electric lights lit our path, and wet stone bricks glistened above us.

When the Americans arrived, Christoph whispered, this tunnel was filled with wine.

Wine?

So they say.

At the end of the tunnel we waited in line to take Hitler's elevator to the Eagle's Nest. Inside, I rested my head against Christoph's shoulder as we throttled upward in the gold and mirrored box. The elevator was crowded with tourists, mostly Americans. Forty seconds later the doors opened and we walked out to the terrace. We leaned against the wooden railing and took it all in: the rocky, blue-gray Alps, high meadows, islands of dark evergreens, cobalt lakes.

The Nazi Neuschwanstein, Christoph said. And a mad king to boot.

Behind us was a busy restaurant full of people eating lunch, drinking golden beer and white wine. Smiling, laughing, enjoying a beautiful day in May. I turned to the mountains and took photos of the Alps from different angles along the terrace. Couples asked strangers to take their picture as they embraced in front of the dramatic backdrop. I wanted to do the same, or at least take Christoph's picture, his face framed by the snowy peaks. But I didn't ask. He had never taken my picture, never brought his camera on our excursions.

We walked along the terrace, then ventured inside the Kehlsteinhaus, into the great room. This was where Hitler had met with his top aides. Now it was full of rectangular wooden tables set with white paper placemats and cutlery standing straight in Bavarian steins. A small bar in the corner sold drinks and postcards. The room was mostly empty. People were outside, sitting in the sun.

I walked over to the maroon marble fireplace my grandfather had told me about, where the GIs had carved their names, and looked up at the space above the mantel where the swastika flag had hung. Now, hanging in its place, was a kitschy alpine painting. I imagined my grandfather's army buddies hoisting him up to grab the flag's corner, the flag falling on them, a deflated parachute. Had they laughed? Were they drunk? The fireplace looked vandalized, hacked. A sign next to it said it had likely been a gift from Mussolini, and that American GIs had chipped off pieces as souvenirs. Christoph stood behind me and put his hands on my shoulders as I peered at the faded names carved into the wine-dark marble. I looked for my grandfather's name, but I couldn't find it.

He was here, I said. Right here.

I photographed the fireplace, and then we walked down a small set of steps onto the adjoining sun terrace. I stood under the high, wood-beamed ceiling and gazed out through the large arched windows overlooking the Alps. Christoph put his hands on my shoulders again, and I leaned back into him.

He was here too, I said. I know it.

Yes. I wonder what he felt that day. This was the top of the world.

I imagined my grandfather sitting in a wicker chair, drinking from a bottle of whiskey, looking out over the mountains.

Lucky, I said, knowing this was true. He felt lucky.

We left the sun terrace and spent a few minutes in a wood-paneled room where, a wall plaque stated, Eva Braun used to hold court. Then we walked back outside, past the restaurant's patio, and up a high rocky trail. Serious-looking hikers with walking poles swept past us.

We sat down on a wide, flat rock overlooking the daggered, snow-capped summits, the deep blue lakes. A light wind blew. We were quiet.

Should we get a beer? Christoph said after a while, his eyes still on the mountains.

I looked over my shoulder, back down the hill, at the bright blue Hofbräu München umbrellas on the patio. The restaurant was crowded.

No, I said. Not here.

Too strange? He looked at me and smiled.

Nobody else seems to mind. Just us.

Just you, he said, gently bumping my shoulder with his. Come, let's have a beer. Your grandfather would want you to. You know he would.

Probably.

I'm sure he and his GI friends had a few drinks up here. Don't you think? He bumped my shoulder again. So come. Let's have a beer. In his honor.

I wanted to stay on that rock a little longer. I suspected I would never be here again, that this would be my only chance to take in this view, with Christoph. That I should let my eyes linger on the Alps for as long as I could. But when Christoph stood up and reached out his hand, I grasped it.

We sat down at a table on the edge of the terrace, and I ordered two beers. Christoph smiled at me.

Did you find any photos of this place in your grandfather's scrapbook? he asked.

No.

Strange. This was a big deal, getting here first. Why didn't he take any, do you think?

Good question. Maybe he ran out of film.

At least he took the flag.

A waiter set the beers down on our table. *Danke schön*, I said. *Bitte schön*, the waiter replied, smiling.

Someday you'll show me, Christoph said. When I come to Boston.

I had been looking out at the view, but now I turned to him.

That's a strange request, I said.

He shrugged. It's my history.

And mine.

Yes. Ours.

He lifted his beer and looked me in the eye.

To your grandfather, he said.

I raised my glass. To Jack.

We clinked our glasses and drank. Christoph set down his beer and looked out over the Alps, the clear blue sky. Then he turned back to me, cocked his head to one side, and smiled. The sun seemed to shine brighter around him at this high altitude, though it could have been a trick of light.

I like this place, he said.

Me too, I admitted. It's been sufficiently desecrated.

By your grandfather.

And capitalists.

He smiled.

I like it that I'm here with you, he said.

I like it too.

What would our grandfathers think? If they could see us here together?

Mine would be happy. And yours?

He gave me a rueful look. Which one.

The one in the picture. Hans. The one in the Wehrmacht.

I don't know. He shrugged. We lost the war.

And yet here we are.

Yes. Here we are.

He raised his glass to me. The light glinted off his watch.

To Jack, he said. Who survived.

And Hans. They were lucky. Like us.

Christoph set his glass down and pushed it away.

No, he said, shaking his head. No.

THE NEXT MORNING we ate a quiet breakfast at the hotel, then drove to Dachau. Christoph told me it wasn't far from Munich. My grandfather had said the same. I remembered his words from my interview: The Germans, they knew. They all knew.

We parked and walked down a tree-lined dirt road, past several school groups, teenagers laughing and flirting. Christoph glared coldly at them as we passed.

They should be more respectful, he said.

They're just kids.

We didn't act like that.

They haven't seen anything yet.

Yes, he said. Maybe they are quieter, after.

We walked in silence for a few minutes until we came to the camp's main gate. I recognized it from one of my grandfather's photographs. I stood where I thought he had stood when he took the photo, the point where the railway line began, and ended, next to a half-ruined platform. Its foundation was crumbling into the dirt. There was a sign about the transports, but I didn't read it. I heard wooden train doors rolling open, barking dogs, crying children. I heard SS men shouting orders in German. I knew these sounds were from movies I had seen. *Sophie's Choice*. *Schindler's List*. For how could I know? How could I begin to imagine? And yet I felt it there, for just a moment—terror, its echoes and vibrations still carried on the air.

I turned away.

Christoph held my hand as we entered the main camp through the open iron gate. *Arbeit Macht Frei*. Beyond the gate, it was quiet. The grounds were vast and empty, apart from the tour groups, huddled together, listening to their guides. Guard towers loomed around the prison's perimeter. They made me afraid.

We walked into an old SS building. Now it was a museum. As soon as I saw the information counter and small bookshop, I felt relief. It was easier to walk through these somber white rooms with their objects and photographs than to stand outside by the train tracks, the ruined platform.

We entered through a room with a floor-to-ceiling map detailing the concentration camp network in Germany, Poland, France, even Belgium. There were dozens of smaller camps, hundreds it seemed, clustered around the bigger camps like Dachau, Buchenwald, Bergen-Belsen, Auschwitz. Satellite camps, the map called them. Black dots, scattered across Europe.

But . . . there are so many, I said to Christoph.

Yes, he said. They were everywhere.

We moved into a cavernous white room full of displays and artifacts. Striped uniforms, political posters, prisoners' art, a wooden handcart, photographs, an enormous SS desk, maps of the prisoners' origins. The walls were white, except for one that had been left in its original state. The plaster was crumbling, the white paint fading to reveal mottled spots of gray underneath. The words *Rauchen verboten*, barely visible, were painted in large black Germanic script.

What does it mean? I asked Christoph.

No smoking, he whispered.

We passed a photograph of Dachau prisoners, some with blankets, walking on a wet, rainy street. I read the caption. It was a death march. A young German man had taken the photograph from his parents' balcony as they passed.

Christoph took my hand. I hadn't realized I'd let go.

We walked into the next room. There were two short, silent films playing on a loop. One was a newsreel of the Americans arriving in Munich at the end of April 1945. I watched the GIs roll into the ruined city atop their tanks. They looked calm and happy. Stone-faced German women, children, and old men lined the road, holding limp white handkerchiefs. White flags hung from windows. German prisoners of war in double-breasted coats walked through the streets, their hands behind their heads in surrender. SS or Wehrmacht, I couldn't tell. Long lines of these surrendering soldiers snaked through the city, under ruined arches into Marienplatz, past the bombed-out Frauenkirche. German women wiped away tears as they watched their vanquished soldiers pass. One of the soldiers gazed straight into the camera with a contemptuous look as he marched by. I startled. He looked just like Christoph.

When the film ended, I watched it a second time and saw him again—the same face, the same build, the same light hair. He was wearing a Nazi uniform and staring, it seemed, at me. This time I shivered. It was Christoph, in black and white.

I looked behind me. My heart was beating very fast. Christoph was reading something across the room. I walked over to him, touched him lightly on the shoulder.

It's the poem, he said. The one I told you about, by Borowski. The love poem. He wrote it here, at Dachau.

I looked under the glass at the tattered manuscript, the tiny, faded letters. Next to it was an English translation:

> *I know you are alive. Otherwise*
> *what sense would there be in the shadow and light*
> *of faraway cold stars, reflections*
> *of a crystal world? The black earth*
> *seems to blaze with dew, the woods*
> *rise up darkly above the horizon*

as if it were the sea's blue depths,
and my blood pulses as if its beat answered
the beat of the waves of all the seas in the universe,
so close to me and yet so far,
pulsing with your blood.
I feel you are here, I know you are.

A plaque below said that Borowski had written the poem to his fian-cée, whom he had last seen alive at Auschwitz. Her name was Maria, but he called her Tuśka. After he was liberated from Dachau, he searched for her for two years. He finally found her in Sweden, and they married.

It's beautiful, I said.

Yes.

I wondered how Borowski had survived Auschwitz, survived Dachau. Had his love for Tuśka saved him? Had poetry? I thought of Adorno. *To write poetry after Auschwitz is barbaric.*

I walked back to the looping films. Christoph stayed where he was. I understood then that he did not want to watch the films. That he could not watch them. I decided to say nothing about the soldier in the news-reel, his ghostly doppelgänger. I decided I had imagined it all. And maybe I had.

The other film was taken on the day Dachau was liberated. I stood behind a small group of German teenagers and watched. This film was in color, and panned over prisoners in their uniforms waving to Ameri-can GIs at the edge of the barbed wire fence. I was surprised to see boys among them, twelve or thirteen. I had forgotten there were children. Prisoners surrounded the front gate, hanging out of windows, pouring out of the camp. A GI stood on a platform, pointing to something, try-ing to keep order.

This film showed the death trains from Buchenwald, the open box-cars, the bodies. I knew these images from my grandfather's photo-graphs. But I had only seen them as black-and-white stills. Now there was color, movement. Now it was real. I wanted to close my eyes, but I didn't. GIs moved among the bodies. Sometimes they looked up at the camera, their hands on their hips, shaking their heads. Then the film cut to a prisoner cooking something in a small pan over a makeshift flame. I remembered the word my grandfather had used. *Emaciated.* Who was this man? Who had he been before Dachau? I was surrounded, in this room, by the things they had worn and touched and drawn and written and still I did not know who they had been. That was what I wanted to know, more than anything. Who they had been.

When the film ended, I closed my eyes. I didn't watch it again, but the German teenagers did.

OUTSIDE, it was getting hot. The sky was cloudless and blue. Christoph and I stopped and stood before a large iron sculpture of skeletal, twisted limbs. He held my hand. I didn't know if I should try to imagine the scenes of suffering that had occurred here, or just stand in silence and pray. But I hadn't prayed since I was a child. The grounds were vast, quiet. I looked at Christoph. He was staring at the sculpture.

After a few minutes we began to walk in silence toward the barracks. We overheard a British tour guide say that the camp had been repurposed after the war, turned into a small suburban development, but that the barracks had all deteriorated by the 1960s. Now there were rows and rows of foundations, scarred into the land. One barrack had been rebuilt. We followed the tour group into it. I tried to conjure sick and starving prisoners in the small, stacked bunks, the open lavatory. The dark, cold mornings before the roll call. But the rooms were clean and empty and betrayed no suffering.

We trailed along with the group, down what the tour guide called the camp road, a wide dirt lane bordered by two tall rows of linden trees. This was one of the only places, she said, where people could gather to pray or exchange information. Dachau had been mostly male political prisoners until late in the war. Then the Jews came, and the women. She said the women were used as prostitutes for the male prisoners. To keep them working. To keep them from committing suicide. Many prisoners threw themselves at the barbed wire fence that surrounded the camp, she said. They knew they would be shot. There were many, many deaths by suicide, she said.

Christoph held my hand as we walked in silence down the long, dusty road, between the linden trees. We fell back and let the group move ahead. We walked slowly. I heard birdsong, felt his presence next to me. He was wearing a white linen shirt, khaki shorts, brown Birkenstocks. I felt the rhythm of our joined hands moving as we walked. The angular green trees swayed in the wind and the thought came to me, sudden and unbidden, that the love I felt for Christoph was a miracle. That a person could feel this way for another. I tried to chase the thought away. It felt selfish and obscene here—a profanity. But the words kept recurring, over and over in my mind. That I had been granted something miraculous—to be capable of such feeling. I don't know why it came to me there, this dawning. It was the last thing I'd expected to feel. I had sensed, when I stood at the ruined platform, that I would not be the same person who left as the person who entered. But I was already failing them, the murdered, with my strange, intrusive thoughts of love. This was no way to honor the dead. And yet all I could think as I walked next to Christoph was that love was stronger than death.

At the road's end, we both stopped and faced a round stone memorial. My love for Christoph in that moment felt like a defiance of his history. I thought of Borowski's poem. *I feel you are here, I know you are.* And I knew then that love moved beyond history. They had loved too, the men and women and children who had died here, prayed here, suffered here. I vowed, silently, that I would always stand in awe of this love, its ferocity and selflessness. I didn't tell Christoph what I was thinking. I never would. But somehow, I suspect, he knew.

WE TURNED LEFT, past another memorial, and crossed a bridge over a small stream. Christoph held my hand as we walked toward the long, low brick building that contained the gas chamber and crematorium. I thought about the murdered Jews and communists and Roma and intellectuals and dissidents. I thought about my nineteen-year-old grandfather, walking through these same hunched doorways fifty years before.

We entered the building in silence. There were photographs on the wall of American GIs walking shoulder-high amid corpses, holding handkerchiefs to their faces. Now everybody was quiet, the British tour group and the German teenagers. I saw the word *Brausebad* in large capital letters above the green-framed iron doorway that led into the gas chamber. I pointed to it, and Christoph whispered, Showers. I don't know why I asked him. I already knew what the word would mean. I saw thin pipes around the doorway. Inside the gas chamber there were grates on the yellow-tiled floor. Holes on the rough plaster ceiling where the fake shower spouts had been. Wall vents for Zyklon-B.

We walked through, quickly, to the death chamber, where the SS had kept the murdered prisoners' bodies. The next room was the crematorium. Concrete floor, white walls, high ceiling, wooden beams. Two brick ovens, iron doors open.

I did not try to imagine what had happened in the gas chamber, the death chamber, and the crematorium.

We were almost at the exit when I saw a photograph on the wall. It showed the townspeople of Dachau viewing the bodies in the crematorium after the camp was liberated. The Americans had forced them to come. To witness. In the photograph, a German couple—he in a hat and she in a headscarf—turn away while a GI looks at the bodies behind them. The German couple was standing exactly where Christoph and I now stood. I could not see the GI's face in the photograph, and I wondered, absurdly, if he could have been my grandfather. I thought I understood, then, why he had taken the photos. Because the Germans had looked away. It was harder to look than to look away.

When we stepped outside, I heard birdsong, incongruous and false. The building was bordered by magnificent green-leafed trees. Some of them, the British tour guide said, had been used as hanging trees.

Christoph leaned into me and pressed his head against my shoulder.

He killed himself, after the war, he said.

Who?

Borowski. The poet.

13

We did not speak on the drive back to Munich. I noticed that Christoph drove slower than usual. As I watched the houses of Dachau pass by, tidy and well-kept, I thought about the photographs in my grandfather's scrapbook. And I thought that fifty years was not a long time.

When we arrived back in the city, Christoph parked near the Haus der Kunst, an art museum close to the English Garden. I followed him to the back of the museum, which looked like a Greek temple. We walked up the steps to the café and sat outside on wood-slatted chairs. It was hot, and the sun was in my eyes. I moved my chair closer to Christoph. He ordered, and the waiter brought us two coffees, two cakes.

Is this the main art museum in Munich? I asked. I didn't know how to talk about what we had just seen at Dachau.

Yes, he said. Hitler built it for German art. Nazi art. There were big exhibits here in the thirties and forties. Nazi parades too. Hitler chose a lot of the art himself. Over there—he pointed some ways in the distance—was the museum that staged the Degenerate Art exhibit, in 1937. Do you know about this?

No. Tell me.

It was mostly abstract painters, Paul Klee, Otto Dix, people like that. International artists. Picasso and Kandinsky. And Jewish artists. There was a whole room devoted to Jewish artists.

I'm surprised the Nazis put it all on display, instead of burning it.

Well, they did that too, a little later. Thousands of paintings. Can you guess how many people came to see the exhibit?

Ten thousand?

Two million people came to see the Degenerate exhibit that summer. Two million. There was a Nazi art exhibit here, in this museum, at the same time. But only half that many people came.

What was the Nazi art like?

He waved his hand dismissively. Classical statues. Strong, virile men. Hitler was a failed artist, you know. He used to live in an apartment near here.

Christoph drank his coffee and looked away from me, over the terrace, toward the English Garden. Neither of us had touched our cake.

No one talked about the murder of the Jews, he said quietly. Adorno wrote to Thomas Mann about it, this silence, when he returned to Germany after the war. It's a very famous letter. Do you know it?

No.

You know Thomas Mann, yes? *The Magic Mountain?*

Not really.

Well, Adorno wrote to Mann, this would have been late 1940s, that during his trip to Germany he didn't meet any Nazis. It wasn't that people *denied* ever having been a Nazi. He expected that. It was that people truly believed they had never *been* Nazis. They had completely repressed their obedience to Hitler. He told Mann how shocking this was because it meant that the Germans would never come to terms with what they had done. Adorno felt there was this . . . amnesia . . . in his conversations with ordinary Germans.

I nodded.

Hannah Arendt wrote about it too, he said, when she went back to Germany after the war. How no one wanted to talk about what had happened to the Jews. People just wanted to talk about their own suffering.

I didn't know that.

Yes. Everyone was focused on rebuilding, you see. Arendt wrote that this obsession with repair resulted in a kind of . . . indifference . . . to what they—we—had done in the war. To the Jews, I mean. She talked about Germans' inability to mourn. That the Germans had been turned into living ghosts. That phrase, it's stayed with me.

But was it an inability to mourn, or a refusal?

Both, I think. There was a sense, after the war, that Nazism had been a kind of . . . drug that Hitler had forced down our throats. That this drug changed us, turned us into addicts. That we were not responsible for our actions because of this drug that was National Socialism. So no one felt the need to make amends for what they had done to the Jews. And the rest of Europe. Sixty million dead because of Germany, yes? They felt they had been . . . possessed by Hitler. *We* became the victims. Because it was war, you see, because everyone had abandoned their morals, not just the Germans. Everyone had been pushed to the brink. Because it was war.

But why were the Germans the ghosts? They were still alive.

Not really. Not in the way that counted. That was Arendt's point. The cities were in ruins. People needed food, shelter, medicine. They decided to deal with what had happened—to the Jews, I mean—later. And the ruins themselves . . . it was like the apocalypse. *Götterdämmerung,* yes? The slate was wiped clean. It was a kind of . . . absolution. A rebirth.

An ironic absolution, you mean?

Yes. I'm not excusing any of it. I'm just trying to explain.

I know. I want to understand.

Arendt talked about how after the war there was no revolution, no uprising against the Nazis. After the Nuremberg trials, people felt that justice had been served because the Nazi leaders had been jailed or executed. And—Christoph gave a desultory puff and shrugged his shoulders—that was that. But *millions* of people had supported Hitler in Germany. Millions. The majority. The *Mitläufer.* There were some trials after Nuremberg for the low-ranking Nazis. But not many were found guilty. There was never a real . . . accounting. Some Nazis even demanded their military pensions from the Allies.

What?

It's true. At first the Allies refused to pay, but then they realized they had a potential uprising on their hands. There were so many Nazis, you see, and they said that the shame of Versailles was being repeated all over again. You know the shame of Versailles? The burden of the war reparations after World War One? The poverty that resulted from all of that?

Yes. That photo of the money in the wheelbarrow.

Exactly. It created so much resentment in Germany . . . it allowed Hitler to come to power. And when France surrendered to the Nazis, Hitler made them do it in the same train carriage where the Germans had surrendered at the end of World War One.

The same carriage?

Just the same. And so that was the feeling, that the victors were imposing these . . . burdens on us all over again. Eventually the Allies realized they would be better off if they paid the pensions. So they did. Even some Waffen-SS were *paid* for their military service. By you! He shook his head. Madness.

But look around, I said. You would never know what happened here fifty years ago. I assume Munich was in ruins.

Yes. All the cities were.

Fifty years is not a long time.

Yes, well, this is all thanks to you. The U.S. rebuilt Germany, as you know.

Have you ever talked with your parents about all this?

Brecht called them *die Nachgeborenen*. The ones born after. They tried to get their parents to face up to their support for the Nazis. They got tired of hearing their fathers complain that the Allies could have bombed the railway lines to Auschwitz, that America could have taken in more Jews. They rebelled, my parents' generation. It was all part of the student movements in the 1960s, the Prague Spring.

I nodded.

A lot of Nazis made up the new postwar government after the war, he said. There was some protest, but the new president understood that the best way to keep the fascists from organizing again was to bring them in. And, actually, it was the right decision. The country stabilized.

So maybe it all served a purpose, I said. The amnesia. If the Germans thought of themselves as Hitler's victims, then they could see the Allies as their liberators. They could reject fascism and embrace democracy.

Yes, but that amnesia came at a cost. It took a long time for ordinary Germans to come to terms with what they—excuse me, we—did to the Jews.

We were quiet for a moment. I heard the low murmur of people around us, speaking German. The sun was in my eyes again. I moved my chair into the shade.

Schoenberg wrote a famous piece right after the war, Christoph said. About the Holocaust. It was the first . . . memorial. Do you know Schoenberg?

No.

He invented a new kind of music. More . . . dissonant. He was the model for the composer in *Doctor Faustus*. Mann's novel.

I nodded.

He was half-Jewish, Schoenberg. He saw all of it coming. All of it. He left Germany for America in the thirties. He asked Mann to help him publish a letter about what was happening to the Jews. This was before Kristallnacht, even. But Mann wouldn't help. He didn't want to get involved.

Christoph drank his coffee, then set his cup down gently.

Schoenberg's piece was short, he said. Just a few minutes. There were lyrics in English and German, about a concentration camp. And a Hebrew prayer. It was . . . a lament. The music was harsh. No one had written anything like it before. When it premiered here, in the fifties, the Germans took out the words about the gas chamber. Just . . . removed them from the score.

He paused.

This is what I mean when I talk about German amnesia, he said.

But that was right after the war.

So what? he said. That's *exactly* when they should have let Schoenberg play music about the gas chambers. That's when the memories were strongest.

He was quiet for a moment.

Waffen-SS men had their blood type tattooed on their arms, he said, his voice low. You could only join the Waffen-SS if you had pure German blood, Aryan blood. So they were proud of these tattoos. Christoph shook his head. They had read Goethe and Hölderlin, but none of that mattered. It was all about blood.

I was beginning to feel out of my depth. I often felt this way with Christoph—I was in awe of his intelligence—but this was different. I didn't know how to meet him in this conversation.

Now it's taught in schools, right? I said. The Holocaust?

Yes. We all visit a concentration camp in high school. That's what the students were doing today. The group we saw.

That's good.

Yes. It is. That all started in the sixties, with the Auschwitz trials. But that was quite late. It took us nearly twenty years to face up to it.

You said before, in Nuremberg, that it was almost too much, the focus on the Holocaust from the time you're young.

Yes, because it absolves us of *really* engaging with what happened. It becomes sanitized. Something in a history book. You saw all the teenagers at Dachau today. Laughing, flirting with each other. They weren't paying attention.

In the beginning. They were quiet at the end.

Yes. But it's distant to them. More distant than it was to us. We paid attention. We wouldn't have dared act like that. All that laughter.

I think you're being too hard on them, Christoph. They were just horsing around by the gift shop.

He shook his head. The gift shop.

I just meant . . . the museum shop. I didn't mean to make light of it. It sold books about the war.

He shook his head again in disgust. *Gift shop,* he said. At Dachau.

I know, I'm sorry. I chose the wrong words. But it's good it exists. It's good they sell history books there. At least it's in your history books. The camps. At least Germany is facing up to it.

In some ways, yes. In others, no.

It's more than we're doing in America. There's no museum about slavery in Washington. I mean, people throw weddings at Southern plantations.

He shrugged, defeated. I don't know what the answer is, he said. But it's something we need to think about, all the time. This capacity in us—in us Germans—for cruelty.

Christoph, you're not cruel.

He looked at me, a little sadly, and paid the bill.

14

We left Munich the next morning. I was exhausted. Christoph was quiet as he drove. I felt the way I did after I had come back from Switzerland, that something had shifted between us. But this time I felt him shifting away from me. I can't explain what made me feel this way. He did not rest his hand on my thigh, as he usually did when he drove, and he kept his eyes on the road. It was a mood, an apprehension. Maybe he was tired of showing me around his country, navigating this terrain for me. Maybe he'd had enough of concentration camps and war requiems. I tried to tell myself that it was all in my head, that nothing had changed, and yet I worried. Part of me always worried when I was with Christoph, that he would choose a woman who spoke his language, who was at home in his world. His beauty dazzled and destabilized me. I was in thrall to it and yet it weighed upon me. Things came too easily for him. I came too easily.

When we arrived back in his university town, Christoph parked near the *Altstadt*. We sat outside at a café and relaxed in the warm May sun. He ordered two weissbiers and some food. I tried not to think about his change in mood or the fact that I was leaving in four days. Instead, I thought about how a year had passed since I met Christoph, how close we'd become. I looked at him sitting across from me in his dark green polo shirt, and he smiled.

It's been a year, I said. Since we met.

He reached across the table and took my hand.

It hasn't been easy, I ventured.

No.

I can't imagine doing it again. The distance, I mean.

He shook his head.

But we'll see each other more next year, I said. Right?

Right.

I looked around at the other happy couples sitting together in the sun, then back at Christoph. My God, he was beautiful in that clear summer light, the sun gleaming on his copper-blond hair, specks of gold in his brown eyes.

You start in September, yes? he asked.

Yes.

I'm going away with Matthias in September, he said, loosening his hand a little. Hiking, in the Alps.

Sounds fun.

We planned it a year ago, he said. Don't be mad.

I'm not mad, I lied.

Our term doesn't start until October, he said.

So you'll come then, to Oxford?

If I can.

I looked at him as if from a different angle.

If you can?

October is the start of term here, he said. It's a busy time.

Uh-huh.

I let go of his hand and took a long drink of my weissbier.

I'll come, *Schatz*. Don't worry. He reached for my hand again.

When?

I don't know yet, but I'll come. You know I'll come.

I don't know, actually. You promised me you would come to Massachusetts in the spring.

I told you, I had to study.

So did I, the week you came to Harvard.

Oh come on, you told me you did fine and you won a prize for your thesis.

I'm just saying, the week you stayed with me at Harvard was the week I was supposed to be studying. You knew that.

Well, you seemed okay with me being there.

I was, but.

But what?

I stayed quiet.

What? he said again.

It didn't feel good when you said you couldn't come to see me, this spring, because you had to study.

He let go of my hand and drank his beer.

I'm sorry it came across like that, he said coldly. But our exams are more important than yours. They determine everything.

I understand that. But mine were important too.

You did fine.

Well, maybe if I hadn't spent so much time with you that week, I could have graduated summa instead of magna.

He laughed. Are you serious?

Yes.

So it's my fault you didn't get the highest degree. You sound ridiculous, you know.

I fumed. That's not what I'm saying.

That's what I'm hearing. Maybe you're just not as intelligent as you think you are.

What?

I *said* maybe you're not as smart as you think you are. You haven't read Goethe, you haven't read Mann. You've barely read Adorno, Habermas.

His meanness stunned me. And yet I thought, *He's right*. There was so much I hadn't read.

My mind was going in circles. I lost track of what I wanted to say. And then I remembered.

This isn't about my exams, Christoph.

Oh no?

This is about us. I hesitated. I always come to you.

It's just the way things have worked out, he said. It doesn't mean anything. He shrugged again. That's why I paid for your ticket. I didn't want you to feel like you were making all the effort.

There was no tenderness in his voice. We sat in silence.

My friends told me to break up with you, I said, after you didn't come.

He leaned back in his chair and crossed his arms over his chest.

Let me guess, he said, Jess and Susie.

Maybe I should have listened to them, I said, brimming with anger, remembering the abortion.

He stared at me but said nothing.

I'm not going to beg you to come to Oxford, I said.

I told you, I'll come.

But you won't say when. It makes me feel like you don't care. Tears began to well.

He reached across the table and took my hand. Of course I care, he said, his voice quieter.

Well, that's nice to know a year into this. Whatever this is. That you care.

Come on.

I need to know what this is, Christoph. What we are.

We're together.

But what does that mean?

He shrugged. It means we're together. What else could it mean?

I'm your girlfriend, I said.

Yes, you're my girlfriend. I thought that was obvious. He sounded annoyed, put out.

Then why won't you say when you're coming to Oxford?

Schatz, let's not fight.

Christoph, we need to talk about this. How often we're going to see each other.

What, a schedule?

Something like that. I can't go home wondering when I'll see you again.

I never expected you to do that.

Well, you don't bring it up. When we'll see each other again. Only I do. And now you say you'll be gone in September, October's busy. I wiped away a tear.

Schatz, I'll come to Oxford.

When?

October. I'll make time for you. For us.

And I suppose there's no chance you'll come to Massachusetts this summer.

He tilted his head. If you want me to come, I'll come.

I want you to come if *you* want to come.

Fine. Yes, I want to come.

I wiped away another tear.

Christ, it feels like I'm begging.

Shh, he said, his voice softer. I want to come. How about August?

I was quiet for a moment. I needed to get my bearings. I had never been this honest or angry with him but I couldn't spend another six months in limbo, wondering what I meant to him, when I would see him again.

August works, I said. But I don't want to talk you into it.

You're not talking me into it.

It feels like I am.

Shh, he said again, squeezing my hand. I'll come to Boston in August, and I'll come to Oxford in October, and then you can come back here in November. We'll go to the Christmas market together. Maybe you can spend Christmas with me in Hamburg.

I nodded, wiped the tears away.

Did you even read the poem? I asked.

What poem?

The poem I gave you, for Christmas.

He shifted in his seat.

Yes.

You never said anything about it.

I liked it.

There were others. That one was the best.

He nodded.

Why did you never say anything?

What did you want me to say?

I don't know. That you had read it.

Of course I read it.

Well, you never mentioned it.

I'm sorry. It felt . . . private.

It was private. I wrote it for you. Just you.

I know. He squeezed my hand. I know you did.

You never played me the Shostakovich. The piece about Dresden. Or the other one.

I will, *Schatz*. I promise I will.

We were quiet for a few minutes. I stopped crying. I knew it was dangerous, crying in front of Christoph. Around us I heard the sounds of happy people, laughing and speaking German. I had no idea what they were saying.

So you want to come, I said.

Of course I want to come.

You're sure?

Yes, I'm sure.

I hate the distance.

Me too.

I hate that I can't speak your language.

That's easy to fix. He smiled.

I'll learn it, I said, suddenly lighter. I'll learn it and I'll read it.

That's my girl, he said. My American girl.

Just then the waitress brought two more weissbiers. He raised his glass.

Prost, he said.

Prost, I said.

We clinked our glasses and drank.

So you'll come in August, I said, wanting to believe him.

Yes, I'll come in August. You can show me all your favorite beaches.

And we'll go out for lobster and mudslides and I'll take you sailing. I'll take you to Boston too. Maybe even New York. We can stay with Jess and Susie.

He gave me a dubious look.

Let's stick to Cape Cod, he said. I've never seen you in a bikini.

What makes you think I'll wear a bikini?

He smiled and shrugged. You'd look good in one.

Well, maybe I will. Just for you.

He smiled and raised his eyebrows.

And you can meet my parents, I said.

I'd like that.

He smiled again, and we were quiet. The sun was lower on the horizon now, and some of the light had left his eyes. I felt like we had passed a crossroads, but, looking at him, I couldn't tell what direction we had taken or whether it was the right one. He had agreed to everything I asked. And yet, I had asked. I was the one who asked.

AFTER LUNCH, we walked around the town center. I told him I wanted to buy some souvenirs and he brought me to a kitschy shop. Inside, he picked up a plastic Viking hat, put it on, and smiled at me. I laughed, said Hold on, and took his picture. I had so few pictures of him. I hoped it would come out all right. I was already looking forward to opening the white envelope and finding his wide smile and deep brown eyes in the stack of photographs within. I would put his photo in the scrapbook I'd made that winter, alongside my photos of Nuremberg and Lichendorf and Hamburg. There were other things in the scrapbook. Dried rose petals from the bouquet he'd given me after Switzerland. Ticket stubs from the Herbert List exhibit and the Dürer museum, the train trip to Hamburg. A sprig of pine from the Black Forest, a linden leaf from Lichendorf. Franziskaner bottle caps. Postcards I'd bought along the way. And then there were the things I had collected in Munich. A cardboard coaster from the Hofbräuhaus, a paper menu from the Augustiner. A brochure in German from the Haus de Kunst. An alpine wildflower he'd picked for me in Berchtesgaden. We'd been sitting in a field of green grass, the snowcapped Alps all around us, and he'd placed the flower, carefully, through a buttonhole in my blue linen shirt. I felt the soft grass on my neck as I lay back and ran my fingers through his hair, opened my eyes and glanced up at the cloudless blue sky, then closed them again to feel his hands on my legs, under my shirt, the warm sun on my skin. I had saved the white wildflower, pressed it in the pages of my journal. It would go into my scrapbook when I got home, the edelweiss, connecting me back to Germany, back to Christoph. Each thing in the scrapbook held its own story. A story only I knew, only he knew.

We should send Josh a postcard, he said. He chose one with hills covered by dark evergreens, and the words *Grüsse aus dem Schwarzwald* at the bottom.

Greetings from the Black Forest, he said, smiling at me.

Perfect, I said, and paid for it along with a small cuckoo clock and marzipan for my parents. Let's send it now so we don't forget.

I found a pen in my purse and gave it to him. *Hi Josh!* he wrote. *There's a beer waiting for you in Bavaria. Wish you were here!* He handed me the pen, and below his words I wrote, *What Christoph said! See you soon, I hope. How about a gig in Boston this summer??* We ducked into a small post office nearby and mailed it.

That only took a year, I said, grabbing hold of his arm as we walked out.

Better late than never.

Did you not want to tell him? About us?

What? No, he said, laughing.

Have you told him?

He knows.

I nodded and leaned my head against his shoulder.

Good.

WE WENT BACK to his flat in the late afternoon and lay in bed for a while, holding each other. We closed our eyes, resting, quiet, as he ran his fingers through my long hair. It was lovely and gentle lying there together under his open window, the cathedral bells ringing. It made me think of Cambridge, the two of us in my bed, the warm spring air washing over us. It was like that again.

I fell asleep in his arms. When I awoke, I reached across his chest and held him tighter, secure in his warmth. My doubts vanished as I lay with him. He was mine and I was his and I thought that maybe, if I was very lucky, it could be like this always.

The sky outside his window began to darken and I saw small shadows inch across his wall. He kissed me. We moved slowly, slower than we ever had, and it all felt new, it always felt new with him. When he kissed my neck I lifted my chin and he said I don't want you to go and I said I don't want to go and then he kissed me again and I closed my eyes and my body became the sea.

WE LAY IN BED, half-asleep. It was dark now.

We should go out, he said. Get something to eat.

All right.

He got up and grabbed a towel from his closet, wrapped it around his waist, and left the room. But then he came back and handed me a clean, folded towel, and said, Come.

I wrapped the towel around my body and followed him down the short hallway into the white bathroom. He opened the glass shower door and turned on the water. When it was warm he took my hand and we stepped in together. I had never done anything like that before and I was nervous. He could see me, all of me, in the water and the light. But then he told me to turn around and he washed my hair and the feeling of his fingers massaging my scalp was like lying in the sun. He took my head, very gently, and tilted it back into the water and the soap ran down my body and he put his arms around me and kissed the back of my head. I closed my eyes. We stood like that in the running water until he turned me toward him.

WE HAD DINNER at a café, then walked to a student bar in the *Altstadt*. There were a lot of people inside who knew Christoph, friends and friends of friends. Some were familiar to me, but most weren't. Christoph spoke German, laughing, gesticulating. I wanted him to myself again as we stood by the bar, waiting for our drinks. I felt edged out, blurred against the pretty, polished girls in short skirts and strappy heels who gave him matching kisses on both cheeks.

I saw Matthias and Saskia come through the door. Matthias caught my eye and waved. I waved back, happy to see him. A table had opened up near the back, and I walked over to it, gesturing for Christoph to follow. He nodded at me but didn't leave the bar. Matthias and Saskia came over and sat down with their drinks. After a few minutes, Christoph came too. Matthias wanted to hear all about our trip to Munich and the Eagle's Nest. Christoph and Saskia stayed mostly quiet.

When we finished our beers, Saskia said they had to go. She'd promised a friend of hers, a ballerina, that they would stop by her party. Matthias asked her a question in German and she nodded. He stood up and said, Okay, see you later. Saskia waved a small goodbye, and they left.

Christoph walked over to the bar, ordered two more beers, and brought them back to our small table. As he walked toward me, one of the pretty blond girls standing at the bar looked at him. A small, quick look. But I saw it.

There was music now. It was getting harder to hear. The lights dimmed. Christoph got up and said he would be back in a minute.

I sat, waiting. I finished my beer and still he had not returned. Where was he? The bar was filling up, the music louder. I waited. Suddenly I became anxious. We'd been drinking for a while. What if he had passed out in the bathroom? What if he was sick and needed me? I bolted downstairs to the basement.

And then I saw them in the dim-lit hallway. He was kissing the blond girl, the one from the bar. The one who had looked at him. Her back was against the wall and his hands were on her hips. Her arms were wrapped round his neck.

My heart stopped.

I backed away, walked up the narrow steps. I reemerged into the dark, crowded bar and leaned against the wall. My breath came ragged as I pushed the heels of my palms into my eyes. I didn't know how this could be happening.

The girl had her arms around his neck. This girl had *seduced* him. I needed to get him away from *this girl*.

And then I remembered his hands on her hips, moving up her waist, up, up.

I WALKED OUT of the bar and found a phone booth down the street. I rummaged around in my bag for my phone card and my address book, then stuck my card into the metal box and called Jess and Susie. Jess answered on the second ring. Across the ocean, I heard the wailing sirens of New York.

I told her, through tears, what had happened. When I finished, my chest tightened and I felt, again, like I couldn't breathe. I was having a panic attack but I didn't know it. Nothing had ever made me feel that way before.

That dirty dog, Jess said.

I heard Susie in the background saying *What happened?* and Jess calling back, *He cheated on her*. Susie said, *I knew it.*

I don't know what to do, I said. Fuck, I can't breathe. I can't breathe.

Anna, listen to me. Listen to my voice. Breathe. Just breathe, okay?

Okay.

Just breathe.

Yeah. Okay.

Okay?

Uh-huh.

You're gonna be all right.

Okay.

Is there anyone there you can stay with?

No.

When does your flight leave?

Wednesday.

Listen, you need to get out of there. Take a train to Berlin. Spend a few days in Paris. I don't know, but Jesus, you need to leave.

I know, I said miserably. The panic was receding. Now I felt disoriented, dazed.

Anna, I know you're really into him, but honestly, you've only known him for a few months.

A year, I said. It's been a year.

But long-distance. How many times have you actually seen him?

I don't know. Four times. Five. It doesn't sound like a lot, but . . . oh God.

Anna, he never came to see you. Not once.

I know. I was starting to see things with a new, bitter clarity.

Look, she said, it's better to find out who he is now. He has a cheating heart. It would have happened eventually. Better to rip off the Band-Aid.

But I love him, I said dumbly.

No, you don't. I told you, this is infatuation, not love. It's not real.

I had no idea what she was talking about.

He's not like American guys, I said. He's . . . an intellectual.

She burst out laughing. Listen to yourself! He's a pretty-boy narcissist who love-bombed you and manipulated you and cheated on you. I saw this train wreck coming a year ago. And here you are, defending him when the truth is staring you in the face. I know you don't want to hear this, but he never loved you, Anna. It was always just about him.

I was quiet. I couldn't believe that I had imagined it all. That none of it was real.

And don't let him make excuses, she said. *I'm sorry, I was drunk,* all that shit. I can already hear it. Don't take him back, Anna. Don't. You have a choice right now. Wake the fuck up.

Another siren wailed. I imagined the streets of New York, the humidity, the yellow taxis and the skyscrapers. I wanted to go home.

Come to New York, she said.

I will. Shit, my phone card is running out.

Listen to me. Do not, I repeat, *do not* sleep in his bed tonight. Pack your bag and find a hostel.

I will.

Promise?

Yeah, I choked. I gotta go. The card is running out.

Come to New York, she said again.

I will.

We'll all get wasted and burn pictures of Christoph.

I laughed a little, and in that moment I knew I would survive him.

We love you, Banana. Call us tomorrow when you're out of there.

I will.

You're gonna be okay. But don't forgive him. Promise me.

Yeah, I choked. Okay. Bye.

I hung up and leaned against the wall of the phone booth and gave thanks for the love of women. I could breathe again. But I knew Jess was right. It was over.

I WALKED BACK to Christoph's flat and pressed the buzzer, hoping Matthias might be home.

Hallo? he called through the intercom.

It's Anna.

He buzzed me in and I walked up the stairs. When he opened the door, he looked behind me.

Where's Christoph?

At the bar.

Oh.

I got tired.

He moved aside to let me pass as I walked toward Christoph's room.

Good night, I said.

Wait . . . Do you want a beer?

I hesitated.

All right.

We went into the kitchen and Matthias grabbed two bottles of Franziskaner from the refrigerator. We sat down at the table.

You didn't stay at the ballet party? I asked him. I was trying very hard to act friendly, casual, like I hadn't just seen the man I loved kissing another girl in a dark corner. I didn't want to discuss any of it with Matthias. He was Christoph's friend, not mine.

Matthias shrugged. I don't really know the dancers. Saskia's still there.

He opened the bottles and handed one to me. I tried to smile. We were quiet.

Bloody hell, I can't do this, he said.

Do what?

Saskia said she told you about Katya.

I didn't like where this conversation was going. I didn't like it at all.

I'm sorry, he said. Saskia shouldn't have told you anything about it.

Anything about what?

Katya, he said. She was there tonight, at the bar. Something happened. That's why you came back alone.

I nodded, willing myself not to cry.

He shook his head, in frustration, disgust, I couldn't tell. Whatever it was, I needed it.

I told him to tell you, he said. I told him it wasn't right.

I looked out the window, into the night.

How long.

He was quiet for a moment, and then said, Autumn. He paused again. But . . . on and off. And never when you were here.

Autumn?

He hesitated. August, after you went back to America.

That's not autumn, I said. That's summer.

He stayed quiet.

But how can she not know about me?

He leaned forward, held my hand, and looked me in the eye.

It's him you should be angry at, he said. Not her.

I let his hand linger on mine, longer than I should have. But it felt good to hear him say these words. I still haven't forgotten them.

I stood up. He let go of my hand.

I'm going to sleep now, I said. I'll leave in the morning.

He handed me the beer. Take the Franziskaner.

I tried to smile. Thank you, Matthias. If I don't see you before I go, thank you.

He stood up and embraced me. Write to me? he said.

I will, I said. But I knew I wouldn't.

I let go of him and turned away and walked into Christoph's room. I cried, hard and quiet, as I stuffed my things into my backpack. Jess was right—we had only seen each other a few times in the last year. And yet he was everything to me. I thought I knew about the treachery of men, but I couldn't understand how this had happened. I had tied my future to him. I had applied to graduate school to be closer to him. I thought he had wanted that too. All of it, I saw now, was foolishness. I began to feel something else besides grief and anger. Shame, humiliation.

I sat down on Christoph's bed and looked at my watch. It was past eleven. I wasn't going out to find a youth hostel and I wasn't sleeping in Matthias's room, though the thought had crossed my mind. I found my Discman, lay down, and listened to my Smashing Pumpkins CD. Billy Corgan's voice calmed me, just a little. *Disarm you with a smile*. I knew Christoph wasn't coming back, that he would end up in Katya's bed. And still I could not leave his room. I was disgusted with myself, at my abasement. I was weak, weak.

Then I heard the door opening and closing, quickly and quietly. It was Christoph, a dark silhouette in the blue-black room. I watched his shadow undress. He let his clothes fall to the floor, then got into bed beside me. I stayed still, facing the wall, and said nothing. He rolled onto his side and put his arm around me.

Es tut mir Leid, he whispered. I could smell alcohol on his breath.

He lifted my hair and kissed the back of my neck.

Bitte.

I closed my eyes.

What's happening? I moaned to the wall.

He reached over, took my hand in his, and I grasped it.

IN THE MORNING I awoke early and got out of his bed. He sat up as I picked my clothes off the floor and put them back on. I had made a mistake, sleeping with him. Jess was right. I couldn't trust my body around him.

What are you doing? he said.

I'm leaving.

But your flight doesn't leave until Wednesday.

I looked away from him and kept packing.

He got out of bed, put on a pair of boxers, and walked over to me. He took my hands in his.

Christoph, what the *fuck*, I said, my voice trembling.

It was nothing, he said, looking into my eyes. I was drunk. I didn't . . .

Fuck you, I hissed.

He was silent for a minute, then he lifted my hands to his face and kissed them.

It won't happen again, he said. Please don't go.

No. No, I can't trust you. You have . . . a cheating heart.

I don't. He gripped my hands tighter. I don't.

You told me we were together. Are we, Christoph? Is this . . .

The word I couldn't say was *real*.

He closed his eyes for a moment. Then he opened them again.

Schatz. I love being with you. Very much. You're so smart. He moved my hair away from my face. And so pretty. I'm lucky.

Tears stung the corners of my eyes.

But you live in America.

I nodded, dazed.

I'll be at Oxford, I said.

Oxford is still far.

I had wanted him to fight for me and he had. He had apologized, said it meant nothing, chalked up his bad behavior to drink. But things were moving in a dangerous direction. *Of course we're together,* he'd said on the train to Hamburg. He wasn't saying that now. Suddenly I was the one fighting for him.

Anna, he said.

We don't have to talk about the war, I said, desperate. I could already feel the cold void, the anguish and the lack, that lay on the other side of this conversation. My intensity had scared him off, just as I had feared. I could hardly blame him. Sometimes it scared me too. I had mostly allowed myself to be the person I was with him.

This isn't about the war, he said.

But I felt that what was happening between us was connected, some-how, to the things we had seen and talked about in Nuremberg, Ham-burg, Heidelberg, Munich, Berchtesgaden, Dachau. That because of me he had opened something up in himself that he wanted closed again. He had said I was the only person he talked to about the war. And I knew then, suddenly and with clarity, that this *was* about the war. He would not talk about the war with Katya. He was leaving me because of the war.

When you're here, he said, I don't want you to go. But I can't see how we make this work . . . for longer.

I nodded, as if I understood.

The distance is too much, he said finally. His words were cold, but his eyes watered and brimmed.

When I look back at this scene, I tell myself to say goodbye, leave his bedroom, take a taxi to the station, and board a train to Prague. Which is exactly what I did that day, but not before I lost all my dignity. I am ashamed that I begged for the love of this man who was, in that moment, destroying me. But the young woman who stood before Christoph that morning was in shock, incapable of acting rationally. She was in love with a man who had probably never imagined that what happened between them in America would extend across the ocean, to Germany, where he would stand with her at the abyss of the twentieth century. How she would find sanctuary in him. How he would find sanctuary in her.

I love you, Christoph.

He put his arms around me and drew me close.

I know, he said quietly. I know.

15

Hans, Early Spring 1943

H e awoke in a field of white. Quiet all around him, as if the snow had muted the sounds he remembered—cannon fire, gunfire, the descending pitch of planes falling from the sky. In battle, noise had the muffled quality of sound underwater. And the things he had seen had been, likewise, blurred. But now everything was clear and silent and still. There were others around him, shadows of figures half buried in the snow. None of them moved.

The wind caught him suddenly, a cold blade cutting the air. He heard the low rumble of cannon fire in the distance and realized that the fighting had moved on. He lifted his head to see if there was movement around him. Nothing. Only silence. Quickly he raised his body off the snow, dragged his leg—something had happened to it—and began moving across the field. He heard the low, accusatory calls of birds circling overhead, and tried to move faster.

When he was out of the clearing, he sat against a tree and looked at his leg. He had been shot but the wound was not serious. He saw the branches of the trees, dark against the white sky. New snow began falling thick all around him, falling on the bodies of the soldiers who had died in the field, erasing the patches of crimson that had seeped from their bodies into the snow.

He lay there for a long time. When he was sure it was safe, he limped back into the clearing. The snow was falling harder now, blanketing the bodies in white. He rubbed snow off the dead men until he found a Wehrmacht officer with good boots. For a moment he was tempted to wipe the snow off the dead man's face, but he didn't.

He unlaced one boot. Gently he wrapped his fingers around the man's ankle, as if he were taking a shoe off a child, and pulled. The boot would not come off. He pulled harder. He pulled so hard the officer's body moved with him and still the boot would not come off. He let go and sat back and looked out at the field. It was almost white again. He could barely see the outlines of the men's dark uniforms, the red of their blood. The battlefield was being wiped clean.

He turned back to the dead man. Only the boots were visible now in the snow.

He tried again, this time twisting the boots back and forth. Finally they came off, first one, then the other. He took the wool socks.

As he limped back to the woods, something compelled him to turn around. All he could see was the snow, falling fast and thick, and the officer's bare feet protruding from the white mound. Someone would find the body, barefoot, in the spring.

He discarded his own battered boots and put on the dead man's. He walked west, limping, through the snow. After an hour he came to a barn, high and dark at the edge of a white clearing. He crept up beside it, his rifle in line with his vision. Increasingly he saw through his rifle now; that was how he gauged distance, decided the fate of those in his sight. For it was hard to distinguish between a peasant and a partisan. His own eyes were faulty, their judgment suspect. Only when he lifted the rifle to his face could he tell the difference between civilian and enemy. The coldness of the metal against his cheek gave him confidence. They had been told they were fighting the great Bolshevik foe, that there need be no trial before an execution if they felt an execution was necessary. That was in the beginning, a year ago. The officers soon made a rule against photographing executions.

He kicked the barn door open and waited for a sound—birds in the rafters, muffled voices, a dog. But there was nothing. He walked inside, the rifle close to his face, and then, when the quiet had surrounded him, he dropped his gun and lay down on the cold ground, out of the snow and wind.

He breathed heavily and saw his breath spill out in a white cloud before him. Suddenly the scene brought him back to his grandfather's farm in Lichendorf, the early mornings, waking in the cold winter night to milk the cows. In a barn not unlike this one, the steam rising off his body, the hot sweat mingling with the cold air. The rhythm he fell into, bent over, not thinking of the day ahead or the day behind but caught up in the motion of his body. He remembered it here, among the broken stalls whose wood had been torn off, maybe years ago, to warm a family, or an army. The barn was empty now.

After he had rested, he stood up and stepped out into the snow. There were trees in the forest all around him, but he had no way to cut them down. He walked deeper into the woods, saw a dead tree lying on the ground, and broke off some small branches. He found the remnants of a bird's nest nearby and brought the branches and the nest back to the barn. He lit the nest with a match and then began to add the small, dead branches for kindling. Slowly he built the fire. He still had a few cigarettes. He smoked one as he watched the smaller branches flare orange and yellow, the color of autumn leaves. It took a long time for the larger branches to catch, but then the flame began to gather momentum, like a wave, and he sat back and exhaled the smoke from his cigarette.

It is difficult to distinguish between a partisan and a peasant. You have every right to commandeer their houses, take their clothes, their food, tear up the floorboards in search of the hidden potatoes—there are always stores of potatoes and grain under the floorboards—and push them out into the snow. You must not pity them.

He had not been near a fire in several days, not since before the fighting. Now he stared at the colors, the red sparks floating up as outside the soft white flakes fell to the ground. He began to feel the pain in his leg, as if the flame itself were burning inside his wound. He found his knife, held it in the fire, then waited for a moment.

When he pressed the scorching blade to his leg, his body retched. And he remembered, suddenly, the pain he had felt in the clearing, firing at the Russians from behind the tank—the moment something had hit his leg, before he had fallen unconscious. The pain had erupted for an instant, then folded back in on itself as it knocked him to the ground. He waited now for this new pain to pass, then brought the knife to the wound again. The knife had cooled down and this time his body did not retch so much. The shrapnel was close to the surface, and he was able to extract it with his knife. He poured some water on the wound, snow he had melted. He found the iodine and field dressing in his pack, dressed the wound, then fell back on the cold ground in the darkness.

HE AWOKE ONCE in the night. Absolute blackness, thick like the white snow he had walked through that afternoon. It was a thing he had not known for a long time, this pure, dark silence.

Jürgen stood before the bonfire, a sheet of paper in his hand. He saluted them and said: Christmas will not take place this year for the following reasons. Joseph has been called up by the army; Mary has become a nurse and is currently on the Ostfront *with the Red Cross; the baby Jesus has been sent to an undisclosed location in the countryside away from the bombs; the three Wise Men could not get visas because they had no proof of Aryan origin; there is no star because of the blackouts; the angels have become sentries and the shepherds are operating the telephones. The donkeys have all been slaughtered and eaten. Again, I repeat, Christmas will not take place this year. You will have to content yourselves with vodka.*

Jürgen pulled two clear bottles out of his sack. Everyone cheered.

A Christmas gift from the partisans, he said.

When he awoke, it was light out. The snow had stopped. He examined his leg and saw that the wound was beginning to heal.

Slowly he limped outside and gathered more kindling. His leg ached more, much more, than it had in the hours after he had taken the boots from the officer in the clearing. He had not noticed the pain then but now it pulsed through his body, a thunderbolt that threatened to crack him open. He would have to ignore it as he had ignored other things that once caused him pain. He needed to focus on something else; that, the army had taught him, was how to move beyond what troubled you.

The last time he had eaten was before the fighting, but he felt no hunger. He would have to hunt. He needed to concentrate on something other than the pain in his leg, to focus all his will on a single goal. He limped slowly, out into the woods, and set up his position behind a tree. He sat down with his bad leg outstretched, brought his rifle to his face, and waited.

The dog walked toward them. It was dressed in a harness with a short pole sticking straight up. One of them called to the dog, Here, puppy, come here.

The dog did not come. It headed straight for the tank. They saw the top of the pole bend as the dog scrambled under the tank, and then the great explosion, the screams of the men inside, one of them escaping, burning, screaming, his hair and clothes on fire.

He waited. Finally a skinny doe emerged from behind the trees and he shot it. He watched its legs buckle, its body sink to the ground.

Hans observed that it fell more slowly than a man.

He dragged the deer into the barn, where he butchered it. It took him most of the day. He kept his hands inside its warm stomach, remembering the feel of hot water against his skin. It required a certain will to take his hands out of the deer's insides and continue gutting and skinning.

Later, inside the barn, he lit the fire and cooked some of the meat. As he watched the venison sizzle and harden, he felt a great hunger rise up in him. He was tempted to bite into the half-raw strip, but he ignored the urge and waited until the meat was cooked. It did not have much taste. Maybe he could not taste now. He melted snow in his cup and drank.

He stared into the flames and thought of how the deer had looked straight at him before he shot it. It was something he had not noticed in the moment he pulled the trigger, but now the image came back to him clearly. The deer had raised its head and looked at him in the same instant he had raised his gun. He wondered why the deer had not run, why it had stood stock-still as he fired.

The mud was so thick it often sucked the boots off the Russian prisoners as they marched. They raised their legs and found their feet were suddenly bare. They were not allowed to stop and search for their boots; they had to keep walking, even in their bare feet. They were marching twenty miles a day and they had to keep to schedule—there was no time to stop and search for boots lost in the mud. This order did not stop the prisoners who lost their boots from yelling for help, falling to their knees and fumbling in the deep mud.

If a German lost his boots in the mud, they were replaced with the boots of a prisoner.

The prisoners without boots were not able to walk as quickly as the prisoners with boots. Prisoners who fell behind, who could not keep up with the march, were shot. The mud was very thick, and they used the corpses as planks. They laid the bodies next to each other, on the mud, and the tanks drove over them. When they ran out of corpses, they shot the prisoners, always the ones without boots first, for it was assumed that they would soon fall behind.

Some of the prisoners asked to be shot. They were refused.

After two weeks he had eaten the venison and most of the rations in his pack. His leg was healing, and so he left the barn and ventured deeper into the woods to hunt and gather kindling. Alone, behind a tree or a mound of snow, he waited for an animal to make its way into his line of vision. Then, the shot. The gun's echoing boom filled the empty forest and the birds, startled, flew up from their branches into the white sky. The branches swung up and down after the birds took flight, and the squirrels scrambled up trees as if pursued by the shot itself. So much motion from a single sound, and then stillness.

He stayed in the woods until he had shot two hares. After the second kill, he began to feel the cold itching against his skin, and so he walked back to the barn. He skinned one of the hares, then packed the other in the snow behind the barn. There was not much meat on the stick after he had cooked the hare over the fire. He gnawed the small body to the bones.

In a few days he would be out of matches. He would have to keep the fire going all the time, for it would be difficult to start a fire with damp kindling. Even when he went to the woods to hunt, he must keep the fire going. He would have liked to stay in the woods from dawn until dusk, hunting deer and rabbit. To do so would set his mind at ease, for there was nothing between himself and the animal in the moment he fired the shot, just a white expanse of snow. It gave him much more satisfaction than shooting a man, for there was a charge in the space between his body and the body of the enemy, an intimate knowledge, the weight of a life and all the other lives that went with it about to end. Fear, too, of his own life ending. The space looked as if it contained nothing, but in truth that was the heaviest space. He had to shoot before the weight of that space held him down and prevented his arm from lifting the gun. After he shot a man, he always expected the space to lighten, but it never did. That was when he felt most alone, the charge between himself and the enemy cut, deadened.

Now there was great satisfaction in the waiting, in hitting the target, bringing the dead animal back to the barn. He was living as he had once dreamed about as a boy, alone in the woods, beholden to no one. He used to take long walks through the countryside around Lichendorf, some-times camping overnight with his friends, telling each other stories of the robber barons who had once lived in the woods. He wondered what had happened to those friends. They had all joined the Wehrmacht, like him. Probably they were dead.

HE AWOKE IN THE NIGHT to the sound of voices. He got up, grabbed his rifle, and peered out of a dark crack in the door.

A small group moved toward the barn, their silhouettes blacker than the night.

He stamped out the fire, spread the ashes into the dirt, and leaned up against the wall of the barn.

Slowly, the door opened. Moonlight revealed men in plainclothes, some of them with guns. He heard a voice say something in a language he did not understand.

The door stayed open. The men spread out through the barn, walking slowly.

Don't shoot, he said in English.

He dropped his rifle and stepped away from the wall, into the moonlight. The men aimed their guns at him, their hands wobbling.

He raised his hands. Don't shoot, he said again. He suspected the men were partisans. I have left the Wehrmacht, he said defiantly, in German.

A tall, thin man approached him in the moonlight.

Where is your gun? he asked in German.

There. Hans pointed to the wall.

One of the other men picked up the gun and gave it to the tall, thin, black-haired man who seemed to be the leader. This man slung the rifle over his shoulder, then asked Hans if he had any food. He spoke German with an accent.

Hans told them about the hare he had packed in the snow behind the barn, and motioned for the leader to follow him. Outside, he pointed to the hare's stiff body on the ground.

The leader bent down and picked up the hare. In that moment Hans could have hit him, grabbed his rifle, and killed him. But he did not. The space between them was too heavy and he could not lift his arms, or even make a fist. He wanted to know why these men had not killed him on sight. The need to know outweighed his need to kill them.

The stranger stared at the hare for a moment, then rummaged in his coat pocket for a pack of cigarettes. He lit one and offered it to Hans. They were quiet for a moment, smoking in the patch of moonlight behind the barn.

So, the man said in German, you have deserted.

Hans nodded.

There are many like you, all over these woods. You were lucky to find this place.

You are partisans?

Not exactly. Come, he said, taking the hare.

Hans followed the man back into the barn. The other men started the fire with the kindling he had stored in one of the empty stalls. They skinned the hare and roasted it. They had shut the barn doors against the cold, and the room was dark now except for the fire and the red glow upon the men's faces.

When they finished roasting the hare, they passed around the meat. Hans was surprised when the leader held the stick out to him.

He took a bite, then passed it on. The next man nodded his thanks. Hans noticed, even in the dim firelight, how thin these men were, how tattered their clothes. More worn, even, than his own. He saw their white, bony fingers protruding from the ends of threadbare socks.

After they had eaten the hare, they sucked on the bones. The men spoke their language in low voices. Slowly, the fire died. They leaned back on their elbows and watched the red embers disappear. For a long time they were quiet. Then they fell asleep.

IN THE MORNING Hans awoke to the sound of the men, moving and coughing. One had lit the fire already and hung a small iron pot over the flames. Hans watched him pour water out of the pot into a battered tin mug.

Just then the leader came in with a bundle of sticks. No one spoke as they stood by the fire and melted the snow. The space in the air felt dense, weighted, as the air before a battle.

He thought they must be partisans.

There were two women inside the house, huddling together, crying. One was old with white hair and a bent back, the other was younger, with blue eyes and pink cheeks. They buried their faces in each other's necks and shoulders. Terrified, they did not look up.

The soldiers moved around the women without touching them. They took food, firewood, clothing. Anything of use. They rummaged through empty drawers and cabinets as the women stood in the kitchen, crying.

Suddenly there was a shot through the window. One of the soldiers was hit, a boy from Munich. He fell to the floor, dead.

They stood there and watched the blood drain from his chest onto the wooden floor.

Another shot rang out. Everyone dropped to the ground.

The women began crying again. Jürgen pulled out his pistol and shot them both in the head.

Jürgen ordered the soldiers to leave the house and find the partisans. But the partisans had vanished into the woods.

While the other men were out hunting, the leader looked closely at Hans's leg.

It's healing, he said in German, but you should rest. And for God's sake, don't touch it.

They were sitting by the fire, inside the barn.

My name is Hans.

Jacob, the man replied.

Are you a doctor?

No, but I was a medical student. In Germany.

But you are not German.

No.

You said yesterday that you were not a partisan.

We are Jews. We escaped from the Vilna ghetto.

The fire cracked and sputtered.

Are there many of you?

Jacob stared into the fire. We don't know yet. There were only a few from the ghetto who made it out. No one believed us, what we knew. The trains, the trucks, the ones they took away. Everybody thought they were going to work. A work camp. The Germans told them to bring towels and soap. And then, one day, there was a girl, she was half-naked and bleeding and her eyes were on fire; she had run through the forest all night, she had somehow found her way back to the ghetto. She told us that the trucks brought them to a clearing in the forest, to Ponary, that everybody was told to kneel at the edge of a deep trench and how the soldiers shot them, one by one, and they fell down into the pit, on top of bodies that had been there for days, they must have, she said, because the smell was the smell of death, but she had only been shot in the arm, they hadn't killed her. She stayed in the pit until it was dark and she could no longer hear the soldiers' voices, then she climbed up out of the bodies. She said there were more bodies in the pit than trees in the forest. This girl, she was buried under the bodies of her neighbors, her family. She climbed out, you see, and ran through the forest, and when she returned to the ghetto nobody believed her—she's crazy, they said, and they put her in the ghetto's hospital so that no one would hear her, no one would see her. But we believed her. This girl, her name was Sarah.

For a moment Jacob was quiet. Then he laughed bitterly. I tell you this. You, a German.

Hans said nothing.

Yes, well, some Germans are different, Jacob said. There was one who helped us in the ghetto. Schmid. He was an officer. He knew what was happening and he helped us escape. Every day he took Jews out of the ghetto in his truck. This was normal, you see, taking Jews out of the ghetto in trucks, hundreds of them. What was unusual was that people were lining up to get into his truck. Because they had got word that this German was not really a German, that he was taking the Jews into the forest and freeing them. And so when the other Germans saw Jews fighting each other to get into this truck, they knew what was happening and they arrested and tortured this man. So I don't know. Maybe you are a good German. Maybe you would have helped us, like he did. That is what I told the others. They wanted to kill you.

You stopped them?

Yes. There has been too much death. But the others do not agree with me. They speak only of revenge now. You would be dead if not for me. These men, they listen to me. Perhaps that is why I saved you— not because I cared about whether you lived or died, not that I cared at all, but because I wanted to be like you Germans. I wanted to have the power to decide who lives and who dies. Yes, now that I think about it, that is the reason. I was searching for it last night, while everyone else was sleeping. I did not stay awake so that I could keep an eye on you, so that the other men would not kill you. I stayed awake because I could not understand why I had not killed you myself. No, listen, this is serious. I wondered, as the others slept, as you slept by the fire, I wondered, was I a coward? Did I not have the courage to kill you as the others did? And then I realized that courage has nothing to do with killing a man, absolutely nothing—this should have been clear to me from the beginning—that those with courage should turn away from death, from killing. Maybe this was what I admired in you, that you had turned away from the killing, and that this was courageous. But now I am starting to think differently about all this. I am starting to think that it is all the other way around. That I spared your life because I wanted to know what it was like to play God, the way you Germans do. To decide fate.

Jacob put his head in his hands. He was silent for a few moments, then looked up at Hans.

You should have seen her, this girl. How can I describe her eyes? The way they burned . . . the way she grabbed my arm and said, *It is true, what I say is true*. Like Cassandra.

Hans looked at the ground. He knew what was happening to the Jews. Such stories were not shocking. They were a confirmation of the truth—the only truth—that everybody was killing each other.

There are many partisans in these woods, Jacob said, after a while. You will be in danger if you stay here.

I know.

Vilna is not too far. About a hundred kilometers to the east. There is a convent on the outskirts of the city. The nuns there are kind. They will hide you, dress you in their habits.

Hans laughed. Jacob began to laugh too.

It's true, Jacob said. They helped us. You should go to them. They will keep you safe, especially if your army begins a retreat.

What will you do?

There is a camp of partisan fighters not far from here. Jews.

I will go to Vilna.

If you make it could you . . . get a message to my sister? She is still in the ghetto. Tell her that you saw me, that I have joined the partisans. Her name is Rachel Glicksman.

Glicksman.

Yes.

I will try.

Thank you.

Just then the other men came back from their hunt, carrying a deer. Together they skinned the animal and cooked the meat over the fire. Each one of them ate their fill, then fell asleep in the firelight.

Jürgen tried to push his men onto the boat. When that did not work he began to shoot at the ones who would not go. One shot, and the man buckled, fell sideways into the water. Another man reached for his pistol but Jürgen shot him first. The cannon fire and the boat's motor merged into one dissonant roar. The shots rang silent, muted by the noise. The men saw bodies falling into the bloody river.

Jürgen shouted something and waved his hands but he was speaking in silence. It was too loud to hear. The rest of the men got into the boat. There was another officer on the boat who was in charge of shooting deserters. The men sat quietly as they motored across the burning river, past bodies floating on the surface of the water. When they approached the far shore the bullets came at them like rain. The officer in the boat was shot dead, and the men began to jump into the river. They swam toward the shore. Some were shot when they came up for air, others drowned. A few reached the riverbank and crawled up into the rubble of the ruined city. But the Russians were ready for them: they had watched them cross the river, they shot at them and watched the bodies fall. They watched their enemy scramble up out of the water, and when they had a shot, they took it.

That night Hans crept up beside Jacob's sleeping body, grabbed his gun, quietly, and shot him. The three other men awoke and tried to fight, but they were weak and disoriented, and he managed to shoot them all. He looked over the bodies and took whatever meager possessions he could use—the tin cup, the threadbare socks—then walked out of the barn and into the snow. He thought about Jürgen, his captain, and the other soldiers he had fought with. He assumed they were all dead. He would walk west, join another unit, keep fighting. It occurred to him that the only ones who would survive the war were those like himself, and the girl, Sarah. The ones left for dead.

Epilogue

Christoph picked me up in a convertible Porsche outside my hotel in San Francisco. It was July 2008, eleven years since I'd last seen him in Germany. The top was down, and as he pulled up to the curb, he flashed that wide, white smile, the same one I remembered from the first time he met me at Frankfurt Airport. He leaned over, pushed the door open, and kissed my cheek as I sat down. I had not expected that, and time collapsed for me then, just a little. He was as handsome as I remembered, maybe more. He had grown into himself, become a man. His hair was shorter, blonder, and he looked sun-kissed and Californian in a white linen shirt, faded jeans, and Ray-Bans. I almost had to look away. But he didn't. I was wearing a beachy white sundress that showed off my tan, and he kept his eyes on me.

Schatz, he said, smiling. He pulled away from the hotel, shifted, accelerated, and turned up Moby's "Porcelain." I noticed he was wearing a Rolex.

He had kept in touch over the years—emails, phone calls, the occasional letter. He sent me postcards from Havana, Verbier, Bangkok, Maui. And once, early on, an article about Madeleine Albright and the Prague Spring that he'd carefully cut from *The Economist*. He always remembered my birthday. When I was at Oxford, he'd called a couple of times from London asking if he could come up to see me there. I told him I was studying.

I was a few years into an assistant professorship in Boston and had just published my first book, on Emily Brontë, when he emailed me from San Francisco. He had moved there to work at an architectural firm, and could he persuade me to visit? He said he'd be happy to fly me out. *As luck would have it,* I replied, *I'll be there for a literature conference in July.* I hit send before I could change my mind. *Great,* he replied immediately, *I can't wait to catch up!* I had tried very hard not to think about him over the years, and I wasn't at all sure it was a good idea to see him again. But it had been a decade.

We drove over the Golden Gate Bridge, a bridge I had never crossed, and he took me to dinner at a lovely waterfront restaurant in Tiburon. We sat outside in the warm air, and as I looked at him and listened to his voice, that slight, familiar accent, I had the strange sensation, again, of time collapsing. Suddenly we were twenty-three, sitting in a Nuremberg beer garden.

That's Angel Island, he said, pointing to the green-and-ocher hills across the bay. It used to be an immigration station. Japanese Americans were interned there, during the war.

I looked out over the harbor.

There's a museum there, he said. I can take you, if you like. Maybe tomorrow, after your conference?

Maybe, I said, my heart racing.

I went a few weeks ago, he said. German POWs were interned there too.

Like your grandfather.

My grandfather?

Yes. Hans. That was his name, right?

Yes.

He didn't desert, I said. He was a prisoner of war.

He looked at me quizzically.

I saw him, I said, in the movie at Dachau. Or . . . I thought I saw him. He was in a line of German POWs walking through Munich.

But . . .

I thought he was you.

Just then our waiter approached with two Negronis. We were silent as he set down the cold ruby cocktails in crystal tumblers, orange twists curling over the rims. The sun was starting its slow descent, and for a moment the glasses became prisms casting colored light on the white linen tablecloth. People laughed and spoke in low voices around us.

But maybe I was wrong, I said. Maybe it was someone else.

Christoph was quiet as I looked out at the sparkling blue water of San Francisco Bay, the long, sleek sailboats, jibs unfurled, cruising out to the Pacific. Sailing calmly on. Beyond the marina I could see the red outlines of the Golden Gate Bridge stretched high across the channel. I heard halyards clinking against masts, echoes of buoy bells and seagulls in the harbor. The sky was beginning to blaze, the ocean turning from sapphire to indigo.

It's beautiful here, I said. You're lucky.

He looked down at his hands for a moment, then stared out at the bay. After a while he turned back to me with a sad smile.

So, Professor, tell me about your ivory tower.

I told him how much I enjoyed teaching, lecturing, but that I could do without the Boston winters. I remember them, he said, nodding, his eyes a little brighter. He told me he loved California, that the sunny weather suited him. We ordered oysters and another round of drinks, and spoke about our work, our friends. Josh was finishing his residency in LA and played in a local band. Matthias was married, as were Jess and Susie. I saw them often in New York. They both lived in Park Slope and had toddlers I adored. Everyone, we agreed, seemed to be married, starting families. I didn't see a ring on his finger and I didn't ask.

We should send Josh a picture, he said, after he paid the bill. Of the two of us. Look, you can still see the sunset.

All right, I said, surprised.

Come.

He stood up and I went to him. He put his arm around my waist as he raised his phone above our heads.

What are you doing? I asked.

Taking our picture. Smile! he said brightly. I felt his hand on my hip, the slight pressure of his fingertips through my thin cotton dress.

After dinner, he brought me to a quiet, dim-lit bistro. My arm brushed against his as he walked beside me in the warm, clear American night.

We sat at a small table in the back and he ordered a bottle of champagne. When the waitress finished pouring, he raised his glass to me, and I to him. I had not forgotten my vow.

Cheers, he said, looking me in the eye.

Cheers.

We clinked our flutes, drank, and set them down in the shadowlight. The years burned as he reached across the table, took my hand in his, and I grasped it.

Author's Note

Though *The Scrapbook* is a work of fiction, Jack O'Brien's wartime route through the Ruhr pocket, Cologne, Munich, Dachau, and Berchtesgaden corresponds to that of my grandfather, who fought in Germany in the late winter and spring of 1945 in the U.S. 86th "Blackhawk" Infantry Division. He arrived at Dachau shortly after it was officially liberated on April 29, 1945, by the 42nd "Rainbow" Infantry Division. My grandfather took photographs of the death trains from Buchenwald and the corpses outside the Dachau gas chamber and crematorium. These photographs ended up in his wartime scrapbook, which his sister made for him after he returned from the Pacific. My grandfather also reached Berchtesgaden and the Eagle's Nest in early May 1945. I never learned whether he was there officially or unofficially, but he spoke of his "squad" having the place to themselves. As far as I know, he took no photographs there. I saw his "souvenirs," as he called them, from the Eagle's Nest when I was a teenager, but I did not see the scrapbook until after his death, at age ninety-one, in 2015.

Jack O'Brien's interview testimony about his first encounters at Dachau, which I have put in quotation marks, is an exact transcription of my grandfather's words as told to a family member in a recorded interview. All other dialogue in the novel is fictional.

The scrapbook is still in my family's possession.

Acknowledgments

To my editor, Deb Garrison, and my late agent, Jacques de Spoelberch, for their enthusiasm and support over many years. I am so grateful.

To Sarah Burnes, for her recent help and guidance.

To Zuleima Ugalde, Stephanie Evans, Rose Cronin-Jackman, and the production team at Pantheon for their guidance, expertise, and efficiency.

To Zeljka Marosevic and her team at Jonathan Cape for their excellent work on the British edition of *The Scrapbook*.

To Rebecca Donner and Samantha Rose Hill for indulging an interloper's interest in German history, and David Rudrum for recommending many excellent books on postwar German identity.

To the New York Public Library Cullman Center for Scholars and Writers, and my fellow fellows, for support as *The Scrapbook* went into production. Special thanks to Jochen Hellbeck for steering me toward two accounts of the Wehrmacht on the eastern front just in time.

To SJ Burton, Abby Santamaria, Lindsey Whalen, Keri Walsh, Eli Trautwein, Grainne Coen, and Adam Plunkett, who cheered me on.

To Ruth Franklin and Mary Dearborn for supporting my work as it has evolved over the years.

To my college roommates for three decades of friendship.

To my family for their love and encouragement.

To my Franconian friends for good conversation, and good beer. And for putting me up in Germany while I was researching *The Scrapbook*.

To my husband, Nate Holcomb, for his love and support over the past twenty-six years, and for bringing his knowledge of German language, culture, and philosophy to *The Scrapbook*. I'm lucky I found you.

Selected Sources

Many histories, novels, and memoirs about World War II, the Holocaust, and Germany's postwar years helped me craft the stories of Hans, Wilhelm, Jack, and Christoph. Christoph's knowledge of music was partially informed by Jeremy Eichler's *Time's Echo: The Second World War, the Holocaust, and the Music of Remembrance,* while Christoph's comments about postwar Germany draw from Harald Jähner's *Aftermath: Life in the Fallout of the Third Reich, 1945–1955* and W. G. Sebald's *On the Natural History of Destruction.* Christoph's discussion about the *Historikerstreit,* German victimhood, guilt, and amnesia draw from several sources listed in the following pages, most helpfully *Time's Echo,* Tony Judt and Timothy Snyder's *Thinking the Twentieth Century,* Uwe Timm's *In My Brother's Shadow: A Life and Death in the SS,* and Frank Trentmann's *Out of the Darkness: The Germans 1942–2022.* In chapter 3, I quote from "Special Orders on German-American Relations," a pamphlet distributed to American GIs in Germany in 1945; an original is pasted in my grandfather's scrapbook. The interview with my grandfather quoted in this chapter was conducted by Joan Clark and filmed by Hannah McCarthy. I also quote, in chapter 3, from pp. 35–36 of G. M. Gilbert's *Nuremberg Diary.* Parts of chapter 5 were inspired by Hans Magnus Enzensberger's experience as a teenager in a German village occupied by the Americans at the end of the war, which he writes about in his 1998 *Granta* essay, "Coming to America." The text of the "Werwolf Oberbayern" flyer that Wilhelm reads in chapter 5 is quoted on p. 157 of Walter Kempowski's *Swansong 1945: A Collective Diary of the Last Days of the Third Reich*. Some of Jack's wartime experiences in chapter 10 were inspired by scenes in Chuck "Bernie" Bernstein's *Blackhawk Mission: From Europe to the Pacific in World War II*, a book that gave me a greater understanding of what the 86th division encountered in Germany, as well as Austin "Red" Goodrich's compilation, *Blackhawk Recollections: 86th Infantry Division Members Remember*. Ruth Franklin discusses the love story behind Tadeusz Borowski's poems in the "Light and Shadow" cycle in her critical study *A Thousand Darknesses: Lies and Truth in Holocaust Fiction*, as does Timothy Snyder in "The World of Tadeusz Borowski's Auschwitz." In chapter 12, I quote Franklin's translation of Borowski's poem, which appears on p. 35 in *A Thousand Darknesses*. Information about stolen Jewish wealth, including antique furniture seized from Dutch Jews, comes from Götz Aly's *Hitler's Beneficiaries: Plunder, Racial War, and the Nazi Welfare State*. Peter Caddick-Adams recounts the French army taking wine from the Kehlsteinhaus down the mountain on stretchers in *1945: Victory in the West*. Information about Waffen-SS blood-type tattoos comes from Timm's *In My Brother's Shadow*. Details about the Wehrmacht on the eastern front in 1942–43 draw from Antony Beevor's *Stalingrad*, the Hamburg Institute for Social Research's *The German Army and Genocide: Crimes Against War Prisoners, Jews, and Other Civilians in the East, 1939–1944*, and Wolfram Wette's *The Wehrmacht: History, Myth, Reality*. Jürgen's Christmas speech in chapter 15 quotes from Beevor's translation of a satirical "spoof order" on p. 45 of *Stalingrad*. The characters of Jacob, Sarah, and Schmid in chapter 15 are informed by Rich Cohen's *The Avengers: A Jewish War Story*, Nechama Tec's *Defiance: The Bielski Partisans*, Wette's *The Wehrmacht*, and Chris Heath's *No Road Leading Back*. Full citations of these works and other selected sources can be found in the following pages.

Aly, Götz. *Hitler's Beneficiaries: Plunder, Racial War, and the Nazi Welfare State*. Translated by Jefferson Chase. Henry Holt, 2006.

Arendt, Hannah. *Eichmann in Jerusalem: A Report on the Banality of Evil.* Penguin Classics, 2006.

Beevor, Antony. *Stalingrad.* Penguin, 1998.

Bernstein, Chuck. *Blackhawk Mission: From Europe to the Pacific in World War II.* iUniverse, 2006.

Borowski, Tadeusz. *This Way for the Gas, Ladies and Gentlemen.* Translated by Barbara Vedder. Penguin Classics, 1992.

Boyd, Julia. *A Village in the Third Reich: How Ordinary Lives Were Transformed by the Rise of Fascism.* Elliot and Thompson, 2022.

Briggs, Richard A. *Blackhawks Over the Danube: The History of the 86th Infantry Division in World War II.* Lulu.com, 2022.

Browning, Christopher R. *Ordinary Men: Reserve Police Battalion 101 and the Final Solution in Poland.* Harper Perennial, 1992; 2017.

Caddick-Adams, Peter. *1945: Victory in the West.* Hutchinson-Heinemann, 2022.

Cohen, Rich. *The Avengers: A Jewish War Story.* Alfred A. Knopf, 2000.

Donner, Rebecca. *All the Frequent Troubles of Our Days: The True Story of the American Woman at the Heart of the German Resistance to Hitler.* Back Bay Books, 2022.

Duffy, Peter. *The Bielski Brothers: The True Story of Three Men Who Defied the Nazis, Saved 1,200 Jews, and Built a Village in the Forest.* HarperCollins, 2003.

Eichler, Jeremy. *Time's Echo: The Second World War, the Holocaust, and the Music of Remembrance.* Alfred A. Knopf, 2023.

Enzensberger, Hans Magnus. "Coming to America." *Granta* 63, 1998.

Ernaux, Annie. *A Girl's Story.* Seven Stories Press, 2020.

Franklin, Ruth. *A Thousand Darknesses: Lies and Truth in Holocaust Fiction.* Oxford University Press, 2011.

Fulbrook, Mary. *Bystander Society: Conformity and Complicity in Nazi Germany and the Holocaust.* Oxford University Press, 2023.

Gilbert, G. M. *Nuremberg Diary.* Da Capo Press, 1974; 1995.

Glass, Charles. *Deserter: A Hidden History of the Second World War.* William Collins, 2013.

Goethe, Johann Wolfgang von. *Faust.* Edited by Cyrus Hamlin. Translated by Walter Arndt. W. W. Norton, 2001.

Goldhagen, Daniel Jonah. *Hitler's Willing Executioners: Ordinary Germans and the Holocaust*. Alfred A. Knopf, 1996.

Goodrich, Austin, ed. *Blackhawk Recollections: 86th Infantry Division Members Remember*. iUniverse, 2008.

Hamburg Institute for Social Research, ed. *The German Army and Genocide: Crimes Against War Prisoners, Jews, and Other Civilians in the East, 1939–1944*. Translated by Scott Abbott. The New Press, 1999. (This book contains documents and photographs included in *The German Army and Genocide, 1941–1944* exhibit that opened in Hamburg in March 1995, and toured Germany and Austria in 1995–96.)

Hastings, Max. *Inferno: The World at War, 1939–1945*. Vintage, 2011.

Heath, Chris. *No Road Leading Back: An Improbable Escape from the Nazis and the Tangled Way We Tell the Story of the Holocaust*. Schocken, 2024.

Hellbeck, Jochen. *Stalingrad: The City That Defeated the Third Reich*. PublicAffairs, 2016.

Hemingway, Ernest. *A Farewell to Arms*. Scribner, 1929; 2014.

Hill, Samantha Rose. *Hannah Arendt*. Reaktion, 2021.

Hofmann, Michael, ed. *Twentieth-Century German Poetry*. Farrar, Straus and Giroux, 2005.

Jähner, Harald. *Aftermath: Life in the Fallout of the Third Reich, 1945–1955*. Translated by Shaun Whiteside. Alfred A. Knopf, 2022.

Judt, Tony. *Postwar: A History of Europe Since 1945*. Penguin, 2006.

Judt, Tony, with Timothy Snyder. *Thinking the Twentieth Century*. Penguin Press, 2012.

Kempowski, Walter. *Swansong 1945: A Collective Diary of the Last Days of the Third Reich*. Translated by Shaun Whiteside. W. W. Norton, 2014.

Kierkegaard, Søren. *Either/Or*. Edited by Victor Eremita. Translated by Alastair Hannay. Penguin Classics, 2004.

Krug, Nora. *Heimat: A German Family Album*. Penguin Books, 2018.

Ledig, Gert. *Payback*. Translated by Michael Hofmann. Granta Books, 2003.

―――. *The Stalin Front*. Translated by Michael Hofmann. New York Review Books, 2004.

Mayer, Milton. *They Thought They Were Free: The Germans, 1933–45*. University of Chicago Press, 1955; 2017.

McKay, Sinclair. *Dresden: The Fire and the Darkness*. Viking, 2020.

Mingarelli, Hubert. *The Invisible Land*. Translated by Sam Taylor. Granta Books, 2021.

Neitzel, Sönke, and Harald Welzer. *Soldaten: On Fighting, Killing and Dying; The Secret World War II Tapes of German POWs*. Simon & Schuster, 2013.

Nossack, Hans Erich. *The End: Hamburg 1943*. Translated by Joel Agee. University of Chicago Press, 2004.

Reese, Willy Peter. *A Stranger to Myself: The Inhumanity of War: Russia, 1941–1944*. Translated by Michael Hofmann. Farrar, Straus and Giroux, 2005.

Sebald, W. G. *The Emigrants*. Translated by Michael Hulse. New Directions, 1996.

―――. *On the Natural History of Destruction*. Translated by Anthea Bell. Modern Library, 2004.

Seiffert, Rachel. *The Dark Room*. Vintage, 2002.

Sereny, Gitta. *The German Trauma: Experiences and Reflections 1938–2000*. Allen Lane/Penguin Press, 2000.

Snyder, Timothy. *Bloodlands: Europe Between Hitler and Stalin*. Basic Books, 2010; 2022.

―――. "The World Behind Tadeusz Borowski's Auschwitz." *New York Review of Books*, September 21, 2021.

Sontag, Susan. *Regarding the Pain of Others*. Farrar, Straus and Giroux, 2003.

Struk, Janina. *Photographing the Holocaust: Interpretations of the Evidence*. I. B. Tauris, 2004.

Tec, Nechama. *Defiance: The Bielski Partisans*. Oxford University Press, 2008.

Trentmann, Frank. *Out of the Darkness: The Germans 1942–2022*. Knopf, 2024.

Uwe, Timm. *In My Brother's Shadow: A Life and Death in the SS*. Translated by Anthea Bell. Farrar, Straus and Giroux, 2005.

Vonnegut, Kurt. *Slaughterhouse-Five*. Delacorte, 1969; Random House, 1999.

Weller, Shane. *Language and Negativity in European Modernism*. Cambridge University Press, 2019.

Wette, Wolfram. *The Wehrmacht: History, Myth, Reality*. Harvard University Press, 2006.